Second Chance
AT
Happiness

Doctor Kultuniak,
Thank you for being there
for me during some dark times
in my life. I appreciate you,
I hope you enjoy the book. ☺

Greta Picklesimer

Second Chance AT Happiness

GRETA PICKLESIMER

Ambassador International
GREENVILLE, SOUTH CAROLINA & BELFAST, NORTHERN IRELAND

www.ambassador-international.com

Second Chance at Happiness
©2022 by Greta Picklesimer
All rights reserved

ISBN: 978-1-64960-112-4
eISBN: 978-1-64960-162-9
Library of Congress Control Number: 2022931719

Cover design by Roseanna White Designs
Interior Typesetting by Dentelle Design
Edited by Katie Cruice Smith

Scripture taken from the King James Version (Public Domain).

AMBASSADOR INTERNATIONAL
Emerald House
411 University Ridge, Suite B14
Greenville, SC 29601
United States
www.ambassador-international.com

AMBASSADOR BOOKS
The Mount
2 Woodstock Link
Belfast, BT6 8DD
Northern Ireland, United Kingdom
www.ambassadormedia.co.uk

The colophon is a trademark of Ambassador, a Christian publishing company.

To everyone who reads this book, may you find comfort, peace, and hope within its pages.

And to my mother, who believed I could get a book published but never saw the fruit of her faith in me fulfilled.

Many thanks to my wonderful editor, Katie Cruice Smith, for her insight and tireless help.

Chapter 1

HARRISVILLE, KENTUCKY

1870

Catherine Reed and her four-year-old daughter, Clair—both wearing simple, matching, black mourning dresses—stepped off the train at 3:00 p.m. in her hometown of Harrisville, Kentucky. Catherine looked at the dark green depot and sighed. It was not a contented sigh, but rather one of heaviness and regret. Standing on the small platform facing the depot, she contemplated her next step. She needed to move, but her feet seemed rooted to the ground. Tears began forming at the corner of her eyes, threatening to spill over onto her cheeks. How would she go on without her dear husband, John, by her side?

It was supposed to be his last run on the river. He had promised. They'd have enough money to buy their own place. Set up a little farm, keep chickens and a few pigs. All that had come crashing to a halt when he fell between the logs he'd been taking downstream on the Cumberland River to Crestville, where they would be sold.

She shook her head as if to shake out the memories. He didn't even make it halfway there. Flicking her shaking free hand to her side, she tried to wipe the memories from her mind.

If only John had worn the old pair of caulk boots, he'd still be here. The new boots had hurt his feet, he had said. Maybe that is what had thrown him off the logs.

Catherine sighed loudly, and her shoulders sank as she gave in once again to sobs. Little arms wrapped around her skirt. Catherine looked down into the concerned face of her daughter. Tears fell on the child's face. Her mother was quick to wipe them away.

"Mommy? Why are you crying?"

"Oh, honey," she said as she squatted down to be on level with the child and opened her arms.

Clair stepped into her arms and asked, "Is Daddy meeting us here?"

"Honey, remember what Mama told you? Daddy . . . Daddy had an accident. He . . . isn't . . . coming back." She choked out the words as she enfolded the child into her arms, stroking and kissing her blonde head as she let the tears flow. Pulling a handkerchief from her sleeve, she dabbed at her eyes. She took her daughter's hand and started to stand. But Clair wouldn't budge.

"I. Want. My. Daddy!" the four-year-old began to wail, her screams becoming louder and louder as people turned to stare at them.

Turning pinker by the second, Catherine knelt back down and tried to hush her daughter.

"Clair," she pleaded. "Clair. Please, honey, calm down. We can talk about this more in private. Please, honey." She rummaged in her purse and found a peppermint. Holding it out to the child, she was relieved when her daughter stopped screaming in order to pop the sticky candy into her mouth. Sighing with relief, she once again took her daughter by the hand and stood.

Turning mechanically, she watched as a tall man with sagging shoulders limped toward them through the steam from the train's engine. Catherine sucked in her breath as she recognized him. She would know that crooked smile anywhere, though the limp was new. Samuel Harris, her old beau, was coming toward her. They hadn't seen each other since she and John had run off together. What in the world was he doing here?

She felt her face warm as he locked eyes with her. Seeing him brought back old memories. *John.* Her heart ached for her husband.

She had fallen head over heels in love with him the first moment she saw him. She was only eighteen when she and John had married. They had moved almost immediately to the lumber camp. John insisted on making his own way in the world and wanted to provide a good future for her and Clair. He had provided for them for several years, and they had lived quite happily in the home provided by the lumber company.

But all that went south when he died. Without a man working, the lumber company had eventually forced her to move out. She had no choice but to move back home and in with her mother and brother. At least by living with them, she could be assured of always having a place. It was good to move back home.

A job would keep her mind busy and off the fact that her husband was dead. And Samuel Harris was the head of the school board. He was just the man she needed to see.

Refocusing her attention on Samuel, she admired her old classmate and friend. He stood tall, even though his shoulders were hunched as if he carried some unseen weight upon them. Striding around piles of baggage and through the crowd of people, Samuel waved one arm in a high arc above his head and called, "Hello."

Catherine mustered a weak smile as she tried to hide the remains of her tears. She swallowed and stood still, holding Clair's hand.

Samuel wore a dark, sackcloth coat over his blue, single-breasted vest. A gold watch chain joined the right side of the vest with the left. His shirt looked to be of white linen, and there was a square-knot bow tie at his throat. He was still dazzlingly handsome with wavy, black hair and piercing, blue eyes. When he was a few yards away, Catherine averted her eyes and looked at the ground.

"Hello," he repeated, coming to a stop before the pair. "Fancy meeting you here."

Catherine examined the face she knew so well—the face she had loved at one time before John set his cap at her. "Hello," she whispered, her throat still choked with tears.

She was lovely with her brown hair tied back in a bun and blue eyes that seemed to sparkle, despite losing John in a horrible logging accident. Or was the sparkle caused by tears in her eyes? What had losing her spouse of four years been like? Was she wondering, even now, how she would go on without him? The stoic expression on her face didn't give her feelings away. When Isabella died, he had cried secretly for days, asking God why He had taken his wife away. But like him, she would find the strength to go on as long as she trusted the Lord to help her.

The little girl held up her rag doll.

"And who is this?" Smiling, Samuel stooped down.

"Her name is Clair," Catherine said in a breath, her cheeks turning a charming shade of pink. "Clair, this is . . . my friend. Mr. Harris."

"Hello, Clair."

Clair stepped closer to her mother and grasped her dress. Turning his gaze to the doll, he asked, "Who's your dolly?"

"Mary," Clair said shyly.

"Well, hello, Mary. It is very nice to meet you."

Clair smiled. Stepping forward, she held out her doll. He shook the doll's hand. Both Catherine and Clair laughed.

"She likes you," Clair said, hugging her doll to her chest.

"I'm expecting my brother, Harl. He should be here soon to pick us up."

A tall, broad-chested man with mousey brown hair and darting, gray eyes walked toward them. The War Between the States had not been kind to him. It showed on his face. Where there should have been a smile, there was a thin line, and his brows pinched together. When he was a few feet from his sister, he nodded his head in greeting to her and Samuel. Turning his gaze to his niece, he stared at her. His lips parted into a weak smile. Clair ducked behind her mother's skirt but kept one eye locked on Harl.

"Clair, this is your uncle Harl Adams come to take us home."

"Is this it then?" Harl looked from her handbag to Clair. "No, here's our baggage tickets. If you wouldn't mind."

Harl took the tickets and wrapped one arm about his sister's shoulders. "I'm so sorry about John," Harl whispered. Turning, he trudged toward the baggage claim area, leaving Samuel and Catherine staring after him.

Samuel looked back at Catherine and cocked his head to one side.

"It's the war. He never got over it."

Samuel nodded. "Let's go see if we can help Harl gather your bags." As they followed after Harl, Samuel said, "Based on your telegrams to the school board, I know you're anxious to interview for the teaching position. I'll let you get settled first, and then we can discuss the matter with the board."

"The board." Catherine appeared nervous. Would she meet with the board's approval? All she needed was a little confidence in herself, and he was sure she would win them over.

Samuel led the way to the baggage claim area. Harl was piling trunks and crates on a handcart beside him. "Here, let me give you a hand." Samuel hefted one of the trunks up on top of the handcart as if it were weightless.

"Thanks for your help. I appreciate it," Harl said.

"Where are we going with these?"

Harl pointed into the street to a team of mules and a wagon. "Over there."

Samuel maneuvered the handcart to the wagon. He lifted the heavy trunk and placed it inside. After all the trunks and crates were piled inside the wagon, Harl smiled. "Thank you. I appreciate your help."

"No trouble at all."

Samuel held out his hand to Catherine, who took it. He helped her up onto the buckboard seat and then placed Clair next to her.

"I'll be out to pick you up at eight o'clock. Will that give you enough time to get settled?" His eyes bore into hers.

Catherine shifted uncomfortably before answering. "That won't be necessary. Harl will bring me into town."

Harl, holding the reins, touched the brim of his hat and nodded. "Will do."

Samuel patted one of the mule's rumps and stepped back. Harl spoke to the mules, and the wagon moved out into the busy street.

They drove the mile or so out to their parents' homestead with hardly a word from Harl. It was a familiar sight for Catherine, and she pointed out the various places to Clair as they rode.

"Look at the pretty apple trees," Catherine exclaimed as the mules tramped along a path that cut through the family apple orchard on the outskirts of the property. Catherine reached out and picked an apple. She held it to her nose.

"Mmm." Offering the apple to Clair, she said, "Take a whiff of that sweet apple."

"I think she'd rather eat it than smell it." Harl smiled. Catherine returned his smile and sighed deeply. It was good to be coming home.

"Go ahead, honey." Clair bit into the skin of the apple. "Isn't that good?"

Clair nodded. "It's good."

"Here, let Mommy have some."

Clair held the apple up to her mother, and Catherine took a large bite.

"Mmm, that is good. Look at all these apples. Looks like they are ready to pick."

"I'm doing the best that I can."

"What? Is it just you trying to get this crop in?"

"For now, it is. I plan to hire help."

Coming out from among the rows of trees, Catherine spotted the familiar two-story, white clapboard house peeping around the corner of the last tree. "Look at the house," she said as the valley opened up before them. "This is the house your mama grew up in."

Catherine kissed the top of Clair's head and looked at her childhood home. The house had a well in the front yard and a variety of colorful rose bushes lining the front porch. Pink climbing roses, in full bloom, twisted their long stems up the plain porch pillars.

Catherine's mother, Hazel—a middle-aged, heavy-set woman—came out onto the porch as they pulled up alongside the steps.

"Catherine," her mother cried holding out her arms to her daughter.

Catherine climbed down and fell into her arms. "Oh, Mama, what am I going to do without him?" She let the tears fall freely.

"It was the same for me when your father died on his way to the war. The Lord'll help you through this. Just take each day as it comes."

Catherine swiped at her eyes with her fingers. "I know He will."

"Don't you worry about it. You're home now, and that's what matters."

Turning to the little girl hugging a rag doll, her mother said, "And this must be Clair."

Clair smiled and held her doll out for her grandmother to see.

"Well, what a fine dolly you have. You want to come see your grandma?"

Clair reached out her arms toward her grandmother, who picked her up.

"Is this your house? Where you live? Are we going to stay with you?"

"Yes, honey. This is my house, where I live. And you're going to stay with me. Y'all come in. Supper is ready."

Inside the home, Catherine looked around. Not much had changed since the last time she was there. The porch led directly into the yellow-painted kitchen—a room happily decorated with shelves and cupboards, a wood-burning stove in one corner, and a table and chairs in the center of the room. The kitchen led into the formal sitting room, which led into a hallway, off of which were two bedrooms. At the end of the hall was a steep stairway that led to a landing and two small bedrooms. The room on the left was Catherine's old bedroom.

Her mother and father's bedroom was across the hall from the sitting room, and Harl's room sat further back in the house just before the stairs. As Catherine passed Harl's room, she glanced into it and saw it was piled high with newspapers surrounding an unmade bed, a table, and a single chair. Harl quickly moved to shut the door.

"Why do you keep all that?"

He scowled and opened his mouth, but his mother cut him off.

"Now, don't you two start. I don't want any arguing. Leave Harl be. I'm just glad he came home from the war safe and sound."

Catherine walked up the steep staircase to the room on the left. Her mother followed her carrying Clair on her hip. "Harl moved a little bed in here in case you wanted to have her close."

"Thank you."

Catherine looked at the two small beds situated near each other in the room as tears rolled down her cheeks. "Oh, Mama," was all she was able to say before a fresh bout of sobs overtook her.

Standing Clair on the floor, her mother opened her arms, and Catherine stepped into them. "Oh, my poor baby. I know it's hard. I had a time after Harl sent word that your father died. Shot through the heart on his way to sign up for the North. I didn't know how I was going to go on without him, but I have gone on these past seven years. I kept myself busy so's I didn't have time to grieve. The Lord'll give you strength to go on. His Word says in 2 Corinthians chapter twelve verse ten, 'When I am weak, then am I strong.' You'll get that teaching job and busy yourself with them young'uns, and that is how you'll go on."

Catherine nodded in agreement and placed her head on her mother's shoulder. "It's so good to be home."

"It's good to have you two here."

Clair bounced over to the smallest bed and sat down. "It's nice here," she said as she danced Mary on the bed.

"There's a good little lamb. Well, I've got dinner cooking. We'll eat after you freshen up. I opened the two windows trying to freshen the room."

"It helped."

The room still smelled musty—a familiar, pleasant scent. Besides the two beds, the room held a low chest and a wardrobe—both of which her father had made—plus a side table with a gray, granite pitcher, water basin, and cotton towels. Off to one side of the furthest back window sat a rocking chair.

Catherine sighed contentedly. It had been years since she had been home—before Clair was born. *Would her mother accept Clair if she knew what Catherine and John had done?*

Chapter 1

Catherine carried Clair downstairs and into the kitchen. She set the girl down and sniffed the air.

"You smell that, honey? That's some of Grandma's roast chicken and fresh bread." Catherine tied on an apron and turned to her mother. "What can I do to help?"

"Set the table. Everything's almost ready."

Catherine set four places at the table and poured a glass of milk for Clair. She sat Clair at the table and gave her the milk to drink. "There, now, that's some fresh milk from Grandma's cows."

Clair drank deeply of the milk, which formed a thick, white mustache on her upper lip. Catherine laughed and wiped it away with the corner of her apron and planted a kiss firmly on top of the child's head. For a moment, she felt like her old self before John died. *He should be here with us.* The emptiness in her heart stung. There was no refusing it. She busied herself by helping her mother set the food on the table.

Catherine and her mother were just taking their seats when Harl walked in. He pulled off his work gloves and hat and hung them on a peg and shelf beside the door. When he saw the table with all the food, he said, "Looks and smells delicious as always, Ma."

Harl sat at the head of the table, folded his hands under his chin, and bowed his head.

"Catherine, you feel up to saying grace?" her mother asked.

"Yes, I'll say grace, Mama."

Everyone bowed their heads. Clair interlocked her fingers and folded her hands under her chin like her uncle had done.

"Dear Lord, thank You for all the blessings You have given us . . . for life . . . and health and dear loved ones. Thank You for this food. Bless the hands that prepared it, and bless it to the nourishment and strength of our bodies. In Jesus' name, amen."

Her mother passed Catherine the mashed potatoes and a long knife and fork to Harl. "If you'd do the honor of carving the chicken. Can't nobody carve a chicken like Harl."

Catherine shrugged and held her plate, waiting for him to place carved chicken breast on it.

As Harl carved, he raised his eyes to his sister's. "I sure was sorry to hear about John dying the way he did."

Catherine's elbows slipped, and her plate clattered onto the table. She looked at Clair, who was stuffing mashed potatoes and peas in her mouth and didn't seem to take any notice.

Her brother laid a large piece of breast meat on his sister's plate. "Sorry."

After a few minutes' silence, their mother spoke. "I'm so glad the school board is considering you for the teacher position. Ms. Whittaker up and quit to get married a month ago, and we haven't had a teacher since. With a new term getting ready to start, it seems like a good time to get one."

Catherine smiled at her mother and chewed her food thoughtfully. She was eighteen when she had entered Millersburg Female College to get her teaching certificate. She had attended only one semester before John came home from the war. *Would that be enough to teach a roomful of students? What would it be like to have a job? To be required to show up early and stay late and plan lessons?* The thought scared and enthralled her all at the same time.

What questions will the board ask when I meet with them later tonight? How will I plan lessons? She had taken one semester of a Normal course at Millersburg. Would that be enough? She still had her primers from her school years. That would help. There were things she learned over the years that she wanted to share with others. It was a start.

This job would be just the thing I need to have a fresh start. Wouldn't John be proud of me? Tears welled in her eyes at the thought. But she would rather have had a life with John than to have to make a life for herself and Clair without him.

"You know, Samuel Harris is on the school board," her mother said, lifting her eyes to Catherine.

"I know he is. We saw him at the train station this afternoon."

Her mother nodded. "He's a good soul. Been our pastor these few years. It was awful hard on him when he lost Isabella last year. Died of complications carrying their child."

"I remember. You wrote me about it," Catherine said. How well she remembered Isabella Green—her rival for the attentions of the handsome Samuel Harris. As girl crazy as he'd been, Catherine was surprised he'd taken and passed the education and exams for the ministry, but Isabella probably helped steady him over their years of marriage. She had been good for him; there was no denying it.

She just wished she had been that solid source of comfort and delight for him. *What a thought,* she scolded herself. John had been a good schoolmate, too, and more than a proper fit as her husband.

He had been quite handsome with his golden, curly hair and blue eyes. He'd been a quiet man, who enjoyed a good joke from time to time and who "only had eyes for her," he'd told her. She believed him. There was no reason not to.

They had been happy together. Then why had the Lord allowed the accident? John knew the job was a dangerous one, riding logs down the Cumberland River. It was the best paying, too. *We would have had enough money to buy our own place if John just wouldn't have slipped off and fallen between the logs.* Shaking her head, she looked over at Clair and marveled at her. "Thank You, Lord, for giving me Clair and my mother and Harl," she breathed in quiet prayer.

Later, after the dishes were done, Catherine and her mother sat back down at the table. Catherine's mother poured tea, filling each of their delicate china cups. Clair sat nearby playing with her rag doll and empty, wooden thread spools on the floor.

"Let's go for a walk," Clair said to her doll. "All right." Taking the dolls hands in hers, she bounced the doll's legs along the floor as she circled the table.

The two women sat in silence for several moments sipping their tea and watching Clair. Catherine's mother finally broke the calm. "Have you given any thought to how you'll handle troublemakers in the classroom?"

"I don't expect there will be any. Why would there be?"

"Not everyone wants their children to learn, and not every child wants to learn."

Catherine raised her eyebrows. "Why not?"

"Children get to learning and growing, and opportunities present themselves. There are those who would want their family to stay ignorant so as to keep them down, so to speak. We're a farming community with plenty of folks who never had formal training."

"I don't believe that. I mean, I don't want to believe that."

"I didn't want to believe it either. As me and your father were growing up here in school together, not everyone sent their children to school. How would you change their minds if you ran into a situation like that?"

Catherine pressed her lips tightly together and mulled over the question before answering. "Present the facts about what an education could mean to the youngster—and to their family if they had a relative that could read and do arithmetic and such."

Her mother poured a little more tea in her cup and sat back. "Well, keep this in mind when you go to see the board tonight. Harl said he'd drive you to the meeting when you're ready to go. And he'll wait the whole time you're in the interview."

"Well, I certainly hope so, or it will be a long walk home." Catherine laughed.

At a quarter to eight, Harl walked into the kitchen and announced the wagon was ready. "You know, you could have just let Sam come out and pick you up."

Catherine brushed the remark aside and kissed Clair goodbye. "You be a good girl and mind Grandma."

"I will," Clair said, nodding her head and holding up her doll for a kiss. Catherine planted a kiss on Mary's cheek.

Outside, Harl helped Catherine up onto the wagon seat. He sat hunched over as he took up the reins and shook them. The mules walked briskly. In no time, they were back in town.

Harl glanced at Catherine. "You, ah, going to be all right tonight?"

"Yes. What do you mean?"

"I mean, with everything being so fresh. I wouldn't want you to . . . you know . . . start crying in front of the board."

"I feel fine. I'm more nervous than anything, and that keeps the tears at bay."

When they arrived at Maude Harris' home, Harl helped his sister down off the wagon. Catherine pulled her shawl closer to her against the chill of the night and walked up the path that led to Maude Harris' home. She knocked softly and waited. Samuel opened the door. "Right on time. Good, good, very good," he said as the clock in the parlor struck eight times. "Won't you come in, Mrs. Reed?" Samuel said, gesturing her into the foyer.

He was taller than Catherine by a head. She looked up at his dark, wavy hair and blue eyes—eyes like a clear sky on a sunny day. She managed a weak smile at her old school chum and sometime love interest—though their love had been as watered down as weak tea. Why she thought of that, she wasn't sure. And there was the smile she remembered so vividly—his crooked smile—something she had loved.

Catherine stepped into the immense foyer of Maude Harris' home. She marveled at the oak, open stairway that led to the second level. In front of her, the hallway ran the length of the house and emptied into a room lit by the glow of firelight. Off to the right and left were enormous, oak sliding doors.

"This way." Samuel directed her to the doors to the right and slid them open. Inside, the room was lit warmly by a fire in a small, white, marble hearth. Kerosene lamps illuminated dark corners. Several men stood around the room across from a petite, gray-haired woman seated on a black walnut, horsehair couch. Across from the couch sat a chair. "Here you are," Samuel said, holding the chair for Catherine, who sat. *Ever the gentleman.*

Limping behind the couch, Samuel introduced each person. "You remember my mother, Maude," he said, gesturing to the gray-haired woman. "And my brothers, Caleb and Benjamin." He directed Catherine's attention across the room to two equally handsome men, each standing with an elbow propped up on the small hearth above the crackling fire.

Catherine smiled and nodded.

"And this fine gentleman here is Henry Frazier, our town's stable livery owner." The white-haired man rolled an unlit cigar around in his mouth as he studied Catherine. "And I don't think you know our doctor, Robert Johnson. He came to town after you moved away. But I'm sure you remember our grocer, Elijah Grant."

With a nod from Catherine, the interview began.

Samuel took a seat next to his mother on the couch and said solemnly, "So, you've come about the job."

Catherine nodded as she said softly, "Yes." Then as if remembering something, she looked at her hands on her lap. Her cheeks grew pink as she studied the backs of her clasped hands.

Samuel studied Catherine's face—or what he could see of it. She was still the pretty girl with brown hair and gray eyes that he remembered from his school days, but this shy person wasn't the Catherine he remembered. The Catherine he had fallen in love with in school had been vibrant and lively. This version was solemn and quiet as if waiting for something terrible to happen to her.

"We won't bite," he said gently, leaning forward.

Catherine snapped her head up to look at the man seated across from her. His blue eyes crinkled as he smiled, and one side of his mouth turned up further than the other.

His gaze was overwhelming and intense. It seemed to burn into her soul. She averted her eyes back to her folded hands. She felt her cheeks flame hotter. Maybe answering the Harrisville board's advertisement for a school teacher wasn't the right thing to do. *What do I know about teaching other than what I learned that first semester at Millersburg?* She had been an outstanding student back in her school days, but that was years ago. *How could I ever stand up to the scrutiny of the board?*

She ventured a look at the others scattered around the room. Each one eyed her with particular interest. Catherine's nose itched, but she didn't dare scratch it for fear of drawing more scrutiny.

"Now then," Samuel said, leaning forward, "tell us why you want to teach the children at Harrisville School. What qualifications do you have?"

Catherine studied her hands and then gingerly lifted her head. She cleared her throat and looked at each of the board members before answering.

"I attended Millersburg Female College for one semester. I studied teaching there."

"Oh, yes, Millersburg. In Georgetown?"

"Yes, that's right."

"But only one semester? Why is that?" Maude asked.

"Well, John Reed . . . my beau . . . at the time . . . well, he was wounded in the war. So, I came home for Christmas break. And we married a month later."

"When was that?" Benjamin asked.

"January the tenth."

"Yes, I remember that day," Samuel said.

"I love children and want to teach them to learn to read and write. I'm teaching my daughter, Clair, how to read, and she's only four."

Samuel nodded in agreement. The other board members looked at her warmly, and she sat up straighter.

"I took all of the finishing exams and passed those when I was in school with Samuel," she said, nodding toward him.

"Quite right, quite right. I remember you were one of the better students in our class."

Catherine nodded in agreement. Samuel raked his hand through his dark hair and smiled encouragingly.

"Go on, dear," Samuel's mother said, gazing intently at her. She opened her hands toward the woman seated across from her.

There was no holding back. If she wanted the job, she would need to prove she could do it. Since she didn't have experience or a normal school degree—only one semester—she would have to rely on her past as a student to prove her future worth as a teacher.

"I won spelling bees and received ribbons for participation in memorization programs in the community." She cleared her throat and tucked her feet under the chair. "I want to teach because I want to instill a love of learning in children—a love that they will hopefully carry with them throughout life."

She paused and looked around the room. The flat gazes that she had been met with when she first started speaking were replaced by warm expressions and smiles.

"There now. That wasn't so bad, was it?" Samuel laughed, leaning back on the couch.

"What about your discipline methods?" asked Henry Frazier, who had seated himself in a wingback chair near the couch. The older, balding man with wispy, white hair stared with eyebrows pinched tightly together at the young woman across from him as he waited for her answer.

"To be honest, I had not given discipline much thought."

"Well, give it some thought now," said Benjamin, stepping forward. "What will you do with unruly children?"

Catherine examined the ceiling. Before answering, she swallowed and licked her lips. She didn't believe in punishment. Many times, she had to redirect Clair away from an activity that could potentially cause her to get into trouble. Clair readily obeyed her parents. The only form of discipline that came to mind was what her former teacher inflicted on his students when they were out of line. "Well, I wouldn't use the cane. Like what we had when we were growing up." She nodded toward Samuel. "I would set them in a corner with their back to the room and make them stand there until I felt the punishment served the offense."

"Would you allow parents to come see what you are teaching their children?" Elijah Grant asked.

"Yes, of course. Parents would always be welcome in my classroom—to come see what I am teaching."

"And what about harvest time? What would you do then? The boys couldn't continue, but the girls could. How would you make sure the boys kept up with their education when they are away from school?" Doctor Johnson asked.

"I haven't given that much thought. The boys would have their school books. I could assign them work to do."

"I'm not sure they would have time to do it what with helping their parents from sun up 'til sun down," the doctor replied.

"Then they will just have to catch up when they return."

A corporate sigh sounded around the room.

Samuel nodded vigorously. "Good, good. Any more questions?" he asked after several moments of silence.

Gazing around the room, Catherine saw the board members smile and shake their heads. She breathed a sigh and relaxed her shoulders. "I have a question," she ventured.

Samuel turned his gaze fully to her. "Go on."

"How many more applicants were there?"

"Just you," Henry Frazier piped up.

Catherine nodded, affirming her understanding. Had she convinced the board of her qualifications to teach the children at Harrisville School? Would she make a good teacher? It all fell into the board's hands.

Samuel stood and limped over to her. He waved his hand, indicating she should follow him back out into the foyer. Samuel slid the heavy doors shut behind them.

He rubbed his dark hair as they walked toward the front door. He had a strong jawline, and his long eyelashes matched the color of his hair—something she didn't remember from years past. He still was as handsome as ever, though a little more aged. She wondered about the limp. Questioning him about it could be saved for another time.

Samuel broke the silence. "It's been good seeing you again," he said softly.

Their eyes met briefly before she turned away.

Samuel walked her outside.

"I see Harl's been waiting for you. I hope we didn't keep you too long."

"No, he's fine, I'm sure. When will I know anything?"

"We will be in touch," he said.

"Well, good evening, then."

"Good evening, Mr. Harris." With that, Catherine walked down the steps and climbed onto the wagon next to Harl.

"Evening, Harl."

"Evening, Preacher Harris." Harl touched a finger to the brim of his hat and then jiggled the reins, and the mules set off at a slow pace.

Inside the foyer, Samuel closed the door tightly and stood for a moment with his hand pressed on it. Her scent lingered in the entranceway, and he wanted to drink it in. It reminded him of something flowery—*a very pleasing aroma for a woman.* There was nothing improper about her scent. She didn't lavish on perfumes or powders. She had an essence all her own. How he wished that aroma would linger longer, but these kinds of thoughts weren't proper for a preacher.

Limping into the parlor, he left the sliding doors open. "So, what do you make of her?"

"A bit nervous, but I like her," Caleb said, brushing his fingers through his dark hair like his brother.

"She was very nervous, wasn't she," Benjamin said, shifting his weight.

"Henry?" Samuel asked, looking across to the man seated in the wingback chair.

"I don't think she's right for the job—too flighty for my tastes—and she doesn't have a proper degree."

"Proper degree." Samuel snorted. "None of us but Doc Johnson and me has a proper degree, and yet we run this town. She has the qualities we are looking for in a teacher—someone who is of high moral character, likes children, and wants to teach them. And it doesn't hurt that she started in school to become a teacher."

"Yes, why did she stop?" Maude asked.

"Her and John got married. She didn't have time to finish a normal school education."

"But she could have continued."

"No, not being married she couldn't. Besides, even if she would have continued, who would have hired a married woman as a teacher?"

"That's true. Most boards require a single person with no romantic connections to teach their children."

"Yes, I see."

"But there is more to it than just letting her loose on this town's children," Frazier said.

"We haven't had another applicant. She's the best we have on short notice," Doctor Johnson offered.

"Short notice," Samuel echoed. "We've had that advertisement in the paper for months now."

"What about offering her the position on a trial basis?" Benjamin piped up. "This way, we'll see what she's made of."

"I think that is best," Elijah chimed in.

"Would you agree to offer her the position if we gave it to her on a trial basis?" Samuel asked Frazier.

"Yes, I would vote for her then."

"Are we all in agreement?" Samuel asked, looking from face to face. Each person nodded.

"Then I'll go see her bright and early tomorrow morning and let her know she has the position on a trial basis. When will the trial end, though?"

"When we are each satisfied that she is teaching our youngsters something they could not learn on their own," his mother asserted.

"Such as . . . "

"Reading, writing, arithmetic. Maybe she could get up a spelling bee or a recital as one way to prove that she is competent to teach our youth."

Samuel slapped his good leg hard. "Very good, then. I'll let her know in the morning what we require of her."

"You being the pastor of the town and living next door to the school, I'm sure she wouldn't mind you keeping abreast of her doings. There's always that back room we built on for a male teacher to live at the school. You could make that into your study and keep watch over her and the class. That way, she wouldn't actually know what you were doing," Frazier said.

"I'll think about it. With my home so close to the school, keeping an eye on her won't be a problem."

After a few moments of silence, the board said good night to each other. Maude walked each person to the door. But she held Samuel back from leaving.

"I remember you were sweet on Catherine long before Isabella came to town. What happened between the two of you that made you court Isabella instead of Catherine?"

"So many things got in the way."

"Like what?"

"Two words. John Reed. He cut in on our friendship before I got around to asking Catherine if she wanted to be my girl; and then Isabella came to town, and the rest is history." His mother studied him.

"Yes, but have you gotten over Isabella? Are you ready to move on?"

Samuel sighed. "Are you over Father?"

His mother shook her head. "You never get over a thing like that. He was a good father and a good husband. Still can't believe he's gone these nine years. Sometimes I wake up in the middle of the night expecting him to be beside me." Shaking her head, she gazed up at her son. "Just tread lightly. Catherine just lost her husband. Be a friend to her before anything else—like you used to be."

"I'll try. That's the best I can do." He bent and kissed her cheek lightly. "Good night, Mother."

Chapter 3

In the morning, Catherine rose early and found Clair seated on her bed watching her. "Oh, honey, weren't you able to sleep?" she asked, changing her out of her nightgown and into her play clothes.

"No, I had a bad dream." Clair shook her head and rubbed her eyes as she allowed her mother to dress her.

"Oh? What about?"

"Daddy—he was in the ground, and they were throwing dirt on him. I couldn't reach him."

"Oh, honey." Catherine hugged the child to her. "I know." Her voice cracked, and she let the tears wash over her face.

"But remember, Daddy's in Heaven with Jesus, and no one's throwing dirt on him now."

Catherine wiped the back of her hand over her face. "Let me get dressed, and we'll go downstairs and help Grandma make our breakfast? How does that sound?"

"And we'll make pancakes?"

"Maybe, but it smells like she already has breakfast underway."

In the kitchen, her mother scooped butter into a large, iron skillet. As the butter melted in the hot pan, she mixed together the ingredients for pancakes. A sauce pan of brown sugar and water bubbled on the back of the stove.

"Mmm, smells good. What are you making?" Catherine asked, tying on an apron.

"Pancakes and brown sugar syrup."

"You hear that, Clair? Grandma is making you pancakes."

"Thank you, Grandma," the child said, wrapping her arms around the older woman's large waist. "I love you, Grandma."

"I love you, too, Child," she said, wrapping her arms around the little girl.

"Smells delicious."

"How did the meeting go last night? I meant to ask you, but you dragged in here late."

"Harl decided to take the long way home so I could get a better glimpse of the property lines and such."

"So, what did you think?"

"I think Harl's right. He'll need several men to help him with the orchard and the cattle. There's just too much for one man to do it all on his own."

Her mother sighed. "No, I meant with the school and the board. What did they ask you?"

Catherine sat Clair at the table and placed apples in front of her. Taking a gray, enameled pan off a shelf and a knife from a drawer, Catherine began peeling the apples. "They asked why I wanted to teach."

"And what did you say?" Hazel said, turning to watch her daughter.

"That I want to instill a love of learning in the children of Harrisville and that I feel I have a lot to offer them."

"So, did they give you the job on the spot?"

"No, they didn't. Should they have?" Was there cause to worry that she had not been offered the job? That her coming back to Harrisville was for a home only and not a job, too? She peeled the apple skins into long strips, which Clair ate. Slicing the apples, she handed the pan to her mother, who added some water to a skillet and slid the apples into it.

"I'm sure you got the job, honey. How could you not have? But let's not think any more on it until you hear from the board one way or another."

Her mother fried the batter and set a stack of pancakes on the table in front of the girls. As they ate, Catherine asked, "Where's Harl?"

"Out in the barn. He'll be in as soon as he smells my cooking."

Before Catherine finished eating her stack of hot cakes, Harl came into the kitchen.

"Smells good, Ma."

Their mother set a stack of hot cakes in front of Harl and added some fried apples on top of his, then drenched it all with the brown sugar syrup.

"Horsey," Clair said, pointing toward the door.

In the distance was the faint sound of hoofs clomping through the orchard.

"Sounds like we've got company." Her mother looked at Catherine. "It must be good news, or they'd come on faster."

Catherine smiled weakly. Her heart beat fast, and her hands shook. She clasped her hands in her lap to calm her nerves and waited for the rider to approach.

Her mother and Harl stepped onto the porch and waited.

"It's Samuel Harris," her mother called through the open door. "Mornin', Preacher Harris."

"Mornin'," he called back.

Catherine watched as Harl stepped off the porch and held the head of Samuel's horse as he swung off it. Harl threw the reins around one of the pillars as his mother invited the preacher into the house. "I hope you came hungry. We have hot cakes."

"Mmm, that's what smells so good. I wouldn't say no to a couple. Is Catherine here?"

"She is. Come on in." Mother ushered the preacher into the kitchen, where Catherine was cutting up a pancake on her daughter's plate.

He took the seat offered him by Mother, who set a plate of hot cakes in front of him with a small pitcher of brown sugar syrup, a plate of butter, and a bowl of fried apples.

Samuel helped himself to the syrup and butter as he watched Catherine.

Surely, he must have good news, or he wouldn't be so ready to accept our hospitality.

Harl returned to his seat without a word and dug into his stack of hot cakes while Mother stirred up a new batch.

"Well, you must know why I'm here," Samuel said, swallowing a few bites.

Catherine glanced at him tentatively. "Yes. Did I get the job then?" she asked softly.

"You got the job. But . . . "

"But what?" She bit her lower lip.

"The board wants to give you a trial period. See how you'll do with the children first. We want you to get together a program to show the community what their children have learned. If that goes well, we'll officially offer you the position permanently."

"The board doesn't have faith in me that I'll do a good job?"

"The board is cautious. You were our only candidate, and you barely have any formal training in teaching. But we are a bit desperate for a teacher, seeing how school is about to start in the next few days. We want to get someone in there right at the start of the year."

"So, if someone more qualified comes along in the meantime, I could be out of a job?"

"Not necessarily. It just depends on how you do. Harrisville isn't big enough to attract a well-qualified candidate, and we haven't time to wait for one. We'd like to have you as our teacher—if you'll have us," he said, looking into her eyes.

She raised her chin determinedly, looking Samuel square in the eye. "I would be pleased to accept the position of Harrisville teacher."

He smiled that crooked smile and thumped the table with his hand. "Good. I'll tell the board of your decision." He finished eating his pancakes. "Thank you for the hotcakes, Mrs. Adams. They sure were good."

"Anytime you want to come for a hot meal, you just come on." Mother smiled.

Samuel turned to Catherine. "I'll expect you'll want to get started preparing your lessons at the schoolhouse. I'll meet you up there this afternoon." He limped out the door and swung up onto his horse.

Catherine washed the dishes hurriedly while her mother dried them. She hummed a bit as she worked.

"Sounds like someone is excited about her new adventure."

Catherine laughed. "Is it that obvious?"

"It is to me," her mother observed. Then she added, "Well, thank the Lord He brought this opportunity into your life. It'll be good for you to get out and do something in the community. Instead of being holed up here with us."

Taking the pan of dirty dishwater outside, she threw it off the side of the porch, being careful not to get it too close to the roses. Her mother carried out the rinse pan and poured it near the rose bushes.

"Think I'll go see if Harl needs any help." Catherine hung the dishpan on the porch wall to dry, took off her apron, and headed to the barn.

The barn smelled heavily of hay, manure, and dusty animals. She spotted Harl in one of the mule's stalls. His back was to her. As she stepped through the door, she let if fall against the weathered wood with a bang.

Harl jumped and spun around, the brush in his hand raised like a knife ready to strike out at whoever made the commotion.

"Harl!" Catherine exclaimed.

Placing the brush against his chest, he asked, "What do you want? Come to scare the stuffing out of me?"

"No. I wanted to know if you needed any help out here." She studied the mules.

"Not from a woman I don't," he said crisply.

"All right." She turned to leave, but Harl called her back.

"No, wait. Here, feed the chickens," he said. Coming out of the mule's pen, he handed her a pail of cracked corn. "You do know how to feed chickens?"

Catherine stepped back. "Harl, you act as if I don't know what I'm doing on a farm. I grew up here, just like you; and just like you, I had the same chores."

"You're right. I'm sorry," Harl said, returning to the mule's pen.

Catherine stepped closer to her brother. "I understand. It's all right. John had the same problem with loud noises, too. It came on him after the war."

Harl nodded his head and continued brushing down the mule. "Just . . . don't let the door slam on your way out."

Catherine stepped out the barn door and closed it carefully, looking around for the chickens that were scattered all over the yard. "Here, chick, chick," she called as chickens from all sides of the barnyard ran toward her as she scattered the corn for them. Once that task was done, she went back into the barn, easing the door closed behind her.

"I'm done feeding the chickens," she said cheerily.

"Well, would you like to go gather the eggs then?"

Catherine collected more than two dozen eggs of varying sizes and colors.

"Some of those chickens sure are sneaky, hiding their nests the way they do," Catherine commented to her mother when she walked into the house with the basket of eggs.

"Are you sure you got all the eggs? There's one or two that I've found nest out in the apple orchard."

"Oh no, the orchard! I didn't even check there," Catherine lamented, unloading the basket of eggs into a small dishpan on the table. She went back out to find any nests in the apple orchard. Three nests and eight eggs later, she walked back into the kitchen and placed all of the eggs back in the basket.

"We'll only keep what we'll eat for today and tomorrow's breakfast. The rest, along with a full milk can, will go to Mr. Grant's store. He'll give us money for the eggs and milk, or we'll trade with him to get what we need for the farm."

Catherine nodded. "I'll go see if Harl's got the milk can ready for us."

Catherine watched as Harl lugged the heavy milk can over to the wagon. Going back into the barn, he came out with a pail of milk. Seeing Catherine, he called, "Bring me a cloth to put over this milk to keep the flies out. I'll hitch up the team, and we'll take the wagon into town. Don't want to spill Mr. Grant's precious milk. 'Sides, we've got another pail going this time."

"Well, hitch up the team, and let's be on our way," his mother instructed, stepping out onto the porch holding Clair's hand.

Harl hitched the team and helped his mother, sister, and niece into the wagon. Catherine and Clair sat on the bed of the wagon on old quilts used especially for cushion. Catherine pulled Clair onto her lap and snuggled the child close.

"We're going into town to see Mr. Grant at his store. If you're good, I'll buy you some licorice."

Harl kept the mules walking at a slow pace so as not to lose any of the precious milk as the wagon wheels lurched into deep ruts and over rocks in the road. Their mother sat on the seat next to Harl and held on for dear life. She kept looking behind her at the girls. "Now, watch out. Don't go flipping yourselves off the sides of the wagon."

"We're fine and dandy here in the middle," Catherine said. "We won't fall off. Will we, Clair?"

"No, we won't fall off. Mama's holding me." Clair giggled as the wagon dipped down into another deep rut.

At the edge of the Adams' property, just past the last apple tree, Harl turned the mules hard right and hurried them up the hill.

"This isn't the way to town," Catherine said over her shoulder.

"We have to drop a pail of milk off for the Fields family. Margaret Fields is in the family way, and she'll be needing the milk," their mother explained. "Harl, don't drive down in them ruts. Try and keep us level."

"I'm doing the best I can, Mama," Harl said.

The wagon cut its way up the side of a hill with jagged outcroppings of limestone. Catherine found herself holding on to Clair, as well as the pail of milk, as the wagon jerked and bucked slowly along.

"Take it easy, Harl, or we'll lose the milk," his mother said.

"I'm trying." He gritted his teeth. "If they'd make a road up here, it would be a heap easier."

"You know they're not going to do that," his mother said.

Finally, the wagon crested the top of the hill, where it was smoother and easier to drive. In front of them, a pretty meadow full of summer's end wild flowers—Queen Anne's lace, milkweed, and daisies—opened up. A weather-beaten, ram-shackled house, which leaned to one side, stood at the end of the meadow. Its tin roof was stained red by years of rain and sun baking it. A dirty, barefoot woman came out onto the porch followed by three equally dirty, barefoot children.

"Hello," Harl yelled, raising his hat off his head. "Hello in the house."

The woman on the porch waved her hand and said, "Hello to you, and come on."

Harl guided the mules toward them.

"Hello, Margaret." Hazel reached down to shake the woman's dirty hand.

"What brings you all the way up here?" Margaret asked.

"We brung you and your babies some milk," Hazel said, gesturing with her thumb toward the back of the wagon.

"Hey, Ma, there's a pail back here, and they brung a basket of eggs, too," the oldest child said.

"Well, don't just stand there, Easter. Take it in. Take it in and bring their basket back," Margaret instructed. "Hershel, come help your sister! And Dorthea can lend a hand, too."

Catherine opened her mouth to say something but clamped it shut seeing how dirty and thin Easter and her siblings were.

Easter and her brother, Hershel, smiled as they handed the youngest, Dorthea, the basket of eggs. She hurried into the house with it. Easter and Hershel carefully carried the pail of milk between them.

"Them are fine children you've got, Margaret," Hazel said. Margaret beamed and rubbed her dirty feet on top of one another.

"Don't I know it."

Pointing at Catherine, Hazel said, "Margaret Fields, this is my youngest—my daughter, Catherine, and her daughter, Clair."

"Pleased to meet you," Margaret beamed, moving toward the back of the wagon to shake hands. She held out her unwashed hand to Catherine, who shook it.

Easter and Hershel returned to their mother's side. Dorthea handed up the empty egg basket to Hazel and ran to stand next to the others.

"These are my young'uns. Here's Hershel, my baby boy. He's nine. And little Dorthea, she's five; and Easter, she's twelve."

"Pleased to meet you," Catherine nodded. "Will all of you be attending school when it starts in a few days?"

Margaret switched her weight from leg to leg and looked at Catherine funny. "It's a school for everyone?"

"Yes, everyone who wants to learn is welcome to attend." Would Margaret consent to let her children attend? Or would she need to explain the benefits of school and learning in general?

"Well, now, that is something. But we ain't got no books. Would books be provided?"

"I'm not sure." Catherine had her own books from her school days that she could share with the Fields' children, but would that be enough?

"Margaret, don't you worry about that. I'm sure Catherine will manage with the books she has. Won't you, Catherine?" her mother asked, turning to look at her daughter.

"I'll do my best."

With the empty milk pail and egg basket back in the wagon, Harl moved the mules along. When they were out of earshot, their mother spoke. "Well, it does me good to see them eggs go to the Fields. They needed it as sure as not. Mr. Grant is usually run over with eggs from folks, so he won't be hurting if ours aren't there this time. We sure do have more things to worry about than a basket full of eggs."

Chapter 4

At Elijah Grant's mercantile store in town, Catherine and her mother marveled over the pretty bolts of blue cloth.

"Would you look at this robin's egg color? And look at this deep blue one," her mother said. It wouldn't do for Catherine to wear anything other than black out of respect for her husband, but Clair should have something new. Maybe a dark blue cotton cloth would help keep her looking fresh when she was at play. Mrs. Tippy Grant cut enough material for a pretty dress and a bonnet for Clair.

"This certainly will bring out the blue in her eyes," Tippy said, nodding at Clair.

Catherine smiled at the woman. "Yes, it will."

She turned toward Clair, who was eyeing the candy counter. "You want some licorice?"

Clair nodded but didn't take her eyes off the jar of candy.

Mr. Grant approached. "So, have you made up your mind, little lady?" he asked Clair.

She nodded and pointed. "I want that one."

"We'll take a penny's worth of the black licorice, thank you." Catherine dug a coin out of her reticule and handed it to the man behind the counter, who gave her a small bag with black licorice whips poking out the top.

"Mmm, licorice. Those are the best tasting, but I'm partial to the peppermint sticks," Tippy said, leaning down and whispering loudly in Clair's ear. "Let me get this wrapped for you," she said, holding the cloth.

Turning to Catherine, Elijah said, "I'm so glad we have you as our new teacher."

Catherine smiled in response.

"New teacher?" a woman's voice behind Catherine said. She turned. Behind her stood a small, delicate-looking woman with light brown hair and glasses. The woman held out her hand. Catherine shook it.

"I'm Gladys Richardson, and I'm pleased as punch to meet you. Are you really our new teacher?"

"What's this? We have a new teacher?" said a tall woman with a squeaky voice, who was looking through the bolts of cloth.

"Yes," Gladys nodded. "And here she is. I'm sorry. I didn't catch your name."

"Oh, I'm Catherine Reed. Mrs. Catherine Reed."

The tall woman came forward, followed by two lanky girls.

"I'm Dosha Clark," she said, coughing into a handkerchief. "And these two are my girls. Minnie and Minerva. They'll be in your class whenever school starts."

"I'm pleased to meet you." A warm smile spread over Catherine's face. "We'll be starting in a couple of days."

Minnie and Minerva looked at each other and smiled. "It'll be nice to get to go to school again," Minerva, the tallest of the two, said. Minnie nodded.

Her mother stepped up beside Catherine and took her elbow. "It was nice seeing you all," she said. "We best be going. Harl will be waiting."

Outside, Harl loaded all their purchases into the back of the wagon and headed the mules toward home.

As they drove, their mother pointed out the school to Catherine.

"That's where you'll be teaching," she said.

"Harl, stop and let me have a look. I'm aching to see inside the school. I'm supposed to meet Samuel here this afternoon. Mama, can you watch Clair for me?"

Harl pulled the reins back, and the mules came to a stop.

"Well, sure."

Catherine hugged Clair and handed her up to her mother. Hazel set the child between her and Harl.

"Now, you be a good girl for Grandma."

Clair smiled, her teeth blackened by the candy. "I will. You want some candy, Grandma?"

"Why, sure."

"Uncle Harl, you want some?"

Harl took one. "You don't want us to wait for you?" he asked.

"No, I'll walk the rest of the way home."

She watched them drive away and then stepped lightly up to the door of the whitewashed, clapboard schoolhouse and tried the doorknob. The door swung open. She stepped inside. The building was hot in the end-of-summer sun. The only form of ventilation were six windows—three on the east side and three on the west—but the windows were closed against the mounting heat of the day.

The schoolhouse smelled of dusty floorboards and was a bit musty. The scent wasn't anything that couldn't be rectified by opening a few windows to let in some fresh air.

She noticed rows of square nails driven into the building. One set was on one side, and another set was on the other wall next to the door so that the children would have a place on which to hang their hats and coats come wintertime.

Her feet squeaked on the plank flooring as she stepped further into the building. Wooden benches sat in neat rows. Here was where the students would sit. Ahead of her on the wall behind the teacher's desk was a large blackboard with plenty of room on which to write. In the middle of the room stood a potbellied stove. It would be put to good use in the colder winter months when the snow was deep.

"The first thing I'll do when I teach here is to open these windows and get some fresh air in here," Catherine said, placing her hands on her hips.

"The first thing?" A deep voice repeated from behind her.

Whirling around, she saw Samuel Harris, who stepped inside the door with hat in hand. He smiled at her. Catherine caught herself smirking as she gave Samuel's face the once-over.

"Well, maybe not the very first thing, but close to it."

"And then what? What comes next?" he asked, stepping further into the room.

She turned and faced the blackboard at the front of the room again. "I'll write lessons on the board for the children to copy and follow along with."

"What about those students who don't have slates to copy down lessons? How can they learn?" She heard his footsteps squeak on the floorboards as he moved closer to where she stood.

Catherine bit her lower lip and pinched her brows. She thought back to the Fields. They wouldn't have money to buy slates or books nor would they have enough even to just buy pencils for their slates. "I haven't given it much thought. I guess those children will have to memorize their lessons instead of writing them down," Catherine said, turning toward him. She placed her hand at her neck and bit her lower lip but held Samuel's gaze, even though her eyes were clouded with thought.

"I think there will be plenty of things that you haven't thought of. Things that will surprise and alarm you."

Catherine's eyes widened, and her lips parted slightly as she gasped. Clasping her hands in front of her, she frowned.

"Don't worry," Samuel said. "My house is right there," he said, pointing out one of the windows to a simple, white, clapboard, two-story home—a perfect place for a man of the cloth. "And I'm within screaming distance," he added, chuckling.

"You really don't think I can do this, do you? You think that I'll be a bad teacher?"

"No, I think that practice makes perfect, and you will have plenty of time to practice."

Catherine scowled. "Why did you and the board agree to give me the job on a trial basis if you felt so poorly about my prospects?"

Samuel held out his hands for her to stop. "Because I know you can do it. You just need to be sure of yourself is all."

Catherine studied his words for a moment and wondered if the board's support was behind her one hundred percent, or if, like Samuel, they were holding onto doubt. If she was honest with herself, she doubted some of her skills as a teacher, too. How could she become a better teacher if not through trial and error? She would give it her best, which is as much as anyone could hope or ask. Besides, she had one semester of a normal school education under her belt. Would that be enough?

Samuel studied her face with her pink cheeks and lovely, ivory skin. He wished he could reach out and touch her cheek, let her know that he had faith in her, but it would be improper for the town preacher to touch a woman. Turning his gaze away from her and back to the front of the room, he pointed out the teacher's desk.

"Came all the way from Lexington," he said, moving forward.

Catherine nodded, acknowledging the desk.

"It's got a bunch of drawers. See?" Samuel said, pulling one out and then jumping back as a green garter snake slithered out and plopped under the desk.

Catherine screamed and jumped onto the nearest bench, which she almost knocked over. "Get it out! Get it out!" she yelled.

The just-as-frightened snake coiled around the leg of the desk and tried to duck out of sight. Samuel ran out the door carrying the drawer with him.

"Come back here and get this snake out of here!" she screeched. "I can't stand it. I can't stand snakes."

Samuel rushed back into the room with a long stick, the drawer still in his hand. "It's just as scared of you as you are of it," he countered.

"I don't care; you get rid of that thing this instant," Catherine yelled, holding her skirts up just above the tops of her boots.

Carefully, Samuel picked the snake up with the stick and tried to place it back in the drawer.

"What are you doing? That thing will bite you," Catherine yelled, her voice growing hoarse from all her screaming.

"No, it won't. It's just a common garter snake. They're not venomous. Look." Samuel held the drawer and stick up for her to inspect the snake, which caused Catherine to stamp her feet and scream more.

She watched as Samuel took the snake outside to let it go. When he returned, Catherine was waiting for him a bit calmer, but still standing, with her skirts pulled up, on the bench.

After replacing the drawer in her desk, Samuel examined the other drawers for more surprises. Finding none, he held out his hand to help her down from her perch. She took it. When her feet were on solid ground again, she gazed around the room.

"I expect you'll want to get yourself settled in your classroom before school starts in a few days."

"Yes. It seems a bit dusty and could use a good once-over."

"It's not that dusty. We use it for Sunday services, too."

"Do you have a broom and dustpan?"

"Yes, there in the corner by the door." Catherine turned her eyes to where Samuel pointed and saw a straw broom and dust pan.

"What about a scrub brush and bucket?"

"Don't have those, I'm afraid," he said.

"Then I'll just walk home and get them. I'm sure Mama won't mind me borrowing hers."

Catherine moved toward the door, followed by Samuel. "I could hitch up the buggy and take you there quicker."

"No, it's a fine day, and I don't mind the walk. It'll do me good."

"Well, then, allow me to escort you home and back."

"Won't your leg bother you?"

"Yes, but the doctor said it was good for me to stretch it out every so often."

Catherine scowled. "I doubt walking as far as the farm can be good for you."

Samuel only smiled in answer and combed his hair back from his face with his hand.

By late afternoon, Samuel and Catherine had returned to the school. Catherine started at the front of the room and swept the dust toward the back door. Samuel sat at the teacher's desk rubbing his leg.

"Sunday morning, we'll move the teacher's desk into the back room and pull out the pulpit. Here, let me show you." Standing, he limped over to a door at the front of the room and opened it.

Inside was a small bed, covered with hand-made quilts; a bedside table with a white wash basin; and a chest of drawers, on top of which sat an oil lamp. In the corner of the room, there was a small, white-washed pulpit with a large, wooden cross on the front. There was another door facing north, which Catherine guessed led outside.

"This would have been your room if you didn't have a place to stay, or we could have boarded you out to community members."

Catherine surveyed the small, sparsely furnished room and smiled. The board had thought of everything—even building a room for a teacher. The room would be too small for her and Clair but would be the perfect size for a single teacher without any children.

Back out in the school room, Catherine finished sweeping and then began scrubbing the floor.

"Careful with that water," Samuel admonished. "We don't want our floor warping."

"There. That should do it." She poured the dirty water out the front door and brushed stray hairs away from her face as she stood in the doorway listening. Somewhere up the hill behind the school, a whippoorwill called; crickets chirped; and cicadas buzzed in the humid air as the light in the sky faded.

"I best be getting home, or Mama will wonder what's become of me."

"It's getting too dark to walk alone. I'll hitch up the buggy and take you. It's too far for me to walk it twice in one day."

"That would be nice. Thank you."

When the buggy was hitched, Samuel helped Catherine climb into it and handed her the brush and bucket.

When they were both situated in the buggy, Samuel chirruped to the horse, which trotted at a good clip until it reached the orchard.

"Remember when we used to play hide and seek among the trees?" he asked.

"And throw green apples at each other. Yes, I remember. Oh, the scolding we got from Harl. He'd run and tell Papa."

"And then we'd get another scolding from your father," he chuckled.

Samuel maneuvered the buggy close to the steps leading into the house.

"Will I see you in church on Sunday?" Samuel asked, helping her down.

"Well, of course, if the good Lord is willing, I'll be there."

Chapter 5

Sunday dawned bright and humid. Catherine dressed Clair and herself in their black crepe mourning dresses. Catherine wound her hair into a tight bun at the base of her neck and thrust two tortoise shell combs into the bun to hold stray strands in place. She gently combed Clair's curls, taking each one in turn.

Breakfast was a hurried affair—toasted bread and jam. Catherine sniffed the air as she ate.

"Smells good, Mama. What's cooking?"

"That's for our lunch. I've got a beef roast, complete with potatoes, onions, cabbage, and carrots straight from the garden."

After eating, Hazel hurried everyone into the wagon. Harl spread out the quilts in the back on which Catherine and Clair sat, so they would not get their clothing dirty.

When they arrived at the church, Harl pulled the wagon as far under the shade of overhanging trees as he could. He helped the women down and lagged behind as they went inside. Already, there was a crowd gathered. Families sat on benches together, while single men stood near the back and around the insides of the building.

At the front of the school—now turned church—stood the pulpit. Gone was the teacher's desk and chair. It was probably in a corner of the little back room.

"Here we are," her mother said. "Here's our spot." She moved into a row in front of Dosha Clark and her family. Turning, she greeted Dosha, who was dabbing at her face with a handkerchief. "Well, how nice to see you again, Dosha."

Dosha leaned forward, looking at Catherine. She opened her mouth just as the door to the little room at the front of the church opened. Out stepped Samuel, dressed in a black broad-cloth suit and carrying a large Bible in one hand. In the other, he held a handkerchief. Hazel instinctively turned to face the front as Samuel stepped up to the pulpit and mopped his brow and face with the handkerchief before speaking.

"It's a warm one today, brothers and sisters," he said.

A chorus of amens rose from the crowd.

"Would the brothers around the room open the windows?" he asked. Men standing near the windows obeyed. When all six of the windows were opened, Samuel raised his voice in prayer. "I thank You, Lord, for this day and for new beginnings. We pray we may be worthy of Your grace and goodness to us. In Jesus' name, amen."

Catherine studied Samuel during his prayer. She had never heard him pray or preach. What a treat this day would be for her. He appeared so solemn and serious—so unlike the cheerful friend with whom she had grown up.

Samuel raised his hands, and the congregation stood. *Just like Moses parting the Red Sea.*

"Does anyone have a song that the Lord has placed on their heart?"

Someone called out a song, and the congregation began to sing. Catherine listened as Samuel's baritone rang out over the crowd.

When the song finished, Samuel motioned for the crowd to be seated and then opened his Bible.

"In Psalm fifty-one, we read in verse seventeen, 'The sacrifices of God are a broken spirit; a broken and a contrite heart, O God, thou wilt not despise.' How many of us feel broken and have a contrite heart?" Samuel raised his hand and looked out at the hands raised in the congregation. His eyes came to rest on Catherine, who raised her hand briefly before quickly putting it back down.

"Have no fear. He sees, and He knows, and He is there for you, even in your brokenness. God is there for you."

After the sermon and just before he dismissed the congregation, he made an announcement. "As many of you know, the school board has been seeking a new teacher for our children after Miss Whittaker left us to get married earlier this year. I'm happy to report a new teacher has been found." He gestured toward Catherine, who stood and clasped her hands in front of her. She gazed briefly at the floor before turning to meet the gazes of the congregation. "This is Mrs. Catherine Reed, who has kindly agreed to fill the role of teacher for us. Thank you, Mrs. Reed."

Catherine sat down. She felt someone pat her back and turned to see Dosha smiling and nodding at her. Beside the woman, her two girls grinned, encouragingly at her.

"Next Sunday, we'll have dinner on the grounds. I'm sure each of you will bring your favorites as I might just want to sample the fare," Samuel said. Several women chortled

After he closed with prayer, Dosha patted Catherine's back again and extended her hand. "I'm so glad we got us a teacher finally," she said. "These two fine girls will be in your class tomorrow. You remember Minnie—she's twelve—and Minerva—she's fifteen." The two lanky girls blushed a deep pink and looked down. "Now, don't go getting' all shy. This here is your new teacher. Say hello, girls."

"Hello," they both said together, not taking their eyes off the floor.

Catherine was interrupted by someone else patting her arm. She turned. Gladys Richardson, the petite woman she had met in Mr. Grant's store, stood behind her. And towering over the woman stood two large boys. "These are my boys. Frank's fifteen." The tallest of the boys nodded. "And James is thirteen." James looked Catherine up and down and smiled fiendishly. "I would introduce you to their pa, Paul, but he don't cotton to church goin'."

By the time Catherine made it outside, she had met her entire class of ten students.

"Catherine, a word," Samuel called from behind her. Limping toward her, he smiled warmly. "What do you think of your students?"

"Looks to be a fine group of children."

"Should be, should be."

"I'm sorry. I have to go."

"I thought maybe you might like to get your classroom in order now that church is over. I can drive you home afterward."

"Well, let me go have some lunch, and then I'll walk back and get started on the classroom."

"You could have lunch with me. I have a roast cooking, and we could sit out of doors so it wouldn't be inappropriate," he said.

She studied him for a moment and then looked over at his home.

"I'll spread a quilt under the chestnut tree in the front yard," he said.

"All right. I'll just go let Mama and Harl know."

Outside, she caught up with her mother. "Mama, Pastor Samuel's invited me to lunch at him house. Would you mind watching Clair?"

"Not at all," she said, holding her hand out to her granddaughter. "Come on, honey. Let's go home and have some lunch."

"Are you going to Preacher's house?" Clair asked, hugging her mother's legs.

"Yes, sweetheart, I am." Catherine bent down and kissed the top of her daughter's head. "You be good for Grandma."

"I will."

Catherine waved goodbye to her family and then walked over to the front of Samuel's home, where he had spread a quilt under the chestnut tree and was carrying out two plates of food with linen napkins and silverware.

"Remember when we used to have picnics out in your orchard?" he asked, handing her a plate.

"With no thought about snakes?" She laughed, seating herself. "Yes, I remember."

"Well, we mostly sat in the trees with our lunches so we didn't have to worry about them." He handed her his plate and sat down cross-legged from her. Taking back his plate, he bowed his head. Catherine did the same. "Thank You, Lord, for friendship and fellowship and for blessing us with all things we need, including this food. In Jesus' name, amen."

"Amen," she echoed.

The plate held roast beef, boiled potatoes, and cooked spinach greens in ample portions.

"You cooked all of this?"

"Yes, why? You think I couldn't cook?"

"Most single men have people who cook for them."

"I'm not like most men."

"That you are not."

"What did you think of the sermon?" he asked, taking a bite of beef.

"I enjoyed it. Where'd you learn to preach like that?"

"I attended Collins Seminary in Cullingham, over in Bell County."

Catherine nodded as she chewed. She was acutely aware that Samuel was studying her face. Turning her head, she smiled. "It's been a long time."

"That it has. What happened to us, Cathy?"

"Two words: John Reed."

Samuel's smile didn't reach his eyes.

"He started showing an interest in me, and the rest is history."

Samuel harrumphed and then cleared his throat. They ate the rest of the meal quickly in silence.

When she finished, Samuel stood and held out his hand for her plate. "I'll be just a minute. Then we'll see about the school."

Catherine stood and folded the quilt. She placed it on a white wicker chair on his porch.

When he returned a few moments later, they walked over to the schoolhouse.

"Mighty hot day today," Samuel said. "Well, let's hurry and get your classroom in order before the day gets away."

Samuel opened the door to the school, and Catherine stepped inside. The men had left the windows open, and a slight, hot breeze stirred the dust in the room.

"Well, at least the air isn't stagnant anymore," Catherine said.

Samuel started arranging the benches in neat rows as Catherine placed the chair behind the desk.

"Looks like you had a good turnout for church," she said. "Is it always that full?"

"Sometimes. Word must have gotten around that we'd hired a new teacher, and everyone was clearly anxious to see and meet her." He smiled.

They worked in silence for several moments. Catherine sneaked a glance at Samuel. It was in this schoolroom where they had first met as schoolmates before John Reed and Isabella Green entered the picture. What a boy John had been—standing tall at the front of the class being introduced by their teacher. What was that old teacher's name? The one that used a cane to punish his pupils?

"What's wrong?" Samuel asked.

Catherine shook her head and shrugged her shoulders as her face warmed. Turning, she hurried to scoot the rest of the benches into place. "I think we're done."

Samuel hitched the buggy as Catherine stood by watching him. His profile was strong with a solid jaw line. He was clean-shaven—something that appealed to her. She felt her cheeks grow hot. *What would John think of me being taken home by the town's preacher?* She wouldn't have to wonder. Placing her hands on her warm cheeks, she closed her eyes and shook her head as if trying to dislodge her thoughts.

It had been an unseasonably warm day when John's body had been recovered. The body had got hung up in some low-hanging branches in the

Cumberland. They'd brought him back and laid him at the site where the logs had been shifted into the river.

"We pulled him out as quick as we could," the foreman, Wilber Watkins, had explained to her as she studied the body. "Used the peavey—you know, that long pole with a hook on the end—to fish him out."

"I'm so sorry you have to see him like this," the foreman continued. Why won't you stop talking? *Catherine wanted to scream.*

She stood gazing down at the lifeless, broken body of her husband. His alabaster-colored face and half-closed eyes testified that he was dead. One corner of his mouth jutted upward as if he had just told something funny and was in the process of laughing at his own joke.

He was always making jokes. She had hoped this was another one. When the wagon with Mr. Watkins came charging up the hill to their house in the camp, she had hoped to find her husband badly hurt, at worst, but this? His chest was caved in, and his legs jutted out from his body at strange angles.

Couldn't they do something about that? This isn't how this part of our story was supposed to go.

After this run on the river, they would have had enough money to buy a little farm of their own. Now, though, since John didn't complete the run, they wouldn't have enough to buy that farm they wanted. What a time to think of buying a farm.

Something wet coursed down her face. Swiping at her cheeks, she felt warm water. Why, she was crying. She needed to think of something else. Pull her attention back to the present. She studied Samuel as he worked, pushing thoughts of John from her head.

Catherine thought about teaching school tomorrow. When she got home, she'd study her readers to find appropriate lessons for all the classes of her students. She'd see how well each one could read and where they were in their lessons, so she could gauge where to start each child.

It was an enormous task, but it would keep her mind off the loss of John, and that would be a welcome relief.

If only he hadn't gotten that job as a logger on the Cumberland River. If only he hadn't slipped as he rode the logs to market. If only someone could have pulled him to safety before the logs crushed the life out of him. If only . . .

Samuel was aware she was watching his every move and wondered what she thought of him after all these years apart. He had changed, of that he was sure. He limped, thanks to a ball to the hip during the war and one in the leg during a dispute with a friend's parishioner. He carried himself much lower now that his wife, Isabella, was gone. Could he start over? Could he find love again? Is that why the Lord brought Catherine back to Harrisville, so he might find happiness again in love?

In no time, Samuel guided the buggy through the apple orchard. "Looks like Harl better get busy and start picking these apples, or they'll go bad."

"He said he's working as fast as he can, but that he needs help."

"I know some men looking for work. I could speak to them and see if they are interested and let Harl know."

"Better speak to Harl first. He might be picky as to who is out in his orchard."

"All right, I will."

At the house, Samuel helped Catherine out of the buggy. Her mother stepped out onto the porch to welcome them, wiping her hands on a flour-sack dishcloth.

Clair shot past her and bounced up to her mother. "I missed you. Did you miss me?"

Catherine chuckled. "You know I did." She tussled the girl's blonde locks.

"Well, there you are. I kept back an apple pie for you all." Turning to Samuel, she invited, "Will you come in for some apple pie?"

He cut his eyes to Catherine, who nodded.

"I can't turn down an invite, what with apple pie," he said. "Is Harl still at supper?"

"No, he's in the barn doing chores."

"I'll talk to Harl after we eat."

After two slices of apple pie, Samuel walked out to the barn. He found Harl brushing down one of the mules in its stall.

"Evening, Harl."

"Evening, Preacher."

"What a fine pair of mules."

"Yep, fine."

"Catherine told me you are in need of a man or two to help with the harvesting of the apples."

"Yes, I could do with a lot of help," Harl said, turning.

"I know of some men looking for work. I'll speak to them if you like and see if they might be interested in helping. How does that sound?"

"I would appreciate that."

"Good. I'll speak to them tomorrow; and if they are willing, I could send them over later in the day. Would that be satisfactory?"

"Sounds good. Gotta get these crops in and up to the mercantile. What Grant can't use, he'll ship down to Middlesboro." Harl went back to brushing.

"How are you faring?"

"Fine. What do you mean?" Harl turned again.

"You know I was wounded in the war, shot in the hip. Laid me up for months."

Harl studied the brush in his hand. "Some wounds you can't see."

Samuel pulled the stool for milking over to him and sat down.

"I . . . we . . . my father and I were on our way to sign up for the war when we ran into a couple of men who were joining up with the other side. Words were spoken. They wanted to know where our allegiance lay. We told them for the North, for sure. They were for the South. 'Draw and fight,' they said as they ran for cover behind some trees.

"We were unarmed. They shot and killed my father. I ducked behind a fallen tree before they could shoot me. I guess once they saw he was dead, they got scared and ran off."

Harl turned back, dropped the brush and grabbed the mule's mane. With his other hand, he wiped at something on his face.

"I'm . . . so sorry," Samuel said.

Harl nodded his head and bent to retrieve the brush.

Samuel saw that the conversation was at an end and so turned and walked out of the barn.

Catherine met him with a glass of lemonade.

"Thank you. It is a hot night, isn't it?"

"Yes, quite. Come sit on the porch and take your leisure before you leave."

On the porch, they sat on two straight-back, cane-bottom chairs. Clair ran out and climbed onto her mother's lap with her doll. Catherine folded her arms around her and kissed the back of her head. Clair giggled.

"Give Mary a kiss, too. She wants one."

Catherine obliged.

"So, how did it go with Harl? Did he agree to help?"

"Yes."

They sat in silence for several minutes, listening to the cicadas buzzing in the trees and the crickets chirping by the house. Samuel swiped the cool glass over his forehead.

"Woo wee! It sure is a hot one tonight," he said.

Catherine felt a twinge of guilt mixed with sadness. She and John would have loved to sit on the porch drinking lemonade, talking and laughing. They hadn't been back to see her parents since before Clair was born. The child had been conceived out of wedlock—something that Catherine wanted to keep secret from her family and, especially, Samuel and the board.

Would they allow me to teach if the board knew the circumstances of Clair's conception? John and Catherine did the right thing by marrying as soon as they found out Catherine was carrying a baby. How would Samuel feel about her carrying a child out of wedlock? Could he forgive her? Could she forgive herself?

Lowering the cool glass from his forehead, Samuel looked over at Catherine as she gave Clair a sip of her lemonade. She studied the front of the barn and sat quietly contemplating some deep secret. Was she thinking of John?

Of course, she would still miss him. Even though his Isabella had been dead well over a year now, he still felt the sting of loss. It was a sting that was not easily healed. How many times he regretted choosing not to be at her bedside as she lay sick and dying. Instead, he chose to be at the bedside of another parishioner. When he finally arrived back home, he found his beloved Isabella dead.

He had prayed about her illness and felt the Lord would heal her, that this illness would not be unto death, and so in faith, he had gone to comfort a sick parishioner instead of staying by his wife's side. He told himself at the time that he was stepping out in faith and that God rewards the faithful, but how faithful was he when he lost the thing he cherished most—his wife and unborn child?

The bitterness of the circumstances surrounding his wife's death ate away at him. He wanted to trust God with his all, but he felt he was holding back trust since the death of his wife. God brought Catherine back to Harrisville. Was this a sign that the Lord was giving him a second chance at happiness? Or was it just wishful thinking on his part? Whatever it was, he was certainly enjoying the company of this woman sitting next to him.

Clair laid her head back against her mother's shoulder. Catherine rocked the child softly and hummed a tune that Samuel couldn't quite place. It was something between a lullaby and a song from church.

Soon, Clair's head drooped, and she snored softly.

"I'd best be going," Samuel said. "Thank you for the lemonade and the supper. It was mighty refreshing. I'll just go put the glasses on the side cupboard."

He reached down and picked up Catherine's empty glass and carried them both inside. Returning to the porch, he nodded his head and said, "Looks like it's time for bed. Good night. I'll see you tomorrow at school bright and early."

Catherine stood holding the sleeping child. Butterflies flitted in her stomach at the thought of seeing Samuel again so soon. Or was it nerves for her first time teaching?

"Yes, bright and early. Thank you for lunch and your help this afternoon."

Nodding, he walked down the stairs and climbed into his buggy.

She watched until the buggy was out of sight, lost among the apple trees. Then she took Clair upstairs and dressed her for bed. She listened as Clair said her prayers.

After returning from tucking Clair into bed, she pulled out her *McGuffy Readers* and other textbooks from a cupboard in her room. Taking them downstairs to the kitchen table, she began planning her lessons for the next day. She worked for hours copying lessons onto pieces of paper, so she would be prepared.

Catherine sat at one end of the table, while her mother sat at the other embroidering a rose motif on a pillowcase. Every so often, she looked up over her glasses at her daughter.

"Does me proud to see you working so diligently on something that you aren't sure about."

"Is it that obvious?"

"Yes, it is. You just need to have confidence to take one lesson at a time and do your best with it. None of them children are going to know if you got it right or not, lessen you tell them or let your face turn all red and such."

Catherine felt her face heat up thinking about how easy it would be for the children to know she was not sure of herself.

"Let's have some tea, and we'll talk about it," her mother said.

Once the water boiled, Hazel added tea leaves to a ceramic pot with painted red roses on it and steeped the leaves in the hot water. She poured a cup for herself and one for Catherine and then sat back down at the table.

"You need to see yourself the way your students are going to see you. You can't let them see you all scared. Those children need to know they can trust you and that you've got their best interests in mind. You need to remember that the Lord brought you here for this job, and He won't fail you. He hasn't failed you yet, even with John's death. There's a reason for that, too."

Catherine bowed her head. "I just wish I wouldn't turn so red. It gives it away when I don't know something or when I'm caught off-guard."

"Well, you'll just have to learn to stand your emotional ground and not let your body show what your heart is thinking." Hazel sipped the hot tea.

Catherine nodded. There must be a way for her to stand her ground without her face showing what was truly in her heart.

As she worked, her mind wandered to thoughts of Samuel. Did he have the same opinion as her mother that she needed to stand her emotional ground and not be so given to showing her emotions? She thought of his strong profile with his chiseled features. *He is handsome, to be sure. He'd make a fine catch as a husband for someone. Is that someone me? What a thought! Where did that come from?* Shaking her head, she chided herself for thinking such thoughts about the local preacher—even if he was an old friend.

It was late when Catherine put the final touches on the lessons she wanted to teach. Her mother helped her pack up her books and notes into a cloth flour sack with a shoulder strap. "I hope you like it. I sewed on the strap, thought it might help you tote your lessons back and forth to school."

"Thank you so much, Mama. I love it. I'll use it every day."

"And don't you worry about Clair. I'll watch her for you."

"Oh, thank you, Mama."

After the dishes were washed and put away, Catherine said good night to her mother and brother, who had just come in from the barn.

She walked up the stairs to her bedroom for the night. What would tomorrow bring? Would her students welcome her, or would there be troublemakers among them? Would she have an easy time teaching?

Chapter 6

Catherine woke to the sound of a rooster crowing. The sun wasn't up yet, but she was certain Harl was hard at work feeding the livestock. Clair slept soundly as Catherine dressed in her black crepe dress—a suitable choice for a teacher. She pulled her hair into a tight bun at the nape of her neck. The dress rustled softly as she crossed to Clair's bed and kissed her forehead.

"You be good for Grandma, little one," she whispered.

Downstairs in the kitchen, she stoked the embers in the stove from the night before and added fresh wood. In a moment's time, a fire was going. She filled the gray granite kettle with water and freshly ground coffee and placed it near the hottest part of the stove. Once the coffee boiled, she poured herself a cup.

"Mmm, that sure does smell good," her mother said, walking into the kitchen. Catherine poured her a cup of the steamy brew, too.

"You want pancakes for breakfast?"

"No. The way my stomach feels right now, I couldn't eat a thing."

"Well, I'm going to get them started for when Harl comes in. He'll be hungry."

Catherine put her empty cup down. She packed a lunch of cold roast beef, some bread, and a small jar of strawberry jam into a basket and then headed out the door with her knapsack on her shoulder.

"Is Harl going to drive you? You should have Harl drive you, being your first day at school and all."

"I hope so, Mama," Catherine called over her shoulder.

Catherine stepped quietly into the barn and found Harl milking a cow in one of the stalls. "Harl, can you take me to school and drop me off?"

"Sure thing. I was planning on it. Just let me run in and grab some breakfast first."

"Thank you so much. How can I help you with the chores? What do you want me to do?"

"I'm almost done here. You can follow me up to the house with this pail of milk."

When the bucket was almost full, Harl handed it to his sister.

"Run this one up to the house. I'll bring the other one."

Catherine carried the bucket and placed it on the side cupboard in the kitchen. Harl brought in his and did the same.

Her mother turned from the stove. "Looks like some good cream's in there. I'll churn it later."

Seating himself at the table, Harl dug into the scrambled eggs and pancakes his mother set before him. He ate quickly. When he finished his plate of food, he and Catherine returned to the barn, where Harl backed the mules out of their stall. He lined them up in front of the wagon and placed their leads on them. When he finished, he motioned for his sister.

"Open the doors and then close them behind us," he instructed. Catherine obeyed. After the doors were shut, Harl pulled her up onto the seat beside him.

"Get up there," he said, speaking to the mules, who moved forward.

As they drove through the orchard, Catherine reached out and picked apples from various trees. She tucked them into her basket; and when that was full, she placed them in her knapsack. "I hope I have enough for all of my students."

"Now, don't go giving away the entire orchard. That's a cash crop right there." Harl laughed.

"There's plenty here, and you won't miss this piddly amount."

When they arrived at the school, Catherine swallowed hard. The sky was lightening in the east, but the schoolhouse was dark. "I didn't think to bring a lamp," she said. "Wait for me while I go in and get the fire going in the stove and light the oil lamp on the teacher's desk, will you?"

Harl pushed his hat back on his head and nodded. He set the brake and helped his sister down.

Catherine opened the door of the school and stepped inside the dark room. She breathed in. The smell of musty pine permeated the space. Striding to the potbellied stove in the middle of the room, she filled and lit the wood in it, which cast long shadows around the room. She was just going to shut the stove door and go light the oil lamp when something on the blackboard caught her eye.

"We don't need no teacher" was scribbled across the board in large, white letters. Catherine's breath caught in her throat, and she wanted to run to Harl, but then she heard footsteps behind her. Turning, she saw Samuel coming in the door. He smiled at her and then caught a glimpse of the board and scowled. Stepping up to where she stood, he opened his mouth to say something and then snapped it shut.

"Who did this?" Catherine breathed shakily, her hand on her heart.

"I can't be sure, but I have a pretty good idea who might have done it. We'll know by who shows up for classes and who doesn't," he said.

Catherine wrung her hands. "Will it come off? Is it painted on?"

"Let's see," Samuel said. Picking up a rag and the bucket for drinking water, he headed outside. Catherine lit the lamp on the teacher's desk and then opened one window and watched him through it.

"Morning, Harl," he said as he rushed to the well.

"Everything all right there, Preacher? My sister didn't start a fire, did she?"

Samuel shook his head and began frantically pumping the handle of the well. A gush of water filled the bucket. Samuel turned and hurried back into the school.

Harl jumped down and followed him. Inside the school, Harl placed his hands on his hips and shook his head. "I thought there might be trouble. You going to be all right, Sis?"

Catherine wrung her hands and looked at him with tears in her eyes. "I was so hoping everything would be perfect today . . . and now this."

"If this is the worst of it, you'll be lucky." Samuel mopped the blackboard with the wet rag. The letters washed off easily.

Catherine turned sharply to face Samuel. "You mean, I should expect more pranks like this?"

"No, not yet, but there are some who don't want to be in school. They'll try everything to scare you away. You'll have a hard time with them."

"Well, *now* you tell me," she wailed, tears flowing down her cheeks.

Samuel stepped over to where she stood and pulled out a clean, monogrammed handkerchief out of his pocket. "Here now. Don't carry on so. The students won't have any confidence at all if they see their teacher crying."

"I'm s-s-s-sorry, but I'm so scared."

"Why? Why are you scared?" he asked gently.

Harl turned his eyes toward his feet and stuffed his hands in his jean pockets.

"Because someone doesn't want me here."

"It doesn't matter if it was you or someone else come to teach. Whoever did this is just trying to scare you off; and from the looks of it, it's working. Are you going to let your students get the best of you without even meeting them?"

"No," Catherine whispered, wiping her face with Samuel's handkerchief. She handed it back to him, but he refused.

"Keep it. You may need it again before the day's over."

"I would say I could stay around, Sis, and keep the big boys in line for you, but I've got to get back to my chores," Harl explained, adjusting his felt hat. "Keep the faith," he admonished; and with a wave of his hand, he was gone.

"Well, thankfully my chores are done. I'll stay if you like."

Catherine nodded. Picking up the basket of apples and the knapsack, she placed them out of sight in the room behind the teacher's desk.

"I see you brought apples for all the children."

"Yes."

"That should win you admirers."

She scowled.

"What I mean is a lot of these children don't have much. They'll be mighty pleased to get a treat from the teacher—and on the first day. It certainly can't hurt."

"How long until the children arrive?"

"Should be in a little while. Do you want me to help you write lessons on the board?"

"No, that won't be necessary, but thank you." She cleared her throat and stepped into the little room. Taking out lessons from her knapsack, she explained how she wanted to set up the board to Samuel. "I'll put the lessons for the smaller children down here because they will be closer to the board. And for the older children, I'll write their lessons up high, so they'll be able to read them easily."

Catherine copied the lessons from the books and her papers onto the board as a thin line of light illuminated the East.

For the small children, Samuel drew two birds near their lessons. Catherine laughed. Near the lessons for the older students, she drew a rose and a deer.

"We make mighty fine artists." He stepped back to admire their work.

"No, he did not," said a voice outside.

"Yes, he did. See? I told ya so," another voice said.

Catherine turned and saw Dosha Clark's girls, Minnie and Minerva, standing just outside the schoolhouse door.

"Hello, girls." She walked down the aisle to meet them. "Come in, come in."

Minnie explained, "Teacher don't never let us come in until everybody's here—"

"And we are all in a line . . . " Minerva interjected.

"Girls on one side and boys on the other. And we got to be real quiet, or we can't come in."

"I see." Catherine smiled. "Well, it's best then if you stay outside until the other children arrive."

The girls wore plain, brown dresses and scuffed, buttoned-up boots. They did not have lunch baskets or pails with them.

"Where are your lunch pails?" she asked.

"We don't got none," Minnie said.

"You mean you don't have any?" Catherine corrected.

"That's what I said—'We don't got none,'" Minnie repeated.

"We don't need none," Minerva interjected. "Come lunchtime, we just run home and eat there."

"Oh."

A tall, dark-haired girl with alabaster skin and blue eyes and wearing a freshly pressed, light blue dress stepped out of the shadows and held out her hand for Catherine to shake. "Penelope Harris. Is my uncle Samuel here?"

"I'm here, Penelope," he said.

He stood at the teacher's desk. Penelope pushed past Minnie and Minerva. She dashed toward him. Turning, she said haughtily, "This is my uncle Samuel Harris."

"You think we don't know that?" Minerva said, placing her hands on her hips.

"Penelope, get back outside with the rest of the students," he said.

She scowled, hugging her lunch pail, books, and slate to her chest in a huff. She walked out the door and joined her brother, Jonathan Harris, who stood under a tree holding the hand of a little girl.

"Gotta watch out for that one," Samuel spoke into Catherine's ear. "She's mighty proud and will run and tell tales to her pa, Caleb, if you give her the chance."

"Well, I best not give her anything to report."

Catherine spied Margaret Fields' children when they arrived. The children wore the same shabby clothing as when she met them the other day. She felt a pang of sorrow. *What kind of life did they live to come to school in what was probably their best clothes?*

Gazing at her watch pinned to her dress over her heart, she stepped outside and greeted her students. "Good morning, Class."

"Good morning, Teacher," the students said in unison.

"My name is Mrs. Reed."

The nervousness she felt earlier was dissipating as she scanned each cheerful, inquisitive face.

"Good morning, Mrs. Reed," all of the students said in response to her introduction.

"That's fine. Now I'd like you to form two lines here in front of the door. On this side," she pointed to the left, "I want the boys, youngest to oldest. And on this side," she pointed to the right, "I want the girls, youngest to oldest. When you get inside, these are the sides on which you will sit."

The student's shifted into two neat lines.

"Now, ladies first," she said, gesturing them into the school. The girls walked in and took seats on the righthand side of the room. "And now, boys." The boys darted in and took their seats.

Catherine walked to the front and stood behind her desk. Samuel stood off to one side. "We have a special guest with us today. Reverend Samuel Harris," she said, waving him forward. "Will you open the school day for us in prayer?"

He nodded and stepped forward. "Bow your heads and close your eyes," he instructed the class. "Lord, I thank You for this fine day. I thank You for sending us Mrs. Reed. I pray a blessing on each one gathered here today and a blessing on their learning. In Jesus' name, amen."

"Amen," Catherine echoed.

Samuel took his hat off the teacher's desk and held it in his hands. "Good day, Class. Learn well." He walked toward the back of the class.

"Good day, Reverend Harris," the class called in unison.

With one last look at Catherine, he smiled, nodded his head and closed the door behind him.

With Samuel gone, Catherine decided to take inventory of what books and supplies the students brought with them. "How many of you brought books? Raise your hands."

A few hands shot up, including Penelope, Jonathan, and Elizabeth Harris.

"Teacher, we have slates, too," Penelope boasted, gesturing to her brother and sister.

"Good, that is good. Does everyone have a slate?" Catherine asked. Many of the children shook their heads. "Well, you will need to have slates so you can write your lessons down, or you will need to memorize your lessons from off the blackboard."

Suddenly, the door in the back of the room burst open, and in walked Frank and James Richardson on their tip toes, held by the nape of their necks by the hulking form of a man Catherine assumed must be their father, Paul.

"And I told *you*, you was going to school to get some learnin' if it killed me." Mr. Richardson threw his sons into the back row on the boys' side. Jonathan Harris slid down the bench, giving the bigger boys a wide berth.

"Now, you sit here and git some learnin'. If I hear anything to the contrary, I'll have your hides." The boys sat quietly, studying the floor as their father ranted over them. Pausing, Mr. Richardson kicked the bench hard. "What do ya say?"

"Yes, Pa," the boys chimed in together.

"Now, that's more like it." Then turning to Catherine, he marched up the aisle and held out his hand. She closed her mouth, which had been standing open while she watched all the commotion, and shook the large hand he offered. "I don't think you'll have any problem out of them, but if you do, you just let me know." He slapped his belt. "I'll tan their hides quicker than not."

"Oh, a-a-all right," Catherine stammered. Looking back to where the boys sat, she saw Samuel standing behind them. Turning, Mr. Richardson saw him, too.

"Them boys won't give you a lick of trouble if the preacher stays over them," he said.

"Well, I really don't think that is necessary, what with your directions to them," Catherine said.

Mr. Richardson pushed his hat back on his head and studied Catherine, looking her up and down. "You look like a mite of a woman. It's 'cause of them two boys back there that Miss Whittaker done run off." He jabbed his finger at them in the air.

"Oh, I didn't know that. I was under the impression that she left the position to get married."

"Only after them two run her off scared."

Samuel bowed his head.

Catherine knew this was a critical moment, and she must position herself in a good light if she was going to show the class she was an able leader. Standing up as tall as her slight frame allowed, she clenched her fists at her sides.

"Thank you very much, Mr. Richardson, but I'll be able to handle my class from here," she said curtly.

"Suit yourself." He shrugged as he walked back toward the door. Walking past the bench where his sons sat, he kicked it again and said, "Behave yourselves."

The rest of the day was uneventful in comparison. Samuel stood like a shadow in the back of the room watching Catherine as she taught the younger children their ABC's. She directed the older children with slates to copy down the assignments from off the blackboard. Those without slates she instructed to memorize the lesson.

At lunch time, she dismissed the students to eat their lunches or to "run home," as Minerva Clark mentioned. Samuel went to his house next door. Taking her nap sack and basket, Catherine seated herself outside under the shade of a tree and noticed that the Fields children did not go home or have lunches with them.

Unpacking her lunch, she divided it among the three children. When they had eaten the cold meat, she spread jam on slices of bread and handed it to them.

"Jam on bread?" Dorthea asked.

"Yes, do you like it?"

Dorthea nodded her head as she chewed. "We don't never get no jam at our house."

Hershel sulked. "We don't never get much of nothing at our house."

"Hershel, don't be telling tales," Easter scolded him, her eyes wide.

"Well, it's true, ain't it?" Hershel said.

Easter licked her lips and pinched her brows together as she glanced from Hershel to Catherine.

When the children finished eating the bread, Catherine pulled apples from her knapsack.

"And apples, too?" Dorthea cried and hugged her teacher.

"From your orchard?" Easter asked.

"Yes."

Dorthea bit into her apple and chewed. "You got anymore?" she asked with her mouth full of apple.

"Yes, we have plenty of apples."

"Dorthea! What a thing to ask," Easter scolded.

"It's all right," Catherine soothed.

"No, I mean with you," Dorthea said, taking another big bite of apple and looking at the lumpy knapsack.

"Yes, I do. Do you want another one?"

"It's not for me; it's for Mama. She'd like to have a taste of apple, too."

Catherine reached into the full knapsack and handed her the largest apple.

"Here's one for your mother."

"Can I have another one?" Dorthea asked.

"Dorthea!" Easter shouted.

"It's all right," Catherine soothed, handing the little girl another apple. "Here, you two might as well have another one, also."

Easter's eyes grew big, and she gasped and stammered out a thank you.

Hershel nodded his head. "Are all teachers as nice as you?" he asked.

"I don't know about all teachers, but I try."

"What are you going to do with the rest of them apples? There're too many for you to eat," Dorthea declared, eyeing the bag.

"I'm going to pass them out to each child at the end of the day, but shhhh. It's a surprise. I don't want anyone to know I brought a treat for them on my first day."

Dorthea lunged at the teacher and threw her little arms around her neck. She planted a wet kiss that smelled much like apple on her cheek. "You're the nicest teacher I ever knowed."

"Well, thank you." Catherine steadied herself under the weight of the child pressed against her.

"I see you have an admirer." Samuel limped over to where Catherine sat in the grass.

"Yes, it appears so."

Dorthea released her hold on Catherine, but not before planting another wet kiss on her cheek. Catherine stood and brushed crumbs off her skirt.

"The children will be returning from lunch soon. I'd like to go talk with those men I was telling Harl about to make sure they want the job of helping on the farm—unless you need me here."

"I'm fine now." She stood tall, clenching her fists at her sides.

"Looks to me as if you are." Then taking her aside out of earshot of the Fields children, he whispered, "You may have to stand up to those boys and show them who is boss if you want to have them mind you."

"I think I'm quite capable of standing up to them." Catherine scowled.

Samuel took a step back. "All right. I believe you. Now, you just need to prove it to those children."

"What makes you think I won't be able to?"

"I didn't mean it like that."

Catherine sniffed in reply.

Turning, she gathered her nap sack and basket and marched back to the school. After replacing the bag and basket into the back room, she stood in the doorway and welcomed the returning students from their lunch. She glanced at Samuel, who was smiling right where she had left him.

Turning her attention to her students, Catherine asked the children to take their seats again. She broke the children into groups based on age and covered the assignments on the board with each one.

When she reached James Richardson, he made a kissing sound at her.

Frank fell on the floor laughing.

"James and Frank Richardson!" She nearly shouted. "This type of behavior will not be tolerated. You stop that at once." She clapped her hands for emphasis as the rest of the class turned to see what all the commotion was about.

"Yes, ma'am." James lowered his head.

Grabbing Frank's arm, she rammed him back onto the bench.

"Now, stay there," she commanded.

Frank stopped laughing and looked around the room. He flushed pink and looked at the floor.

There were no further incidents from James, Frank, or any other student for the rest of the day. Catherine felt she had proved to the class that she was an able leader. Hopefully, she could convince the board of the same, so she could stay in her post.

By the time Catherine said the closing prayer and dismissed the class, she was tired. She handed an apple to each of the students as they left. The students thanked her as they filed out the door.

When she handed an apple to Frank Richardson, he paused in the doorway and looked at her with brows pinched. "An apple for me, too? But I wasn't good."

"Yes, an apple for you and your brother." She handed one to James, who stood behind Frank. "Besides, tomorrow is a new day, and I'm sure you'll be on your best behavior." The boys stared at her, their mouths agape. "Now, run along home."

The boys stepped mechanically out the open door.

Back in the classroom, she hooked several stray strands of hair behind her ears as she tidied the room and put the benches back into rows. She hummed as she worked and didn't hear the footsteps at the door until someone spoke.

"Looks like you rallied the troops." Samuel smiled.

"Looks like." She straightened.

"So, how did your first day go after I left?" he asked, taking a seat on one of the benches.

Catherine sat on a bench a row up from him.

"Well, James Richardson made a kissing sound at me, and his brother fell on the floor laughing, but I quelled their enthusiasm. I don't think they will brave doing it again."

"I'm driving out to see how Harl got on with the crew I took out to him this afternoon. Can I offer you a ride?"

"I would appreciate that. Just let me gather my things."

Catherine placed her satchel with her books on her shoulder and her empty dinner basket on her arm. She banked the fire in the potbelly stove. When she stepped out of the schoolhouse, she was surprised to see Samuel driving a wagon instead of the buggy.

"I'll have to take the fellers I found to help Harl back home tonight," Samuel explained, seeing her perplexed look. "I'll bring them back tomorrow if they suited Harl's needs."

Catherine nodded as he helped her up onto the seat next to him. She gazed at Samuel's face and tried to memorize his once-familiar features. Turning, he caught her studying him and smiled.

"Something on your mind?"

"Not in particular."

"Enjoying the view then?"

Catherine turned her head, her cheeks warming.

When they reached the orchard, she was surprised to see many of the trees were bare along the path they took.

"How many men did you bring Harl?"

"Only three."

"It looks like an army came through here."

Samuel laughed heartily.

When they neared the barn, Catherine was surprised to see three black men sitting in the grass dipping tin cups into a water bucket and drinking.

"Is this the crew then?"

"Yes, it is."

"Well, it looks like these men know what they're doing when it comes to apple-picking." Harl walked over to the wagon and nodded his head in greeting to his sister and Samuel before pushing his hat up on his head.

"You brought me a good crew, Preacher, and I'm obliged to you for them."

"It was no trouble."

Samuel climbed from the wagon seat. He limped over to Catherine's side and helped her down. Placing her hands on his shoulders, he lifted her easily out of the wagon, and she marveled at how solid he was and felt her cheeks warm.

"There's the girl I knew." Samuel laughed.

On the ground, Catherine looked up at him and could not hide the embarrassed smile on her face. She diverted her attention to the crates of apples stacked neatly by the barn.

"Looks like they got a lot of work done," she observed.

"Yes, they did. They worked up a storm. Never seen men work as fast as they did."

"I knew if you gave them the chance, they would help you out."

"They didn't just hurry through the job, but they was real careful handling each apple. I expected them to plunk them down in the crates, but they didn't. They handled them as if each one was a baby." Harl laughed.

"Mommy, you're home!" Clair shouted running to her mother and throwing her arms around her legs.

Catherine smiled and patted the girl's back. "Did you and Grandma have fun?"

"Uh-huh. Look at what I drew for you," she said, revealing a crumpled piece of paper.

"Show your ma the picture you drew for her."

Clair turned the paper for her mother to see. On it was a drawing of a stick woman and child in black dresses with a schoolhouse in the background.

"Oh, Clair!" Catherine exclaimed. "Did you draw this for me?"

"Yes, I did. All by myself. Grandma didn't help me. Did you?"

"No, I sure didn't, Child." Hazel laughed.

"What a beautiful picture. I'll pin it up at school, so everyone can see what a good little artist I have." She kissed the top of Clair's head.

"With that picture up at the school, you'll have every other child wanting to draw one, too," her mother said, as they walked into the house.

"What a good idea. I could have my students decorate the room. We could go on a nature hike and bring back items from our excursion for the classroom. The students who want to would be welcome to draw pictures or write a poem or a story about our adventure outside."

"Well, just don't let them get out there and run wild."

"Of course, I wouldn't let them run wild, would I?" Catherine motioned to Samuel, who was standing just outside the door.

"I believe she'll be able to handle whatever comes her way." He smiled at her. Pausing, he sniffed the air. "Smells good, Mrs. Adams."

"Well, sit down both of you, and I'll get you a plate," Hazel said.

"I would, but I'm driving Harl's men back home tonight, or else I'd be pleased to stay for dinner. Thank you for the invitation."

"Anytime, anytime. Reminds me of when you were growing up. I fed you right along with my family," Hazel said, setting four plates on the table.

"I remember," Samuel recalled with a laugh. "We'd eat here or up at my mother's house. Those were good times. Well, I better be going." Samuel limped down the stairs and over to his wagon, followed by Catherine.

"Will you be coming by the school tomorrow?"

"I will if you don't mind."

"I would appreciate it. And I was serious about taking the students on an outing. You could come with us."

"It would be my pleasure." Then to the men sitting near the barn, he said, "Let's load up, so I can get you home tonight."

The men climbed into the back of the wagon and seated themselves.

Samuel hobbled up onto the driver's seat and spoke to his horses. The wagon bumped through the orchard and was soon out of sight.

Catherine returned to the kitchen and seated herself at the table where Harl, Clair, and her mother waited. Harl asked the blessing.

"Thank You, Lord, for good help in the orchard today. I pray a blessing on those men for their health and safety. I thank You for this food and the hands that prepared it. In Jesus' name, amen."

Harl reached for a hot roll and the plate of butter. "Preacher brought me a good group of hard workers. I could probably pay them in apples, and they'd be satisfied," he said through mouthfuls of dinner roll.

"Yes, but you are going to pay them, right, Harl?" his mother said.

"Already did. And will do every day they come to work for me." Then changing the subject, he looked at Catherine and asked, "How was your first day at school?"

"It was a fine day. I feel the students are eager to learn and willing to put forth the effort. I enjoyed myself and look forward to tomorrow."

"I'm so glad to hear that." Her mother refilled Clair's milk glass. "I was praying that the Lord would settle you in."

"I would say your prayer was answered. I even stood up to the Richardson boys. One of them was making kissing noises at me."

Harl chuckled. "You have any trouble with them, just tell their pa. He'll take care of any misbehavior."

Her mother gasped. "Those big boys? Don't you let them bother you. You stand your ground is what."

"I'm thinking if they give me any more trouble, I'll make them my helpers and let them take on some extra assignments—keep them busy and out of trouble. Tomorrow, they should be able to help with the little ones as we hike through the woods gathering items for the classroom."

"Do you really think that is a good idea?" her mother asked. "I'd be afraid they'd tease them or push them down."

"Maybe all they need is a little authority to help them. We'll see tomorrow."

Outside in the distance, thunder rumbled, and the wind picked up.

"Feels like a storm is comin'," her mother said.

Clair covered her ears at the sound of thunder. Frowning, she looked at her mother. "Make it stop, Mommy."

"It's okay, honey," Catherine soothed, patting the child's arm. "Come and sit on Mama's lap." The little girl slid off her chair and held her arms up to her mother.

Catherine picked her up and held her tightly as thunder rumbled again. "There now, it's just thunder."

"Good thing we got as many apples picked as we did," Harl commented. "Sounds like that storm is going to be a big one soon as it gets here. I better go out and cover over those crates."

In bed that night, as she listened to the rumbling of the distant thunder, Catherine thought of the events of the day and planned for the coming morning. She needed to make the Richardson boys mind her and not give them opportunities to misbehave. Giving them responsibility with the little ones might be just what they needed.

Chapter 1

Morning came too soon. Distant, dark clouds predicted the coming of rain, but Catherine wasn't worried.

"By the time that storm gets here, we'll have our excursion finished and be safe back in the schoolhouse. Besides, it might miss us altogether," she told her mother over breakfast.

Her mother nodded.

"Well, I better get going." Turning to Clair, who was finishing a glass of milk, she kissed her. "Be good for Grandma while your mama is away."

The little girl nodded. "I will."

"I better take a hearty lunch today. I'll probably be sharing it with some of my students again."

"Good idea."

Taking her knapsack with books and a lunch basket with plenty of bread, jam, and dried meat, she headed off to school.

When she arrived, she lit the oil lamp and looked around her. The blackboard was bare. She breathed a sigh of relief and then busily filled the blank board with the lessons for the day. Stepping back, she surveyed her work.

"Looks like you have a full day planned," Samuel said, stepping into the room.

She whirled around on her heels and smiled when their eyes met.

"Yes, I thought we'd have a lesson this morning out in nature. We can pick up some items to decorate the classroom with and then have the afternoon session in here."

"I think that is a fine idea. But it's looking like rain."

"It's still quite a ways off; besides, we'll be back in the classroom before the storm hits. Will you go with us?"

"Of course, I will. I know a good spot for collecting specimens up at Johnson's Point behind the school. It's a bit of a hike, but there's a cave and a river. If we have time, we could go fishing for our lunch."

"That sounds wonderful."

"Me and my brothers used to play up there all the time. I'll bring the wagon to haul the children. It'll be easier than walking all that distance."

Catherine nodded her thanks as the first students arrived.

When everyone was gathered into the classroom, the preacher opened the day with prayer and then went to ready the wagon. Catherine explained about their outing. Frank and James Richardson exchanged looks and smiled. Catherine saw the exchange and warned, "There'll be none of that."

"What?" Frank asked.

"We didn't say anything," James added.

"You didn't have to. Your guilt is written on your faces. As it is, I'll need your help with the younger children, and I want you to set a good example for them to follow."

"Them? Set an example?" Penelope Harris hissed.

Frank made a hissing sound, and James slapped his knees. "Guilty before even committing the crime." James laughed.

"I expect you to help out, too, Penelope."

Penelope sat up a little straighter. Clasping her hands on her lap, she nodded. "Yes, Mrs. Reed."

"Let's gather your lunches; we'll take them with us and have a picnic on the mountain."

Catherine grabbed the quilts off the bed in the little room. The children could sit on them for the ride up to Johnson's Point. The jingling of tack let Catherine know the preacher was back and ready to go.

The children lined up beside the wagon in two single-file lines.

"Are you sure you want to do this today?" he asked. "It's starting to cloud up."

"We won't be gone that long, an hour at the maximum. Besides, I have my heart set on it."

Once all of the children were safely seated in the back of the wagon on the quilts, Samuel helped Catherine up onto the seat beside him. She felt a warm sensation course through her arm when she took his hand.

Some of the girls giggled.

"Now, there will be none of that, girls." Catherine turned to face them. "All right. Everyone in? Good. Let's go."

Samuel turned the horses and briskly headed up a path behind the school that Catherine had not seen before. It was well-hidden among the tall pine trees. The wagon bucked over bumps and ruts in the road.

"Oh, yeah, did I tell you it would be a bit of rough going?" Samuel grimaced.

"No, you didn't." Catherine stared straight ahead while holding the sides of the seat. "Are you children all right back there?" she called, afraid to turn her head for fear the motion would throw her from the wagon.

"All right," several called back together in chorus. The children giggled and whooped as the wagon pitched from side to side through the ruts.

Soon, the wagon crested the hill. Before them was an open valley with a shallow river curving through it. The road ran through the river and back up into a dense, tree-lined hill. "Oh, it's lovely."

"Wait until you see where we're going."

The wagon bumped along down into the valley and through the shallow part of the river. As it climbed the dense, tree-lined hill beyond the river, Catherine marveled at the sun streaming through the trees. Distant thunder rumbled behind them.

"Here we are. Johnson's Point," Samuel said, pointing to a jagged outcropping of limestone rock that came to a point at the highest spot. He pulled the wagon under the overhanging rock slabs and helped Catherine down. "This looks like a good spot."

"Frank and James, help us unload the little ones," Catherine instructed as they jumped down.

Both boys reluctantly helped the little ones off the wagon.

"Now, let's see what we can find," Catherine said.

"What're we lookin' fer, Teacher?" Dorthea asked.

"Well, we are looking for leaves, and branches from trees, and rocks and such to identify and to decorate the schoolhouse with."

Dorthea reached down and picked up a leaf. "You mean like this?"

"Well, yes."

"There's a whole bunch of leaves all over here," Dorthea said. "Looks like it will take us a while to pick them all up."

"We aren't picking them all up. Just a few of each kind for the classroom."

"Oh," Dorthea said with understanding.

"Now, let's see how many we can gather from the different trees."

As the children worked picking up fallen leaves and small rocks, Catherine felt the wind pick up.

"Them clouds sure are boiling," Hershel said, looking up.

Catherine followed his gaze as the first big raindrops hit her face.

"Children, let's gather under the overhang. Quickly." She rushed to the wagon and grabbed the quilts, tucking them under her arms as she ran under the limestone outcropping.

Frank and James Richardson were already under the overhang inspecting an opening as the wind picked up.

"What's so interesting, boys?" Catherine asked.

"Look." James pointed to an opening at the back of the overhang.

"It's a cave," she said.

Samuel joined the party at that moment. "Ah, yes. My brothers and I had many good times exploring it years ago."

"How far back does it go?" James wondered aloud.

"Well, we aren't going to find out. I don't want you getting in there and breaking a limb," Catherine said.

"It's quite safe and goes back quite a ways," Samuel said. Catherine furrowed her brows, and Samuel clamped his mouth shut.

"Whatcha lookin' at?" Dorthea asked.

"It's a cave," Frank explained.

"It's a prison for bad, little girls." James grabbed Dorthea's arms.

"James, stop it," Catherine reprimanded, throwing James a stern look.

Thunder rumbled overhead, and lightning flashed, causing some of the smaller children to scream and run to their teacher for comfort.

Catherine dropped the quilts and held the children to her sides and soothed them. "There isn't anything to be afraid of. We are safe under here. The storm will pass."

As if in answer to her statement, the rain came down in torrents. Thunder boomed overhead, followed closely by flashes of lightning.

"Let's get the children into the cave," Catherine yelled over the downpour. She scooped up the quilts and ushered the children near her into the cave as another boom of thunder sounded.

"Hurry now, children. Come with me. There's plenty of room back in the cave, and we'll be safer in there than out here."

The air around them was cool with a heavy scent of wet dirt and mustiness. Catherine motioned for Penelope to come to her. "Here, help me lay these quilts down along the wall. That's where it's driest."

Penelope obeyed, and soon, Catherine and she had the smallest children sitting on the warm quilts as the older boys stood around.

"Where are we supposed to sit?" Frank asked looking around him.

"You can sit here on the quilt," Catherine offered.

"There isn't enough room."

"There are rocks," James Richardson observed.

"Dirty rocks," Penelope commented, taking a seat next to Catherine.

"Well, then, stand if you want to," Samuel said. "I need to go unharness the horses and move them farther under the overhang."

The air near the cave opening was electric as lightning moved closer. Catherine watched Samuel rush to unharness the horses, who nickered with fear at the sound of the storm. Samuel patted each one and spoke softly to them as the storm raged around them.

Catherine watched Samuel as he calmed his team. She wished he was calming her instead of his horses. *Where did that come from?* she wondered. *We're just friends.* The thought surprised and confused her.

Once the team was well under the overhang, Samuel limped back into the cave, where he chose a spot on a blanket. A flash of lightning momentarily blinded Catherine as she peered out at the storm. She heard a crack and then a loud crash outside.

She watched as Samuel limped out of the cave. The horses nickered their nervousness with the storm so close. Limping back in and over to her, he whispered in Catherine's ear, "We're trapped. There's a tree fell over the path. We'll have to move it if we plan to take the wagon back with us."

"We can't very well have the children walk all that way back. The rain will stop soon, and then we'll get out," she whispered back.

Dorthea scrambled onto Samuel's lap when he sat down. "Preacher, pray and make it stop that thunderin' and lightnin'."

"God makes the thunder and lightning, just like He makes the sunshine. If we didn't have thunder and lightning every now and then, things wouldn't grow."

"Can't you make it stop? My ears hurt."

"I can't make it stop, but you might want to plug your ears."

Dorthea stuffed her fingers in her ears.

"You seem to be very good with children," Catherine observed.

Samuel sighed; he folded his arms around the small child, bent his head, and then looked up at Catherine. "Isabella died carrying my child."

"Oh, I'm so sorry, Samuel." Catherine placed her hand lightly on his arm.

"The one thing Isabella and I never had was children. I wish we could have had at least one, if not a whole house full."

Catherine nodded. "I was so sorry to hear about Isabella dying last year. My mother wrote to me of her passing."

Samuel held Dorthea closer and sighed, looking out at the storm.

After a while, the thunder and lightning subsided, taking with it the torrential rain.

"Finally." Samuel set Dorthea on the quilt next to him and rose. "Let's get this tree moved and get back to the school." Calling to James and Frank, he said, "I'm going to need some help moving that tree, boys. Come with me."

Frank and James hopped up and followed him out of the cave.

The girls protested. "What about us?" Penelope and Minerva Clark asked.

"I have a job for you in here," Catherine said. Both girls turned their attention to their teacher. "Let's get the lunches out of the back of the wagon, and we'll eat before we head back." Catherine grabbed her basket and several lunch pails. "Here, hand these out to the children."

The girls helped gather and pass out each child's lunch. For the ones who hadn't brought anything, Catherine cut slices of bread, spread them with jam, and handed it out, along with dried meat. Before the students finished eating, Samuel and the boys moved the tree out of their path. Once they were finished, Frank and James ate their lunches. Catherine handed Samuel some dried meat and a slice of bread, for which he thanked her. He ate quickly.

"Let's get these children home."

Once all the students and Catherine were back in the wagon, he started down the road back toward town. As he drove, heavy drops of rain fell off the overhanging trees, wetting him and the students afresh. The warm air hung heavy with humidity.

By the time they reached the river, it was dusky dark. The river was swollen with the rain making it move fast and high.

"We can't go through this."

"Why not? We have to get through—get these children back home." Catherine's voice was frantic.

"The river is too swollen; it'll cart the horses and wagon and us all away. We'll have to wait it out."

"How long will that take?"

"It could be all night."

Catherine gasped and looked at the faces behind her. "We can't just sleep out here under the stars," she said. "Their parents will be so angry with me and worried. We have to get them home."

"And get carted away downstream and drown?" Samuel asked. "We'll have to get back to the cave and make camp up there. That's the safest place for us."

"Can't we just go around it?"

"No, this river cuts us off from the town."

Catherine knew further protesting would not accomplish anything. She clamped her mouth shut and watched reluctantly as Samuel turned the horses back around and headed for Johnson's Point once more.

When they reached the overhang, it was dark. Samuel guided the wagon by moonlight. Under the overhang, Catherine instructed the students to bunch together in two groups in the wagon. She handed out the quilts and hoped they would be enough to keep them warm in the cool night air.

"I know my brothers and I used to build campfires under here. We kept a pile of wood in the cave. It should be good enough to light a fire with," Samuel said. Limping into the cave, Samuel was gone only a few minutes when he came out dragging a large tree limb. "Here, boys, help me break this up."

James and Frank Richardson and Hershel Fields all hopped out of the wagon.

"You tend this, and I'll go back for more."

"My pa is going to be so mad," Penelope Harris cried. "And I ruined my good dress in all this rain and dirt."

"It can't be as bad as all that," Minerva Clark interjected. "It still looks fine to me."

"How can you tell? You can't see straight in this moonlight," Penelope countered.

"Well, maybe if you weren't so worried about your dress, we wouldn't be in this mess," Minnie Clark argued.

"Now, girls, that's enough. Try and get comfortable. Move closer together because this will be our bed for the night."

"Oh!" Penelope cried.

"Hush up now. You're scaring Dorthea," Easter Fields said. The girls moved closer together. Dorthea hugged her sister Easter as the boys built a fire near the wagon.

"We'll sleep by the fire," Samuel said to Catherine and the boys.

As her students drifted off to sleep, Catherine thought of the parents waiting for them back at the school. How angry and worried they must be.

What would the board think of her out in the wilderness with not only her students but also an unmarried man? Who cares if it happened to be the reverend and a board member. This was serious and could lead to her removal from her position as teacher. Tears welled up in her eyes at the thought of losing her position so quickly. *If only I hadn't insisted that they decorate the room with natural things. If only I would have waited a day or two to drive up into the mountains. If only I would have told their parents my idea, so they could have gone along with us.*

Samuel lay with his back to the fire and Catherine. How would he explain their outing to the parents waiting back at the school sick with worry? How would he explain their overnight stay to the board? How could he explain it to the town?

He'd been in trouble before because of his oversight. His wife and unborn child died because of it. He didn't believe at the time that God would allow his wife to die. He thought she would pull through and get better; but allow it or not, she still died without him by her side. He shook the thought of his wife's death from his mind. There were more pressing matters on which to think. Such as, would the board ask for his resignation?

Would the town people ask him to step down as their pastor in light of the scandal of him being out alone with an unmarried woman and vulnerable children? Surely, the town wouldn't want to keep him on after such a scandal as this.

He thought of Catherine and her love of the children she taught. What would become of her if he left? How could she survive this scandal? She might have to leave town. Surely, God would forgive him for his blunder in bringing the school and its unmarried teacher out into the wilderness—even if the school board and the town didn't.

By the time morning came, Samuel was up. He roused Catherine and the boys and had everyone back in their seats as he pulled the wagon out from under the overhang. Humid air met them as they headed back down the mountain. The day dawned clear and bright as he drove. Looking ahead once they were out of the tree-lined mountain, he saw that the river had returned to a normal level and would be easily crossable.

As the wagon bumped through the river, Samuel looked up and saw someone riding toward them—his brother, Caleb. His face was bright red.

"Thank goodness." He breathed a sigh of relief, riding up alongside the wagon. "I thought you might have come up this way. We didn't know where you or the children were. What were you thinking coming out all this way?"

Samuel shook his head. Catherine felt her face grow hot under Caleb's gaze. She cast her eyes down at the ground beside the wagon.

"Papa!" Elizabeth exclaimed.

"Look at my dress; it's ruined," Penelope cried.

"Well, at least everyone is all right," Caleb observed, turning his horse to ride alongside the wagon as it moved back toward the schoolhouse.

"I'm so sorry about this. We got caught in the rain; a tree fell across our path; and the river rose, and we couldn't cross it," Samuel explained.

"I knew it was something like that. I know you wouldn't keep these children away from home unless it was an emergency. All the parents are gathered at the schoolhouse. I told them I might know where you were and to sit tight."

The wagon bumped along the rutted road leading down to the school.

"Oh, my goodness!" Dosha Clark said, holding her stomach and hurrying to meet the wagon. "I thought you was killed."

When they saw their mother, Minnie and Minerva Clark shouted in unison, "Mama!"

Paul Richardson hurried to the wagon, looking for his sons. "What ails you, Preacher, taking our children out to who-knows-where and for who-knows-what?" he spit out angrily.

"There's my babies," Margaret Fields cried, hurrying to meet the wagon. "My babies!"

"Mama, we had to sleep in the wagon," Easter explained.

"I'm hungry," Dorthea cried.

"We'll get you home and get you fed."

The children jumped off the wagon as soon as it stopped near the door of the schoolhouse. Each one hurried away with their respective parent as Samuel and Catherine sat watching from their seat.

"That was a fool thing I did taking them all the way up the mountain like that," Samuel said. "I don't know what I was thinking. I wanted to show you and the class Johnson's Point. I was so proud to show you all that place that I forgot my head."

"You were just following my desire to decorate the classroom with natural things—to allow the children to gather them. I'm so sorry for that."

"That was a fool thing to do," Henry Frazier agreed, stepping out of the schoolhouse, chomping on a lit cigar. "What were you thinking?"

Samuel just shook his head. Catherine looked at her hands clasped in her lap.

"We called an emergency meeting of the board to discuss this matter tonight at seven at your mother's place. We'll see you both there." He stomped away. The heavy smell of the cigar lingered in the humid air like a bad omen of things to come.

Catherine started to get down off the wagon, but Samuel held her back. "We need to talk about this. I'll drive you home."

As he drove, Catherine began to sob. "It's all my fault. If only I hadn't wanted to decorate the schoolhouse with nature, this never would have happened. It was going to be such a nice lesson, too. The children were going to draw pictures and write about their time outside."

"No. It's not your fault. It's mine. I never should have taken those children up to Johnson's Point. It was my oversight."

"What are we going to tell the board? How will they ever see reason now?"

"We'll tell them the truth and hope they forgive us and can forget this oversight of judgment on my part."

"What if they can't?"

"Then we both lose our positions," Samuel said soberly.

Catherine hiccupped and cried afresh. Her shoulders shook with the weight of her emotion.

They rode the rest of the way in silence as Catherine occasionally blew her nose on the handkerchief she kept stuffed up one sleeve.

When they arrived at her home, her mother was waiting for them at the bottom of the stairs with Clair beside her. "Land sakes, what happened to you two?" she asked.

Catherine began to sob afresh as she hurried down from the wagon and ran to embrace her daughter. Clair threw her tiny arms around her mother's neck as Catherine covered her face in kisses.

"Did you go see Daddy?" Clair asked.

Catherine's mouth fell open. "No, we didn't go see your daddy. We're home now."

"We got caught in the storm," Samuel explained. "We were up at Johnson's Point when the storm hit."

"Johnson's Point? What were you doing way up there?"

"I wanted to show the class the overhang and cave." Samuel added, "We saw it all right. Up close."

"Well, at least you're all right. No harm done."

"I'm not sure the board will see it that way," Samuel said glumly.

"Well, the Lord knows what's best, and He'll see you through."

"I wish I had your optimism."

"Can I invite you in for some breakfast?"

"No. I think it's best if I go on home and study what my next move is going to be. I might have to start packing."

"Surely, it's not as bad as all that," Hazel exclaimed.

"It might be. I'll pick you up a half-hour before the meeting."

Catherine nodded silently.

As he turned the horses around and headed away from the house, Hazel turned her attention to her daughter.

"He's right. We might both have to start packing."

Her mother sucked in her breath. "No matter what the board says, you'll always have a home here with me and Harl."

Chapter 8

Catherine removed her mourning dress and surveyed the damage. The hem of the skirt was covered in dirt from being in the cave. She draped it over the cane-bottom chair in the corner of the room and took out a navy blue dress from the chest at the foot of her bed. She would wash her black mourning dress that afternoon and hang it to dry. Hopefully, it would be dry by the time she went to meet with the board.

She took the dirty dress outside to the large cast iron pot reserved for washing clothes and making lye soap. It took several trips to the well to get enough water to fill the pot before she started a fire under it and placed her dress in it to soak.

As she watched the water simmer and then boil, she thought of what she might say to the board—how she would explain herself to them. What could she say? It was a mistake to take the children so far out of town. The weather had changed faster than she thought it would. She didn't think the venture would take all day and so chanced it. But she was wrong. What if one of the students had taken ill or been hurt?

Surely, the board could see that she and Samuel did the best they could. It wasn't like her to act so rashly. She kept reminding herself that she intended for the outing to only be for an hour. The rain caught them off-guard. If it hadn't been for the rain and the tree falling, blocking their path, she and the children would have been safely back in the schoolhouse before the afternoon. They couldn't outrun the rain, and she didn't want a lot of wet children catching colds, even in the heat of early September. It had rained buckets.

She thought through what she could have done differently as she swirled the dress around in the boiling water with a long stick. She added some homemade lye soap flakes to the water and continued stirring and thinking.

She should have waited a day and told the parents what she planned to do. If she just would have waited, none of this fuss would have happened. Samuel would have still gone to Johnson's Point; the class would have gathered items to study in the classroom; and they would have made it back in plenty of time for the afternoon session. The children would have told their parents how much fun the class was that day. The parents would have praised her for her innovative thinking, and everyone would have been happy—including the board. Instead, here she was, thinking of what she would say to defend herself before the wrath of the board, who possibly now saw her as irresponsible and short-sighted. No one could have anticipated how intense the storm would be. If she just would have known, she never would have taken the students out on a day like that.

She fished the dress out of the water with the long stick and draped it over the clothesline for it to cool. When the dress was cool enough, Catherine wrung it out and took it inside to hang near the stove to dry.

Samuel thought about the day and how it could have gone differently. For one, he could have refrained from offering to take the children all the way up to Johnson's Point, some five miles away from the schoolhouse. The children could have found plenty of items just up the road from the school if he just would have stayed out of it. They didn't need him, but somehow, he always wanted to be around the school teacher. He admitted to himself he enjoyed her company.

What could he say to the school board to explain their misstep in such a way so as not to get them both fired on the spot? It was an oversight on his part that led them out into the wilderness in the first place. His horses were a good, strong team, and he wanted to show Catherine and the class a place that was meaningful to him. It was yet another opportunity to get close to the teacher—his former love interest. *Could she be my love interest now?* Not likely, now that the board was going to throw her out of her position.

Would the townspeople run him out of his position? If the board did throw her out, and the townspeople removed him, they could have a life together far away from Harrisville. He could raise Clair as his own, and she would be the wife for which he longed. It would be a good arrangement—the three of them together, starting over in a new town or city. It might be best to go to a city where there were plenty of people—too many to care about your past. It was decided then. If the board moved to remove her from her position, and the townspeople asked for his resignation, he would ask for her hand in marriage and move on with her to another place, where they could start over. But what if the board only wanted to remove her from the teaching post? What would he do then? Would he resign? He wasn't sure.

When he arrived home, Samuel spent the rest of the day in his study praying for the Lord's direction and grace for both of them.

At 6:15 p.m., he was in his buggy on his way to Catherine's to pick her up for the meeting. He noticed she had changed her clothing and now wore a clean, navy blue dress, which suited her eye color.

"Come in for a bite of dinner," Hazel offered. "Catherine didn't eat a thing."

"I couldn't eat anything either," he said. "Not with my stomach in a ruckus over this meeting."

Catherine climbed in next to him, and when they were down the road and out of earshot of her mother, Catherine spoke. "I don't think you have anything to be worried about. It's me that should be worrying."

"Frazier called us both to the meeting, so it can't be good for either of us."

They rode the rest of the way in silence to his mother's home, arriving with several minutes to spare.

Two horses stood sentry along the porch. "Benjamin and Caleb are here already. I expect the rest to be along shortly. Let's go in."

Inside the house, Samuel led Catherine into the sitting room on the right. The same room she was interviewed in for the position as teacher. She paused at the door and took it all in. Benjamin and Caleb Harris sat on the sofa talking with their mother. They stood when Catherine walked into the room. None of their faces gave any indication of what was to come.

"You're early." Benjamin looked as the clock on the mantle, which showed 6:45 p.m.

"It's better than being late." Samuel limped over to his mother and placed a kiss on her cheek.

"Frazier, Grant, and Doc Johnson should be here on the dot," Caleb said.

"Won't you sit down," Maude offered, waving Catherine into a seat across from her—the same seat she had sat in during the interview. Samuel pulled a chair over and took a seat next to her. The five of them sat in silence, waiting. The only sound was the ticking of the clock.

Close to seven o'clock, the sound of several hoof beats broke the silence.

"They're here." Samuel rubbed his hands together, then raked his hand through his dark hair.

Henry Frazier, minus his usual unlit cigar, walked in without knocking. He strode into the sitting room as if he owned the place and took a seat near the couch in a wingback chair. He scowled at Samuel and Catherine. Catherine looked down at her hands in her lap as the clock chimed seven times.

Mr. Grant and Doc Johnson followed shortly.

"Well, let's get to the matter at hand," Frazier said. "We can't allow a teacher as irresponsible as you to continue to teach our children. It just ain't right."

"Now, hold on there, Henry," Samuel interjected. "She was content to pick up items near the school. I was the one who drove them out to Johnson's Point. Blame me for the mishap if you blame anyone."

Henry Frazier licked his lips and scowled. "Even so, we can't permit a teacher who would allow her students to be taken so far away from their classroom and for so long to continue teaching."

"I was the one who encouraged her to go to Johnson's Point. If it hadn't been for me, she never would have ventured that far or had to sleep out with her students. I can tell you that nothing unseemly happened. The students can attest to that."

"Oh, ho, ho," Frazier laughed. "Nothing unseemly? Well, what do you call spending the night out in the wilderness with students and an unmarried woman? I would call that very unseemly."

"But we couldn't help it," Samuel said.

"It really couldn't be helped," Catherine said, raising her eyes to Henry. "We were trapped, and the only thing to do was to spend the night out of the weather and hope the water level went down in the river so we could cross it in the morning."

"Surely, you don't expect me to believe that you tried to get across that river? Why, there are plenty of places where you could have safely crossed," Frazier countered.

"No, there aren't," Benjamin chimed in. "I've been out that way when there's come a big storm all of a sudden. There's no getting through that river once you are on the northside of the hill."

"I don't believe it."

"Are you calling me a liar?" Benjamin asked, rising.

"Now, listen, everyone, and let's hear what happened so we can make an informed decision," Maude Harris said, glaring at the men. "I trust my son when he says there wasn't anything unseemly that happened between him and the school teacher." Henry Frazier stood, but she waved him back down. "We at least need to hear them out. It's only fair, Henry, and I know you want to be fair in this matter."

Doc Johnson blew his nose into a handkerchief. Mr. Grant cleared his throat as if he was going to say something. He opened his mouth but then snapped it shut, casting his eyes down at his feet.

"Proceed then," Frazier said with a gleam in his eye.

"I offered to drive Mrs. Reed up the mountain to Johnson's Point to show her and her students the cave where Benjamin, Caleb, and

I used to play. I wanted them to see the overhang, too," Samuel explained. "So, we drove up the mountain."

"Knowing full well there was a storm coming," Frazier interrupted.

"Let them tell their tale, Henry, and stop interrupting," Maude Harris contested hotly.

"We didn't think the storm would come on us so quickly," Catherine continued. "I thought it would be a quick trip up the mountain and back to the school within a couple of hours. I knew we could travel fast in the wagon, and the storm was way off when we started."

"You see," Samuel affirmed. "It was only supposed to be a quick trip, but by the time we reached the overhang, we had to take cover out of the rain. We did the best we could with what we had."

"I see," Frazier said. Catherine wondered if he really did see the situation for what it was—a mistake.

"We pulled the wagon under the overhang and then took cover in the cave," Catherine said. "I thought the storm would pass quickly. It eventually did pass but not without felling a tree in our path, which the boys and Reverend Harris removed so we could return to the schoolhouse."

"The rain had raised the water level of the river so high that it would have been dangerous for us to attempt to cross it. I was afraid I'd lose the horses, wagon, and all the children if we tried to cross," Samuel explained.

"So, we did what any sensible person would have done," Catherine offered. 'We turned around and spent the night under the overhang out of the weather."

Henry Frazier hissed over his teeth. "And I suppose you are going to believe them." He turned to face the others.

"I do," Doctor Johnson said. "There's no reason not to."

"I do, too," Mr. Grant said, shifting uneasily in his seat. "Why wouldn't we? What have they said to prove they are lying?"

"Yes, Henry," Maude said.

"What else can we do but believe them?" Caleb said. "It's not like they are deliberately trying to pull the wool over our eyes. The facts are there. A mistake was made. Can we really make them pay for this mistake as if a crime had been committed?"

"I don't think you are seeing this clearly." Frazier motioned to Catherine. "Her reputation is ruined. We can't let a teacher with a ruined reputation continue teaching at our school."

"And who ruined that reputation?" Maude asked. "The local preacher? So why should we allow him to continue preaching if he is the one who ruined our teacher's reputation?"

"Don't be silly. No one is going to question the preacher's integrity. His is solid."

"And why wouldn't mine be solid, since he was the one who supposedly ruined my reputation with children all around us—children who won't keep their mouths quiet if there was any impropriety going on?" Catherine asked.

"Enough. I won't hear another word from you. I move that we discharge the teacher on the spot." Frazier raised his hand as if to vote.

"Oh, Henry, enough already," Maude said crossly. "Can't you see she didn't do anything wrong? We all make mistakes."

"Yes, please be quiet, Henry," Doctor Johnson said. "A mistake of judgement is all the crime that has been committed. If we are finished here, I have a patient to attend to." He slid forward in his seat and started to rise.

"I say, let the parents be the judge," Caleb offered. "If the children don't come back to school, then we'll know the jury has decided that the teacher must go. But if most of them return, then your findings are unfounded, and we let her continue teaching."

Mr. Grant raised his eyes to Catherine. "I think that's an excellent idea."

"Fine," Henry said with a roll of his eyes. Then pointing at Catherine, he said, "Let the parents decide. And when you see that only the Harris children are coming to school, you pack your bags and get gone."

"She lives here with her mother, so getting gone isn't going to happen," Samuel said.

"You know what I mean. She'll need to be prepared to pack her teacher things and go home."

Samuel turned to Catherine, who stared at Henry Frazier. "How does that sound to you? If the children don't return, then you have your answer."

"All right. As long as Mr. Frazier doesn't interfere with them making it to school tomorrow," she countered.

"Of all the notions!" Frazier burst out. "I wouldn't interfere with your students coming to school, but don't come crying to me when they don't come back."

"Sir, of course I wouldn't come crying to you," Catherine said, irritated. Turning to the rest of the board members, she said, "Thank you for giving me another chance to prove myself. There won't be any more problems, I can assure you."

Doctor Johnson took his pocket watch out of his vest and opened it. "I need to be going," he said, standing. "Keep the faith," he said to Catherine and Samuel. "I believe everything will work out." With that, he let himself out through the way he came.

Samuel stood, followed by Catherine. "I'll see to it that there aren't any more problems," he said, pinching his brows together. "The next time we decide to take the students on any field trips, we'll make sure to let the parents know first. Maybe they might like to go with us."

"Better not be any more fool trips out to Johnson's Point—or anywhere else, for that matter." Frazier ground his teeth.

Catherine bowed her head. "Thank you," she said simply.

Mr. Grant rose and came forward, holding out his hand and smiling. "So glad that's over," he said. "Well, well, good night then." He turned and scurried through the open sliding doors.

Samuel leaned over and whispered, "Let me drive you home. We have things to discuss." She nodded and managed a weak smile. She followed Samuel out of the parlor.

As they drove, Samuel said, "Don't let Frazier scare you. He may be the owner of the livery stables in town, but he isn't much to suffer fools."

"You mean us?"

"Yeah, unfortunately. We better not take any more trips with the students. We should have gotten their parents' approval first before we ventured out."

"I never thought we'd go so far, or I would have."

"You're not blaming me for this debacle?"

"No. I think we both had equal hands at the rudder."

Samuel thought for a while before answering her. "What we need to do now is show this town that you are a serious teacher for their young 'uns."

"How do you plan to do that?"

"Well, you were doing a fine job before all of this came crashing down on our heads. So, just go back to what you were doing. Keep those children in their seats, busy learning, and keep your back to Frazier. I don't want him scaring you by rolling his eyes, which he has a tendency to do."

"I hadn't noticed."

"Good. Maybe he'll be more of a gentleman now that he's had his say and not put on airs that he kept the teacher on by the goodness of his heart."

"Ha!" Catherine laughed cynically. "If he would have had his way, I would be thrown to the side of the street for another teacher."

"Good thing you were our only applicant. By the way, I got you something. Call it faith," he said, pulling a box out from under the seat.

Catherine untied the string holding it closed and opened the lid to find a large, brass bell with a wooden handle wrapped in a flour sack.

"Oh, it's beautiful."

"Thought you might need some help calling the students back to school," he smiled.

"Thank you so much for having faith in me. I appreciate it more than you know, Reverend Harris."

"Samuel. Call me Samuel—like you used to when we were in school, Cathy."

"All right, Samuel. But as I remember, I used to call you Sammy."

"That was when we were little, but I wouldn't mind you calling me Sammy," he said, his eyes shining.

"It would probably be more proper to just call you Samuel."

"Suit yourself." He turned to gaze at her.

Catherine looked away, noticing Harl's apple trees as they made their way through the orchard. What would tomorrow bring? Would her students return to school? Reaching out, she plucked two apples from a tree. She handed one over to Samuel, who nodded to his right pocket. She raised the flap and slipped the apple inside his jacket. She held hers in her lap, feeling the smooth, red-and-yellow-striped skin. Looking up, she noticed her mother standing on the front porch, wiping her hands on a flour sack dish towel as she waited for them.

"Well, how'd it go?" she asked when they were close enough to hear her.

Catherine scrambled out of the buggy. "It went as well as could be expected. I'm still employed," she said. "But I think I've made some enemies by not allowing caution to be my guide."

"Well, thankfully, you're all right, and them children are all right." Turning to Samuel, Hazel said, "I've got apple pie. Come in and have a slice before you leave. It'll be a nice finish to the evening."

"That it would be," he said, climbing out of the buggy. Catherine smiled as he approached. "I hope it's not an imposition."

"It never is." She led the way into the house.

After eating a large slice of pie, Samuel said his goodbyes to Hazel and Clair. Clair wrapped her arms around his legs, and Samuel patted her back.

"I believe I have an admirer."

Walking outside with Catherine, he said, "You know, we really did just scrape by the skin of our teeth and the grace of God."

"Let's hope His grace continues to get us out of scrapes in the future."

"It always will," he said.

Chapter 9

Early the next morning, Catherine rose and met Harl in the kitchen eating a breakfast of eggs, ham, and bread. He looked up from his plate when she entered.

"Sounds like you had a close shave last night," he said. "Going in early to make up the time?"

"No, I'm going in early to prepare my classroom for my students."

"If you have any students, you mean."

"They'll be there. I have faith." She poured herself a cup of coffee.

But Catherine wasn't so sure. What would happen if the students decided not to return?

Their parents might keep them home an extra day, but even they had to see that there was no helping it. They'd gotten stuck out in the wilderness and made the best of it. What else could they have done? Not gone at all? The damage was done. It was time to face the consequences and survey the results. She'd go to school like normal, prepare her lessons on the board, and then wait for her students to arrive. She hoped they would all show up. She couldn't stand the thought of Henry Frazier being right about them and about her. She wanted to—needed to—prove him wrong.

Maybe if she hurried, she could catch Samuel before daybreak, so he could be prepared to help her round up the students who didn't show up.

She quickly packed her breakfast and lunch of cured ham, bread, and jam. She wrapped the bell in a dishcloth flour sack and placed it in the basket. She'd pick apples on her way through the orchard and put them in her knapsack for the students who did venture to school. In a few minutes, she was on her way.

When she arrived, she lit the lamp and was relieved to see no one had written any disapproving messages on the blackboard. She washed the blackboard and then wrote the day's lessons on it. Stepping back, she surveyed her work.

"Looks good," someone said from the doorway behind her. Turning, she found Samuel looking at her with his hands on his hips. "This'll teach Frazier not to doubt his choice in a teacher."

Catherine smiled. "I was going to come speak to you."

Samuel held up his hand. "Let me guess. You'll need me to drive around picking up students who aren't here by the start of class."

"Exactly. Do you mind?"

"Mind? Not at all. I planned to do this very thing the moment I drove away from your house last night. We can't let Frazier win."

Catherine sighed and then laughed. "No, we can't."

"I know Caleb will send his children, and so will the Fields and the Richardsons. I'm not so sure about Dosha Clark's children. She might want to keep them out another day, just in case they caught cold or something," he said. "I'll drive out there and encourage her to let her daughters attend school."

"Yes. Good."

He turned to leave and then swung back around. "You know, Henry Frazier will be paying you a visit sometime today to check on things, right?"

"Ugh!" she exclaimed. "It's to be expected."

"Don't worry. Have faith. We'll see to it that he doesn't have yet another bad report on the schoolteacher." Readjusting his hat, he strode out of the room.

Catherine listened to the sound of the buggy bumping along the road until she couldn't hear it anymore. She stood in the doorway of the school and watched the day break in the east.

"Such a beautiful sight," she murmured. Out of the shadows walked Jonathan and Elizabeth Harris, led by their sister Penelope in a new dress.

Catherine wanted to shout as she watched them approach carrying their school books, slates, and lunch tins. She settled for a hearty, "Good morning, students."

"Good morning, Mrs. Reed," they chimed.

"My pa said last night was a humdinger of a meeting," Penelope said with her nose in the air.

"Don't repeat such things," Jonathan scolded.

"Yes, it was," Catherine agreed. "But we won't be having any more meetings like that one."

As she spoke, three more students stepped out of the shadows. Catherine clapped her hands together as she recognized Hershel, Dorthea, and Easter Fields. Next came Frank and James Richardson sulkily, followed by their father.

"Get on in there, boys," Paul Richardson commanded. His beady eyes watched as his boys stepped past the teacher into the schoolroom before turning his attention fully to Catherine.

"That was a fool thing to do going all the way up to Johnson's Point. Even on a good day, it still would have been foolhardy."

He pushed his hat back on his head and stood with his thick hands on his hips, waiting for Catherine to say something.

She smiled determinedly and raised her chin.

"You are right, Mr. Richardson. It was foolhardy and won't happen again."

"Harrumph. See that it don't." Satisfied, he yelled into the school at his boys, "You all come straight home after school and don't be dilly-dallying. We got crops to get in."

He waited for a response. When none came, he shouted, "Did ya hear me?"

"Yes, Pa," the boys sang.

Pushing his hat back down on his head, Mr. Richardson strode away.

All that was left were the Clark sisters, and Catherine would have a full schoolhouse again. As she waited, her thoughts turned to Samuel. *He stood up for me at the possible cost of his own job. Why would he do that? He very well could have been sacked if the meeting went south. Why was he so bent on keeping me on as their teacher, besides the fact that there were no other candidates? Was there something more to his insistence that I remain in my post?*

The jingle of a harness brought her out of her thoughts. She watched the dark buggy approach. Realizing that all of her students were now accounted for, she stepped out of the doorway to ring the handbell, took another look at the buggy, and stopped. It wasn't Samuel returning with the Clark girls. It was Henry Frazier come to check up on her.

He guided the horse to the side of the building and jumped down.

Quickly counting heads, he sneered, walked toward her, and said, "Well, it looks like *some* of your students are missing."

The Richardson boys poked their heads out the door and then hurried out to join the rest of their class in lines in front of the teacher.

"Yes, but the majority are here."

"But they *all* have to be here in order for you to have a full school."

"There are only two missing out of ten children."

"Still, you'll need to wait before you ring that bell and call your class in."

Catherine fumed. She held her tongue, but what she wanted to say was, *Don't tell me how to run my classroom, and I won't tell you how to run your livery stable.* Instead, she tapped her foot and folded her arms over her chest. Where was Samuel? He should have been back by now. Could something have happened on the road to slow his return? Did the girls agree not to return, and even now he was trying to persuade them to go with him? Minutes passed as Henry Frazier chomped on his unlit cigar.

"Doesn't look like the Clark girls are coming to school today. Which means you don't have a full schoolhouse. Which means all these children should return home, and we'll call another meeting of the school board."

"We ain't having school today?" Penelope asked.

Wherever could Samuel be? Catherine stood on tiptoes gazing over the heads of the children to get a view of the road Samuel had taken.

"We'll just have to wait to see about that. Reverend Harris is still out there; and until he returns, these students aren't going anywhere," she said firmly. "And I'd like it if you didn't put thoughts into my students' heads."

"Just speaking the inevitable." Frazier stepped away from her and leaned back against the school.

Catherine heard the faint jingle of harness rings. Surely, it was Samuel returning with the Clark children. She waited and listened as the sound drew nearer. The sun was now up and illuminated the road between the mountains—the road Samuel took to retrieve the Clark girls, the road on which he now drove. Catherine was relieved to see Samuel returning and even more relieved when she saw the heads of two little girls bobbing beside him on the buggy seat.

"I believe I have a full schoolhouse now," she said, turning to Frazier, who scratched his back against the whitewashed boards of the schoolhouse.

"Hmph," he grunted as he stepped away from the school. Catherine noticed that the back of his black jacket was covered in white dust. She stifled a laugh as Samuel pulled his rig right up to the schoolhouse door. The students scattered to make way for him.

"Delivered as promised." He looked at Frazier.

Catherine was so excited to see the girls, she held out her arms and gave them both hugs as they disembarked from the buggy.

"Now, that's the way to come to school," Minnie Clark remarked.

"Can we do that every day?" Minerva asked.

Samuel laughed. "This was a one-time ride, I'm afraid. After this, you'll need to get yourselves to school the old-fashioned way."

"The old-fashioned way?" Minerva asked.

"Walking," Samuel said. Turning toward Frazier, who still stood off to the side of the door, Samuel remarked, "Let's get these children into the schoolhouse out of this cool morning air. Our teacher has some teaching to do."

Catherine rang the bell as a gleeful Samuel and an angry Frazier drove away. The students lined up, the boys on one side and the girls on the other. They followed their teacher into the classroom and waited for their first lessons to begin.

Chapter 10

At lunchtime, Catherine handed out the apples she had brought to each thankful student. Samuel walked over from his house to see how she was faring, and she gave him an apple, too.

"They say Harl's apples are some of the sweetest around." He held the apple up to look at it.

"That's what they say," Catherine agreed.

Samuel took a large bite and chewed.

"So, how has your day gone so far?"

"It's been normal. Reading, writing, reciting, and arithmetic. The students are putting forth quite an effort."

"Think they know how close they came to losing their teacher?"

"No. I don't think they would ponder such things."

"Maybe not. How are the Richardson boys acting? Are they behaving themselves?"

"As smooth as cream. I think they actually want to learn, or maybe their father gave them another talking to and set them in order."

Catherine looked out over the soft grass surrounding the school. The day was bright and warm. Margaret Fields' children sat under a poplar tree, eating their apples and some of the ham and bread Catherine brought for her lunch. It did her good to share the bounty that the Lord had given her. Out of the corner of her eye, she saw Samuel looking at her. Turning, she asked, "What's on your mind?"

He shook his head and shrugged his shoulders. How could he explain his growing feelings for her? A day ago, she proved her worth by not falling to pieces under dire circumstances—circumstances brought on mainly by him. How could he ever forgive himself for putting her and her class in harm's way? He would be there for her always, he decided. That would be his penance. No matter where she was or what she was doing, he would be there with her.

Samuel waited until she called her students in for their afternoon session before taking her hand briefly and letting her know she could count on him. "Whatever you need, I'll be there for you. Just let me know."

She quickly dropped his hand and stared at him. "Have you gone mad? Taking on so and in front of the children?"

Samuel's cheeks flamed red. "I'm sorry. I wasn't thinking. I just want you to know that even though you couldn't count on me at Johnson's Point, you can count on me now."

Catherine took a step back. "You can't go on blaming yourself for what we didn't know. Without you, who knows what would have happened? You need to stop blaming yourself for that."

"Easier said than done."

Catherine nodded. There were things in Catherine's past that she had trouble forgiving herself for—the death of her husband, the conception of Clair—but those weren't things she wanted to think about right now, so she excused herself as the last of her students walked by her. "I must go," she said, turning to leave. But hesitating, she turned back and said, "Will you come for dinner later tonight?"

"Of course. I'd love to."

The rest of the afternoon passed quickly. Catherine felt a bit jittery as she looked forward to the evening with the preacher.

After school let out, she didn't have long to wait for his company. He limped into the school with a bucket of water and a rag. "To clean off the blackboard," he explained. While he wiped the blackboard with the wet rag, Catherine set about grading papers, catching little glimpses of Samuel as he worked. It was easy work for him. He was tall enough to reach all the way up the board. She used a chair to reach those spots to utilize the full blackboard for lessons.

He wiped the board clean and dumped the dirty water out the door. "Are you ready to go?" he asked.

"Yes."

"I want to get over to Harl's and make sure the men I lined up for him showed up today, since they didn't get a free ride there."

"Oh, yes. I'm sure Harl is happy for the help now that apple-picking is under way. We have a large crop this year."

Samuel's buggy waited outside the door of the school. Alongside it sat Henry Frazier in his rig.

"Evening, teacher and preacher," he greeted them with a sly smile.

"Evening," Samuel said cautiously.

Catherine merely nodded.

"Warm night for a drive," Frazier observed, mopping at his brow with a handkerchief.

"That it is," Samuel agreed.

"Did all of your students return from their noon meals? You didn't have to go looking for any of them lost lambs, did you?" he asked, chomping on his unlit cigar. The condescension in his voice was apparent.

"They were all accounted for." Catherine shut the door to the school and climbed into Samuel's buggy.

"Wouldn't want any of them to get lost on their way back to school."

"Certainly not," Catherine said with a sniff.

"Well, we better be on our way." Samuel snapped the reins over the horse's back. The buggy moved forward and away from Frazier.

"Don't pay him any mind. He's still trying to intimidate you from yesterday."

If only Catherine could "pay him no mind." There was just too much of him not to mind.

As they made their way through the orchard, Catherine picked an armload of apples. "In payment for the ride home," she explained.

"You don't have to pay me. I enjoy doing it."

"Even so, I want you to have something for your trouble."

"It's no trouble at all." His blue eyes pierced her. She turned away, feeling her cheeks warm under his gaze. "Ah, there's Harl and his men."

Catherine glanced up and saw Harl talking to several dark-faced men.

"Look at all those crates of apples," she observed. "Looks like they outdid themselves today."

Harl waved at them as they drove up. Samuel stopped the horse beside him.

"How would you like to do a man a favor?" he asked Samuel.

"If it's in my power to do it, I certainly will."

"I need another wagon to help take these apples up to Grant's store. Feel like hitching up your wagon and coming on back here tonight?"

"Oh, Harl, the preacher was coming for dinner. He doesn't want to be carting apples up to Grant's," Catherine said.

"Now, it's no trouble at all." Samuel held up his hand. "I'd be pleased to help out. I see all of your helpers, and a few more showed back up."

"They're the best hands to work. They're real gentle with the apples, too."

Samuel helped Catherine down from the buggy. "Come in and have a little something first," she said.

He shook his head. "Gotta get these apples to market while they're fresh."

Samuel turned the buggy around and headed back through the orchard the way he came.

In no time, he was back with his wagon. The men loaded the crates of apples into the back and climbed onboard. Harl climbed up onto his loaded wagon and led the way out through the orchard to Grant's Mercantile.

Once the apples were delivered to Grant's store, Harl and the preacher turned back for Hazel's. Harl bid his workers a good night, paid them, and set back off for home.

When they arrived back at Hazel's, she had chicken and dumplings, biscuits, and apple pie ready for them. The group sat at the kitchen table and ate their fill. After Clair ate her meal, she jumped down from her chair and climbed up onto Samuel's lap. "Well, now. It looks as though I have a friend." He chuckled. "Hello, Clair."

She giggled and snuggled into him, playing with her doll.

He held her securely on his knee as he finished eating the slice of apple pie set before him. Putting down his fork on the empty plate, he patted his distended stomach and commented, "More of this treatment, and I will be busting out of my clothing."

Catherine hid her laughter behind a napkin. Hazel and Harl chuckled.

Once the dishes were done and put away, Catherine and Samuel went out on the front porch to sit. "Sure is a nice, clear night," Samuel observed. "Look at all those stars."

Catherine nodded, smiling to herself.

"What?" Samuel asked.

"Clair. She doesn't take to people the way she's taken to you."

"Oh, that. Well, she probably misses her pa."

Catherine bowed her head.

"I didn't mean to say anything amiss."

"No. No. It's true. We all miss him, especially me. I keep a photo of him on the dresser in our room, hoping she won't forget what her father looked like."

"That's good. You want to keep his memory alive in her."

She nodded. "I want to keep his memory alive in me, too."

"As you should."

They sat in silence, listening to the frogs down by the creek and the crickets chirp.

"How do you keep your memories of Isabella alive?"

"I keep her picture on the mantel. I remember the special little things that she used to do for me, like having supper ready when I came from my study. She was always there for me until she got sick . . . " His voice faded away as he spoke. "Well, it's getting late. I better be getting home and let you go to bed, so you'll be rested for tomorrow."

"I'm glad you stayed." Catherine rose with him. "I'm always glad for your company." She looked at the hem of her skirt and was glad that the night covered her reddening face.

"Thank you. I always enjoy your company as well." He hurried off the porch. Donning his hat, he climbed up on the wagon and road off into the orchard and into the night.

Catherine watched him go and stood listening to the sounds of the frogs and crickets. A sudden gust of cold air blew by her. She pulled her shawl around her shoulders, suddenly feeling a chill in the night air. She wondered if Samuel was the answer to her prayers for a husband for her and a daddy for Clair. The child obviously liked him. But how could he be the answer when he didn't even know the truth about her? When would she ever be able to tell him the secret she carried in her heart? How could she tell him something like that? Even if Samuel forgave and accepted her, she'd still lose her job, her standing in the community, and her good name. What's more, once it got out into the community, her mother and brother may suffer, too, because of her mistake.

If only she and John hadn't spent that one night together over Christmas when she had returned home for the holiday from Millersburg.

There was no way to recover from a secret like that, and Samuel must never know. Her family might have guessed, but he must never be told the truth if she wished to remain on friendly terms with the preacher. He was an ally she couldn't do without. He stuck up for her during the board's scrutiny over the Johnson's Point fiasco. He recommended her for the job. Would he still recommend her if he knew the truth?

As Samuel drove, he thought about Isabella and how much he missed her company. He was driving to an empty house. How he longed to have a wife again, but what woman would want him for a husband if she knew the nature in which his wife died? He'd left her to die by herself. She'd died alone while he visited with a sick parishioner.

A neighbor lady who had helped care for her spread the rumor that he deliberately left his wife to die. He did no such thing. If he had known that his wife was that ill, he never would have left her side. He would have been there holding her hand and praying for God' help. What was done was done; now, he must pay his penance for his neglect. Surely, God could forgive him if he asked, but he wasn't done persecuting himself enough yet. His dear Isabella died with only a neighbor beside her.

What if he could do it all over again? He'd stay with her. Mind her himself and hold her while she died. She'd seemed so strong. He was certain she would pull through. He thought this was only a test from God to see how strong his faith was. He was wrong, and he had failed God's test. He didn't only have himself to forgive, but also the Lord for allowing his Isabella to die of complications while carrying their child.

As tears poured down his face, he rode home in silence. Even so, his thoughts concerning his mistake churned on inside. How could the sting of losing a spouse still feel so fresh a year after her death? He brushed the tears off his face. Pulling his handkerchief out of his back pocket, he blew his nose loudly. How long could he keep up the farse that all was right between him and the Lord without someone taking notice? Catherine might be the only person close enough to him to see the cracks in his façade and what lay beyond it.

At his home, he put the wagon away and brushed down the horses while they ate. A tear rolled down his cheek. He wiped it away angrily with his thumb. He thought of Catherine. *Could a woman like that forgive me for my oversight?* If he were her, he would not after the Johnson's Point fiasco. How could she trust him with her life if she couldn't even trust him to keep his wife alive and the children out of harm's way? No one was hurt. True. But the children were shaken up. Sure, they all came back to class, but not without his help in driving the Clark sisters to school.

When he finished brushing down the last horse, Samuel trudged into the house. A knock sounded on the front door. Opening it, he found his mother and brothers.

Maude Harris stepped over the threshold and into the house, followed by his brothers, Caleb and Benjamin. Maude looked around.

"You've kept the place up nicely. Your father would be proud of you," she said.

"But you're not?"

She dipped her head, pushed her glasses up on her nose, and raised her eyes to her son's.

"How are you getting on?" she asked.

Samuel motioned for them to follow him into the parlor off the entranceway. He waved them into seats on the couch and chairs. When they were seated, he sat and folded his hands in front of him.

"I'm fine," he lied.

"Really?" Caleb asked leaning forward.

Samuel looked at the concern etched on his mother and brothers' faces. "What exactly is your concern?"

"You've been spending a great deal of time with Mrs. Reed—or so Henry Frazier told me," his mother said.

Samuel sat back in his chair. "Is that a problem?"

"She almost lost her job, Samuel. I know you miss Isabella, but don't you think you're rushing things the way the two of you are always together?"

Samuel gasped. "She's an old friend. We're friends. That's all."

"I know. I remember," his mother said. "I just don't want you to go too fast and get your heart broken by her again."

"We're just friends. There's no call for concern."

Maude nodded. "All right. I believe you."

"Hey," Benjamin said, "remember when we would play out in the Adams' apple orchard?"

"I remember I couldn't shake you two until we hid up in the trees," Samuel said.

Caleb laughed. "Those were some fun times."

"Your father would get so mad at you boys when Harl tattled to him that you were throwing apples at each other."

Samuel smirked. "Well, it's getting late."

"Oh, don't let us keep you," Caleb said, throwing his arm over the back of his chair.

"Come on, Boys. Walk me home and let's leave Samuel alone."

"Well, at least one of you understands when a man's tired."

The group stood, and Samuel walked them to the foyer. Opening the door, he held it for his brothers. His mother paused, turning to him.

"You've done well for yourself and kept our old home up nicely. I'm sure if your father were alive, he'd tell you how proud he is of you and what you've become."

"You mean, he wouldn't have minded that I really did become a preacher instead of a businessman like him?"

She chuckled and touched his face.

"You are a credit to the Harrises."

"Thank you for that, Mother." Walking forward, she joined her sons out in the street. Turning left, they waved as they walked away back toward town.

Chapter 11

John Reed stood at the front of the class being introduced by their teacher. Catherine's heart warmed as she stared at the blond-haired boy with mirth-filled blue eyes. Suddenly, a large tree grew beside him, clapping him in its branches. He struggled to get free. Instead of the school, they were at their home in the lumber camp. Water poured all around them. She reached out to take his hand but found herself pulling leaves off the tree. Where was her John?

Catherine woke with a start. Something had woken her out of sleep. In the dim, morning light, she looked over at Clair's bed and found it empty. "Clair!" she called, rising and lighting a lamp. "Clair?"

She looked under the bed and found the child stretched out, holding the framed picture of her father. "Clair, what are you doing down there?"

"Where's Daddy?"

"Come out from under there," Catherine commanded. Taking the child's hand to help her out from under the bed, she drew her daughter onto her lap and enfolded her in her arms.

"I dreamed of Daddy."

"Everything all right up there?" Hazel's voice sounded at the bottom of the stairs.

Catherine hurried to the landing with the child in her arms. "Yes. I couldn't find Clair."

"Well, where was she?"

"She was sleeping under the bed with her father's picture."

"Oh, dear. Poor child."

Clair sniffed and wiped at her eyes.

"I want Daddy."

"You want to come down and sleep with Grandma?"

Clair nodded. Catherine walked the child, still holding the portrait of her father, down the stairs to her mother's waiting arms. She kissed Clair on the cheek and admonished her, "Be good for your grandma."

"I will."

When Catherine climbed back into bed, she couldn't sleep. She lay awake thinking of Samuel and Isabella. Did he miss her as much as she missed her husband, John? A lone tear slid down her temple. She brushed it away with her finger.

"Oh, John, if only . . . "

She waited in bed until the sky began to lighten. She rose, donned her black mourning dress, and headed down the stairs. The hem of the dress swished as she walked.

In the kitchen, she fried eggs, cured ham, and cut slices of bread to toast on the wood-burning stove.

Harl came in from the chores and saw her pouring coffee into his cup. "Where's Ma?" he asked.

"She has Clair sleeping with her, and I thought she might need her sleep. You don't know how Clair can kick."

Harl smiled and took his place at the table. He folded his hands in front of him and cut his eyes to his sister, who had just sat down at her place. "You want me to ask the prayer?"

She returned his smile. "If you like."

He bowed his head. "Dear Lord, I thank You for bringing my sister and niece all this way safely. I pray You'll bless this food to our bodies and bless the hands that prepared it. In Jesus' name, amen."

Catherine passed the platter of fried eggs and ham to Harl. He speared some ham and offered it first to his sister, who placed some on her plate.

"You want eggs?"

"Yes, please." Catherine held up her plate as Harl raked eggs onto it.

The pair ate in silence for a moment before Harl asked, "Those big boys behaving themselves?"

"I think I've got a handle on the situation."

"Good. Don't want to see my little sis frightened off."

"Oh, no. Not me." She smiled and then sobered. Looking at her brother, she said, "I'm so sorry you got stuck here taking care of the farm and watching over Mama when Pa died.

Harl shook his head and shrugged. "It was my duty. After Pa died . . . well, I just couldn't leave Ma alone, you know."

Catherine reached out her hand and placed it on her brother's arm. "I don't know what you went through when you saw our father get killed right in front of you. I know that tore you apart. Tore us all apart, you coming back on that wagon so soon after you and Pa left to sign up for the war. And there he was, dead. I'll never forget that day."

"Neither will I," he said, flicking a tear off his cheek.

"But you could have had a life afterward."

Harl jerked his head around to look at his sister. "I did have a life. I mean, I do have a life here with Ma and the farm. You don't need to feel sorry for me. There's nothing to feel sorry about. It's been a good life."

"But you never married."

"Ha," he said. "I'll get around to it sometime. Ain't nobody caught my eye as such."

He finished his breakfast and stood. Placing his hand on his sister's shoulder, he said, "Good talk." And walked out the door.

After finishing her meal, Catherine filled a lunch basket with ham, a few boiled eggs, and some bread and jam. She peeked in the door to her mother's room. Clair looked at her. She placed a finger to her lips as she listened to the soft snores of her mother.

Creeping into the room, she brushed her fingers through Clair's soft hair and whispered, "Mama's got to get to school. Love you, sweetheart." She bent and kissed the child, who reached up and hugged her neck and kissed her back. She waved as she went out of the room and shut the door quietly.

Heavy, cold dew lay on the ground as she walked, which wet her leather boots and the hem of her dress. She would light a fire in the potbellied stove once she arrived at school, she decided. Hopefully, her dress and boots would dry by the time school started. She didn't need to come down with a cold on top of everything else.

By the time she arrived at school, the sun was just visible on the eastern horizon. She lit the fire in the stove and carried in more wood in case the day grew cool. Wrapping her shawl around her, she rubbed her hands over the black stove as it warmed. The fire popped and crackled.

She pulled off her boots and socks and laid them beside the stove to dry and then went about writing that day's lessons on the blackboard.

"So, the teacher went barefoot," said a deep voice from the doorway of the schoolhouse behind her.

Catherine spun around to see Samuel standing with his hands on his hips laughing at her.

"I don't see anything funny about catching cold. Do you?"

"No. Not at all." He sobered. "Your shoes and socks should dry quickly." He limped into the room and ran a hand through his hair before picking up one delicate calf-skin boot and examining it. "See? Look. It's almost dry. Your socks, on the other hand, are dry." He held them up.

"Please drop my stockings," she commanded him.

"There." He dropped the socks next to the boots. "Do you want me to help you put them back on?" He tried to look serious, but she saw the twinkle in his eye.

"Of course not." She stepped lightly toward the stove. Picking up her stockings and boots, she carried them to the front of the room. Samuel turned his back to her. She put them back on under the cover of her desk.

"Better?" he asked when he heard the gentle swish of her skirts on the floorboards behind him.

"Better."

Turning, Samuel's eyes twinkled. "I'll go fill the water bucket."

Catherine returned his gaze. "That would be nice. Thank you."

The first students to arrive were the Harris children. They were followed by Margaret Field's children, then the Clark sisters, and finally, the Richardson brothers.

"Well, it looks like all of my students are here. Time to get some learning done."

"I'll leave you to it." He donned his hat and walked out, greeting the students as he left.

"Preacher sure is here a lot," Dorthea observed.

"Shh." Easter yanked on Dorthea's hand. "You ain't supposed to say things like that."

"Well, it's true, ain't it?"

"Yes, it's true. Just you ain't supposed to say."

Catherine's face grew hot. She hoped the children didn't see it. Stepping from the doorway to the porch, she rang the bell to start school. The students hurried into lines.

"Anyone can see that the preacher is sweet on teacher," Dorthea said.

"Shhhh," Easter hissed from the back of the line.

"Thank you, Easter," Catherine said. "Now, children, come in and get seated."

The class filed into the room. Each student who had a lunch basket or pail put it under the bench where they sat and picked up their slates. After Catherine prayed, the students copied the lessons off the board and began working.

Catherine thought about what Dorthea had insisted. Was the preacher sweet on her? They were friends long ago. Could he have feelings for her? She wondered at her own feelings for him. He was a warm, caring man. Clair took to him like a chicken to a June bug. Was there something more to his interest in her other than friendship? He took her side twice before the board. He was quick to offer rides home. Yes, but he offered to find Harl help when he needed it and didn't easily turn down Hazel's cooking. He was more like another brother to her than a love interest, but could he be more? Would he be more if he knew the secret that she held deep inside? Could he love a fallen woman? Catherine's mind drifted back to the classroom when she saw Minerva Clark's hand shoot up.

"Yes, Minerva."

"I need help with this problem."

Catherine's skirts swished on the floor as she walked back to where the girl sat. Looking over Minerva's book and slate, she pointed out where the girl went wrong and showed her how to correct the problem on which she worked.

Stepping away from her student, she put more wood into the stove and stood warming her already warm hands, trying to put Dorthea's words and her own thoughts out of her head.

At lunchtime, she shared her lunch with the Fields children, who ate outside under one of the many trees while Catherine ate at her desk. She stared out the window lost in thought.

"Preacher is sweet on you, ain't he?" Dorthea asked, returning to the classroom by herself.

Catherine turned her attention to the child standing in the doorway.

"I don't know. We are good friends."

"That's how love starts, Ma always said—like friends—and then you git to liking your friend more and more, and that turns into love."

"Your mother is right," Catherine agreed, turning her attention back to the book on the desk as she felt her cheeks grow warm.

"I thought so." Running out the door, Dorthea called to Hershel and Easter, "I was right. He is sweet on her."

Easter hushed her sister, but the damage was done. Catherine's thoughts returned to Samuel. She felt the heat rise higher in her cheeks. *Could he consider me more than a friend?* Why was it that thoughts of him as more than a friend still caused her to blush? Was she considering him more than a friend?

She wanted to sit at her desk and ponder her rekindled friendship with Samuel, but it was time to ring the bell and bring the students in from lunch.

After school let out, Catherine washed the blackboard. The day had turned hot, and she draped her shawl over her arm as she closed up the school.

Samuel met her in his wagon. "Care for a ride home?" he asked.

She gazed up at him and those piercing blue eyes of his and answered, "Yes."

Samuel pulled her up into the wagon. She felt her arm tingle with electricity as he helped her up beside him. Their eyes met. *Did he feel it, too?*

She turned her face away from him.

"Why so quiet?"

"Oh, just something one of the students asked me today made me think."

"What did the student ask you?" he said, releasing the brake and speaking to the horses to "git up."

She felt her face warm under his gaze. She sat in silence for a few seconds before answering. "Well, that's a conversation best left for another time."

"Yes, but it has you so quiet."

"Why do you take me home every day? And why would you stay for dinner?"

"Well, Hazel is an excellent cook, and I want to check on those workers I sent to Harl."

"So, you are just doing your neighborly duty then?"

"More or less, yes."

Catherine looked straight ahead, her mouth pulled into a tight line. What glimmer of hope she had that maybe there was something more between her and Samuel was gone. He was only a friend, after all. Even so, knowing he would only be a friend did nothing to squelch her growing feelings for him. She sat in silence, pondering his statement. She thought she saw a glimmer of hope through all of their times together, but if all he wanted was to be a friend, it might be best not to let Clair get too close. She didn't want to break the girl's heart, or her own.

Tears began to well up in her eyes. She brushed them away quickly and kept her head turned away from Samuel. She stifled a sob. Were her feelings for Samuel more than she intended?

"Here now. What seems to be the matter?" he asked, pulling the horses to a halt on the edge of the orchard.

Catherine didn't dare look at him for fear that her resolve would break and she would let her tears and anguished sobs loose. Samuel touched her hand. All the hopes she held that she was finally finding love again came gushing out in tears and sobs.

"Tell me what's the matter," he said, concern sounding in his voice.

"I can't. I just . . . " Catherine hurried down from the wagon and ran toward the house.

Samuel sat looking after her, his mouth open. He lost sight of her among the trees before he remembered himself and spoke to the horses to go forward again. When he arrived at Hazel's, he didn't see Catherine anywhere. *She must have gone into the house,* he thought. Hazel stood on the porch wiping her hands on her apron. "Everything all right, Preacher?"

"Not really sure. Where's Catherine?"

"She came tearing through here just a minute ago, ran right up the stairs to her room."

"Hmmm," Samuel mused.

"Ready to load up?" Harl asked, walking toward Samuel.

"What? Oh, yeah. Sure."

In a few minutes, Harl and his team of workers filled Samuel's wagon with crates of apples. Samuel sat still and thought of Catherine. What did he say to make her go off like that? Did she have feelings for him that he did not know? Could she be in love with him? Their love was superficial when they were younger. Did she forgive him for marrying Isabella? He thought that only his heart was at stake in their friendship. Did her feelings run deeper than just friends?

He shook the thought out of his head as he waited for the last crate to be loaded. There was no way he could take on a wife and a child and give them the type of undivided attention that they deserved when he couldn't even forgive himself for leaving his own wife to die. If Catherine knew the truth, she wouldn't forgive him either.

Maybe it would be best if instead of returning for dinner, he just went on home and ate alone. He didn't want to upset Catherine anymore tonight, and he knew his presence would upset her. How could he partake with the family at dinner and not show his thanks by courting Catherine? Was that what she was expecting? Is that what her tears and sobs were about? That she felt scorned because he could never be more than her friend—would never allow himself to be more than a friend to her and her family?

When the last crate was loaded, Samuel turned his horses around and slowly followed Harl's wagon into town. He'd drop off the load at Mr. Grant's mercantile and then head for home. It had been a long day already.

As Samuel unloaded the crates of apples from his wagon with Harl and his workers, he saw out of the corner of his eye a petite woman, holding a string tied package and sauntering toward him. Turning his gaze to her, he recognized his mother. He shook his head and put out his hand to halt her approach. She stopped.

"Samuel, dear, whatever is the matter?" she asked.

Samuel shook his head again as the last crate was unloaded. He watched as Harl counted out coins to each worker. The men loaded into the back of Harl's wagon. Samuel waited until Harl was out of earshot before speaking.

"I've made a terrible mistake," he said, gripping the side of his wagon.

"What do you mean?" she asked, walking toward her son.

"Somehow, someway, I made Catherine upset, and I don't even know what I did or said." He scrubbed his hand over his face.

"Tell me what happened," she said placing a delicate, gloved hand on her son's arm.

He turned and looked at her, shaking his head again.

"One minute, she's fine. We're riding along in the wagon headed to her place. The next minute, she's jumping down and tearing through the orchard toward the house."

"What did you say to her?"

"That's just it. I don't know what I said to her to get her so upset. She seemed out of sorts, and I asked her what was the matter."

"And what did she say?"

"She broke down in tears and said she couldn't tell me and then ran off toward the house."

Maude nodded and pressed her lips together.

"I was afraid something like this would happen," she said, sighing heavily.

"Something like what?"

"She must have feelings for you. Can't you see?"

Samuel's mouth fell open, and he looked at the sky.

"You've been spending so much time together. It's only natural that you two pick up where you left off," she said.

"But she's not over John yet."

"That doesn't matter. She'll always love her husband, but that doesn't mean she can't make room for someone else in her life. And maybe that scares her."

Samuel's smile was slow, like the sunrise.

"I hadn't thought of that."

"The question is, are you ready to get on with your life?"

Samuel gazed at the ground for a moment.

"I'm not sure she'd want me for more than a friend."

"No? Why not?"

"Because Isabella died without me by her side."

"It's high time you forgive yourself for that."

Samuel sniffed and looked away.

"Yeah, it is. Well, it's getting late. I need to get home."

"Come home with me and have dinner."

He shook his head. "I'd be poor company. But I can offer you a ride home."

"All right."

Taking her parcel, he placed it on the seat of the wagon and then helped his mother up onto the seat.

He smiled at her and then chirped to the horses to "walk on."

In her room, Catherine sobbed into her pillow and wondered how she could have been so blind. Samuel Harris wasn't interested in her; it was plain now. He was only being friendly—rekindling their old friendship once more. She misjudged all of his actions for more than what they were. *How could I be so blind?* A knock sounded lightly on the door.

"Come in."

Her mother walked in holding Clair. "She wanted to see her mama." Catherine sat up and took her child. Holding Clair, Catherine pulled a handkerchief out of her sleeve and dried her eyes.

"Why are you crying, Mama?" Clair asked. Catherine pulled the child into a hug.

"Because sometimes what we think is, isn't."

Mother sat on Clair's bed and faced Catherine. "Want to talk about it?"

"Oh, Mama." Catherine's tears started afresh. "I've made such a fool of myself. I thought there was a glimmer of hope starting between the preacher and me, but I was wrong. How could he love someone like me? I've been so blind."

"Well, the Lord don't fault us for blindness. It's good to have hope. Without hope, we couldn't go on."

"My hope has been dashed. All I want is a father for Clair, and all I got was a friend."

"Don't you want a husband for you?"

"It wouldn't hurt."

"That's how love starts—or, at least, how it's supposed to start—with friendship that turns into something more. That's how it was for me and your father. We started off as schoolmates. We loved to play out in his daddy's orchard, just like you and the preacher used to. Remember?"

Catherine sniffed and nodded.

"We used to have such a time playing hide and go seek out there," Hazel laughed. "We'd chuck green apples at each other and get a scolding from his father if he caught us. We loved being together no matter what we did. As we grew, we discovered our like had turned to love. There wasn't anything your father couldn't do for me, except live through the war." Hazel was silent for a moment before continuing.

"The preacher probably doesn't know his own mind right now. He's like you—so addled over the loss of his loved one, he can't even think or see straight. Give him time. If it's the Lord's will, he'll come around."

"And if it isn't?"

"Then it wasn't worth having to begin with. Honey, you still got a lot of grieving to go through. Don't rush things. It's all in God's timing."

Catherine nodded, hiccupped, and hugged Clair. "You're right, Mama. I forget that from time to time."

"Now, come on downstairs and have something to eat. Harl already ate, so it's just us."

Catherine carried Clair and followed her mother downstairs. Their skirts swished on the staircase. In the kitchen, the comforting smell of fresh apple pie and roasted chicken tickled Catherine's nose.

After dinner, the women washed the dishes and put them away. It was sometime before Harl returned with an empty wagon.

"Think I'll go help Harl put the mules away for the night," Catherine offered.

Walking into the barn, Harl looked up from his work. "I've already eaten."

"I thought I might be of some help with the mules."

"Well, I'll never turn down help, but don't you have books to study?"

"Yes, but I wanted to help you first."

"Thank you. I appreciate that."

Catherine reached up and grabbed the halter of one of the mules and led him to his stall. Picking up a brush, she began rhythmically brushing the mule's neck, shoulders, and back. "I see the preacher didn't come back with you. Did he decide to go home?"

"I guess so. I invited him back to eat with us, but I guess he just didn't have a taste for Hazel's apple pie tonight."

"No, I guess not."

Catherine smoothed her hand over the mule as she brushed. "Was he mad?"

"Mad about what? You? Not that I know of. Why? Did you do something to make him mad?"

"No. I just wish I knew why he didn't come back for dinner."

"Well, you running in the house crying didn't help matters much."

"Oh. You saw that?"

"We *all* saw that. What were you crying about anyway?" he asked softer.

"It's not important now."

"It made you come crying, cutting through the orchard like a rat on fire, and it's not important?" Harl put down his brush and turned to her. "It sure as shootin' was important to you, sis."

"Have you ever been in love, Harl?"

"Oh, don't tell me this is about love," he said, picking the brush back up he turned his back to her.

"Well, have you?"

"What?"

"Been in love."

"Once, a long time ago, I thought I was, but she didn't have the same feelings as me. I think her father didn't like the thought of her being courted by an apple farmer. And that is that."

Catherine waited for him to go on. He didn't. "Never mind then. I think I'm finished here." Catherine turned to go out the door.

"You can run as far as you like, but your problems will always find you," he said, turning to her.

Catherine spun around and said hotly, "I'm not running anywhere."

"Just remember that the next time you come tearing through the orchard with Samuel Harris on your heels."

"He wasn't on my heels." Catherine turned toward the door with a sniff. She stepped through the door, making sure to not let it slam, and headed for the house.

Inside, she picked up Clair and walked up the stairs to their room. She readied the child for bed and tucked her in. "Now, say your prayers." Catherine shut her eyes and bowed her head.

"God bless Mama and Grandma and Uncle Harl and the preacher. Amen."

"The preacher? Why the preacher?"

"Because he made you sad, and maybe he's sad, too."

Catherine didn't want to hope that Samuel could be sad for making her cry that afternoon. She wanted him to forget what his words—or lack of them—did to her. She wanted him to love her without reserve, but it seemed that neither one of them was ready to give up their grief in exchange for love. Who knew when either one would be ready to love again? Catherine felt a warm sensation in her chest. Maybe her time to love was coming sooner than she thought.

She sat with Clair until her breathing became rhythmic, then hurried back downstairs to the kitchen and opened her knapsack where she kept her books. She looked over the lessons for the following day, took notes, and closed her books. Satisfied that she had a handle on the next day, she went to bed.

As she lay in bed, she thought of Samuel and what he must have thought of her outburst that afternoon. Was he thinking of her? Wondering about her? Did he care if she was all right? Did he wonder if her personal storm had passed?

She soon drifted off to sleep and dreamed of riding through the orchard in full bloom with the handsome preacher at her side. They were laughing about something one of them said. The dream changed, and they were sitting on the front porch of the house drinking sweet tea and listening to the birds chatter in the trees as the sun came up.

She woke abruptly and smiled to herself. Balling her fists over her heart, she wanted to remember such a good dream and keep it close to her. It gave her hope again. She would just have to wait and see if it came true.

Chapter 12

In the morning, Catherine scooted her books into the knapsack on the table in the kitchen as Clair watched, chewing on a piece of buttered toast with apple butter on it.

"Aren't you going to stay and play with me today?" Clair asked.

"No, honey. You know I have to go to work at the school."

"I want you to stay and play with me."

"I can't. You be a good girl for Grandma today, honey," Catherine said, bending to kiss the top of her daughter's head.

Clair frowned and her chin quivered.

Catherine moved to her daughter and squatted down. "Come here," she said, opening her arms.

Tears rolled down Clair's cheeks as she fell into her mother's embrace.

"I miss Daddy."

"Oh, honey, I miss your daddy, too," Catherine whispered against the child's hair.

"Now, don't you fret, Clair. I'll play with you," her grandmother said.

Catherine rose and brushed a tear from her face. Clair returned to her seat.

"Are you going to eat a bite?" Hazel asked, standing at the stove.

"The way my stomach is in knots? I couldn't eat a thing."

"Well, take something with you, anyway," her mother said, buttering some freshly toasted bread and wrapping it in a cloth napkin. She handed it to Catherine. "Why the rush all of a sudden?"

"I need to get to school early to apologize to Samuel for my outburst yesterday."

Her mother nodded.

Catherine slung the bag over her shoulder. "See you this afternoon, Mama." She kissed her mother and ruffled Clair's hair. "And you and me will play then." Clair smiled at her as Catherine headed out the door.

As she ambled through the orchard, picking apples to give to the children, her thoughts turned to Samuel and how she would go about apologizing. Maybe he would stop by the school to check on her, and then she could apologize. If he didn't stop by the school, she would be forced to go to his home and knock on the door. It wouldn't be very proper, but she didn't want her outburst the previous day to cause him any more grief than it already had.

As it was, she didn't have to wait long for Samuel to come check on her once she entered the school.

"I was watching for you. I wanted to come over and apologize for upsetting you yesterday," he said.

Catherine spun around from writing assignments on the board.

"No, it's me who should be apologizing. I had no right to assume that you had anything other than friendship for me."

Samuel sighed. "It's not that. It's too hard to put into words . . . "

Catherine turned her attention to the board again and began writing lessons on it.

"Here, let me help you."

They worked silently side by side. Placing the chalk in a box on the desk, their hands momentarily brushed. Catherine felt a tingle of excitement course up her arm and raised her eyes to Samuel's. He studied her face for a moment before speaking.

"Catherine . . . I . . . "

"I know," she whispered. "I felt it, too."

He stepped closer to her and held out his hand.

"Preacher sure is here a lot," Catherine overheard Dorthea say just outside the door.

"Hush up. They'll hear you," Easter reproached her.

Dropping his hand, he stepped back.

"I better go let them in."

"I should go then. I'll see you later?"

After Samuel left, Catherine lined the students up and prayed for the day before letting them into the schoolhouse.

As she worked with her pupils in individual grades, she remembered her dream and the way Samuel laughed—as if he didn't have a care in the world. Could his frozen heart be thawing? Could hers be, too?

She clasped her hand to her chest and thought of the jolt of excitement when their hands touched.

At lunchtime, Easter came back into the schoolhouse and approached her teacher seated at the desk. "Can anyone come to school and learn to read?"

"Why, yes, they can if they have a mind to," Catherine answered. "Why?"

"It's just that my ma can't read, and she was wondering if you'd teach her how."

"You tell your mother to come on. I'd be pleased to help her learn to read and write."

"Thank you. I'll tell her."

The thought of having another student thrilled Catherine, but she wondered how her class would take it having a much older person learning in their midst. If Margaret Fields couldn't read or write, Catherine would have to start her on the basics such as the ABCs. She would begin devising a course of study for her tonight at home. She was deep in thought about how to teach an older student to read and write when a deep voice sounded from the doorway. She jumped at the sound of Samuel's voice.

"Oh, I didn't mean to startle you," he said, holding his hand in front of him.

"No, it's fine. I was just lost in thought."

"I see that. Lost in thought about what?"

"I'm going to have a new student. Margaret Fields. Do you know her?"

"Yes, I know the Fields." Then he leaned over the desk and whispered, "Her husband is a drunkard."

"Oh, that poor woman and those children. How is it they have survived?"

"I hear their neighbors take them milk and eggs from time to time." He winked.

"I hear that, too," Catherine said, smiling up at him across the desk. "Learning to read and write would turn her world right-side up, I'm sure. Well, lunchtime is almost over. I better get ready for the afternoon work."

Samuel bowed slightly and left.

Catherine stood and watched him go. She felt the same warmth in her chest as she did when she balled her fists over her heart after waking from the dream. She followed Samuel out the door.

"I told ya he was sweet on you."

"All right, Dorthea, you shouldn't say such things; they may not be true."

"Oh, it's true all right," she said. "Easter tell you my ma wants to come to school?"

"Yes, she did."

"Can she sit by me?"

"You're in the front row. She might not be comfortable there. We'll see where she would like to sit when she gets here."

"That's a fine plan, Teacher."

"Thank you. Now, let's get ready to go in for the afternoon session."

The afternoon session flew by. Catherine was so excited at the prospect of a new student that she hurried the students through their lessons and let them out early.

"Have a good weekend," she called to them as they left. Turning to the blackboard, she erased the lessons. A few moments later, someone spoke from the doorway.

"Letting them leave early?" The voice of Henry Frazier grated on her nerves. "Tsk tsk. I would say we aren't doing our job very well."

The hairs on the back of Catherine's neck stood up as she turned to face him. "I'm getting a new student Monday, and I want to be prepared."

"Good thing you aren't getting two new students; you might have let the children go home at noon," he teased, removing his hat. He fidgeted with the felt brim.

"What brings you out this way, Mr. Frazier?" Catherine asked, changing the subject.

"Just checking up on Harrisville's favorite teacher."

"Is that all?"

"No, I saw the children leaving and thought something was wrong, so I wanted to check on you. Make sure you were all right."

"As you can see, there is nothing amiss."

"Fine, fine," he added, turning his hat over in his hands before clearing his throat loudly. "Perhaps you might like to join me for dinner some evening."

Catherine's mouth dropped open. Was older, confirmed bachelor Henry Frazier asking her out for dinner? How impertinent. Of course, she didn't want to go to dinner with Henry Frazier—board member or not. But she answered civilly, "No, thank you."

"Suit yourself." He shrugged. "It might be good to have another ally on the school board is all."

"She does have an ally on the board. Me." Samuel stepped into the room behind Frazier.

"Ah, yes," Frazier observed. "Well, carry on then." With that, he donned his hat and rushed from the room.

"Hmmm, I'm going to need to keep a closer eye on you."

"Why is that?"

"Allowing wolves into your classroom. Not good for the children."

Catherine laughed.

"Care to allow me to escort you home?"

"Of course." She felt her cheeks warm under his intense gaze.

She packed her books into the knapsack and closed the school door for the weekend. Samuel helped her up onto the wagon and then seated himself next to her. They rode in silence all the way to the farm, stealing glances and smiles at each other as they drove.

Catherine felt warm inside, just like the fall day. She understood why she smiled, but why was Samuel? Could he have unspoken feelings for her? Had he felt a jolt of excitement course up his arm, too, when their hands touched?

At the farm, Samuel held Catherine's hand as she climbed down. She gasped when her arm tingled again. Their eyes momentarily met. Samuel opened his mouth.

"Dinner will be ready by the time you get back," said Hazel, who had stepped out onto the porch. "I've got fresh apple pie."

Samuel closed his mouth and then smiled, releasing Catherine's hand.

"Now, how could a man turn down such fixin's?"

Hazel smiled, and putting her arm around her daughter, they headed into the house as the men loaded crates of apples into the back of Samuel's wagon.

"Now, don't you worry about a thing. He's coming back, and that's a good sign," Hazel said.

Clair ran to her mother and wrapped her tiny arms around her skirt.

"Now, who's ready to play?"

"Me," Clair said, jabbing her thumb toward her chest.

Catherine laughed as she picked up her daughter and spun around.

When Samuel returned, he ate dinner and two helpings of apple pie.

"I'm stuffed like a Sunday after-meeting chicken dinner," he said and laughed.

After the dishes were done, Catherine called to Samuel, who was seated on the front porch. "There's something I'd like to discuss with you. Let's go for a walk."

"All right."

"Mama, we're going for a walk out in the orchard."

"Go right ahead. I'll watch Clair for you."

When they were out of view of the house, Catherine spoke. "Today, Easter asked me if anyone could learn."

"What did you say?"

"I said yes. I didn't know it at the time, but she was speaking about her mother and whether she could attend school. I told her she could and would be welcome, but I wasn't thinking straight. I should have brought this up to the board, but since Henry Frazier came by and got me all addled, I'm not sure I can. That's why I'm asking you if it would be all right for a much older student to attend school with the children."

"I don't see why not, as long as they aren't disruptive or keep the students from learning their lessons by taking too much of your time."

"I don't see that happening with Margaret Fields."

They walked on through the high grass surrounding the apple trees. The night air was warm and fragrant with the scent of sweet, ripe apples. Deer ran ahead of them as they walked, and crickets chirped around them. Fireflies dotted the darkening sky. The night air stirred loose strands of hair framing Catherine's face. Pausing, she brushed them behind her ears and smiled up at Samuel, studying his face. He returned her smile.

"Remember when we used to play hide and seek out here in the summer?"

He chuckled at the memory. "Yes, I do. That was a long time ago."

"We used to climb the trees and eat our fill of green apples."

"And be so sick, we couldn't eat dinner. Yes, I remember those times. Harl used to scold us for eating the green apples and tell your pa on us. Said we were eating the fall crop and to stop it."

Catherine laughed. It felt good to chuckle at the memory of their misbehavior. It felt good to feel like laughing again. Her brows pinched together. *What would John say if he could see me? Am I moving on too fast? Shouldn't I still feel the weight of grief instead of the lightness of mirth?* She shook her head as if to let go of the past.

When they came to the end of the row, they circled back around the outer edge of the orchard. Samuel clasped his hands behind his back as they strolled.

It was good to hear Catherine's laughter. It was good to feel like laughing with her. So much had changed since the last time they had hidden among the trees eating apples. They had grown up and married. Even though their spouses were dead, Samuel was surprised by the stirring in his heart toward this woman beside him. Had she felt a spark when their hands had touched at the school? There was a definite jolt when he helped her down off the wagon a few hours ago. But had she felt it? Was it the beginning of something? What was the Lord saying in all of this? Was it time for her to throw off grief like a cloak?

He looked down at the silent woman walking beside him. Her grief was new. His was old. His heart was healing. Was hers? Was she ready to be more than just friends? He opened his mouth to ask if she felt the spark, but all that came out was, "What types of apples do you grow?"

"We have Maiden Blush, Pineapple, MacIntosh—though they come in early—Northern Spy and Newtown Pippin. There are some others that Harl is working on, but I don't know what they are called. Besides taking them to market, we can and preserve as much as we are able to for the winter months. Mama makes apple butter and cans slices with spices for making apple pies in the winter. We make apple sauce, too, and apple jelly."

It was too late. The moment had passed. He'd have to save the question of sparks for another time.

"I'd love to try some of your mother's apple butter."

"I'll bring some to school on Monday for lunch."

"All right. I'll plan on meeting you then."

They walked all the way around and ended their walk at the barn. The door stood open, and a light shined.

"Think I'll go see what Harl is up to. Offer him some help if I can."

"I think he'd like that," Catherine said as she headed back up to the house.

As Samuel entered the barn, he was greeted by Harl.

"Sister done dragging you around the orchard?"

Samuel chuckled. "Seems so."

"Doesn't seem right to be dragging a wounded man all over creation."

"Well, this wounded man let her."

They fell silent as Harl worked at repairing a harness.

"Need a hand with that?"

"No," Harl said, keeping his eyes on his work. Samuel turned to go. "But you can brush down the mules."

Samuel limped over to the stall of one of the mules, picked up a brush, and began brushing.

Samuel felt Harl's eyes on his back as he worked.

"Looks like you healed pretty well, except for that limp."

"A bullet in the hip'll do that to a man."

"How'd it happen?"

"I always say someone didn't like the topic of my sermon and shot me," he said with a laugh. Harl didn't laugh but sat patiently waiting for the story. Samuel turned and faced him.

"I was a chaplain during the war and was out in the field ministering to the fallen when someone shot me in the hip from across the way. I think he was aiming for my heart. Good thing he was a poor shot, or I'd be dead."

Harl nodded his understanding and waited.

"I sure have had some close calls in my life. Once my hip healed, I went to Bell County visiting a dying woman with a circuit preacher—a friend. We prayed with her and hoped that God would see fit to heal her; but He didn't, and she died—just as soon as we left. Her man came storming after us, gun in hand. He said we should have done more. That it was our fault his wife had died. We tried talking to him, but talk was no good. He wound up shooting my friend—killed him on the spot—and shot me in the leg as a reminder that God doesn't always answer prayer according to what we hope, I guess."

Harl put down the tack and gaped at the preacher.

"A doctor over in Pineville pulled the slug out of my leg, but I've had a limp ever since. Good thing I got hit both in the same side."

"What happened to the man?"

"Hung for murder." Samuel looked at the brush in his hand. "Wish I could have saved him, but the judge and jury had their minds made up. He would hang for his sin, and that was that."

Harl picked the harness back up and began mending it again. The two men worked in silence as Samuel brushed down both mules.

"Well, my job's done here." Samuel put the brush away. "'Night, Harl."

"'Night, preacher."

Outside, Samuel turned his wagon around and headed back out through the orchard and into the night.

Inside the house, Catherine dug through the shelves of canned goods until she found a jar of apple butter. "Mind if I take this?"

"Sure, help yourself to whatever you need or can use." Hazel said, playing with Clair on the kitchen floor.

"Samuel has a hankering for some of your apple butter."

"Does he now? You know, maybe you should make the apple butter this year. Give him a taste of your cooking instead of mine all the time. He must think you don't know how to cook, since all he's ever eaten is my cooking."

"Of course, he knows I can cook. I was married, you know."

"I'm just saying that a fella needs to know what he's getting himself into before he goes in too deep."

"Ma!"

Her mother chuckled and studied the ceiling. "I remember cooking for your father when we were courting. I invited him to dinner one Saturday afternoon. I was so excited, I nearly burned the chicken. It was mighty crispy, though." She laughed again. "I watched him crunch his way through that dinner, smiling the whole time as if it was the best thing he'd ever eaten. I sure do miss your pa."

"After all these years?"

"Of course. Missing someone you've been married to for seventeen years doesn't change your yearning for them when they are gone. Goodness," she said, studying the ceiling again.

"He's been gone seven years now." She shook her head. "It's probably the same for you."

"I miss John every day. Working at the school keeps me busy and keeps those feelings in check. I still miss Papa, too. The way he died . . . " She dipped her head.

"Yes, he was a good father to you and a good husband to me. We'll always miss them 'til we see them in glory, but you still need to cry and let it out. Like steam setting the kettle to boil, you need to vent it and let it go."

"I do, Mama. Just because I don't sob in front of you doesn't mean I don't cry every so often. I cry in my heart."

Her mother nodded.

Catherine smiled, tears threatening to spill from her eyes. "Remember when I was little and Papa and me would dance around? I'd put my feet on his, and he'd dance a jig with me holding on for dear life, laughing."

Hazel grinned. "And you falling off every so often and him waiting patiently until you put your feet back on his. And then he'd start the dance all over again."

"He was always there for me. When I fell out of one of the trees in the orchard and bumped my head, he came running and carried me all the way to the house. He helped doctor me and sat up with me all through the night. He was a good father."

Catherine wiped tears from her eyes at the memory. After a moment or two, she said, "The only time I could cook supper would be on Saturday or Sunday."

"Well, invite him home then. You know, we do have that dinner on the grounds after church this Sunday. You could show off your cooking then."

Catherine studied the door frame.

"That is a good idea. I'll make us a picnic basket to be envied."

"'Pride goes before the fall.'"

"Well, I'll make up a good one, anyway."

"So, what are you planning on serving Sunday?"

"Hmmm . . . I think I'll fry some chicken and cook cornbread with honey to sweeten it. I'll make white bread with a jar of your apple butter and take some plain butter in a jar and an apple pie for dessert."

Her mother nodded.

"At least, we know he isn't a picky eater, so those things should be good choices."

"I just wish I knew what his favorite dishes were."

"Oh, honey, when a man likes a woman, any dish is his favorite. Just like me and your pa and that awful chicken dinner. He thanked me afterward. I turned as pink as a cooked-down beet, knowing that it wasn't that good, but he still ate it. It was so bad, I gave the rest of it to the hogs after he left."

Catherine laughed. "Oh, Mama. It wasn't that bad, was it?"

"Yes, it was." Her mother chuckled.

"I want to keep the dishes easy so they'll carry well in the basket. I don't want them to be too cumbersome."

"They'll be fine. I'm sure if the basket is too heavy, you could always ask the preacher to help you carry it."

"Mother! I would do no such a thing. Half the town would be talking; and after getting stuck overnight at Johnson's Point, I don't want to give them anything else to discuss."

It was her mother's turn to laugh.

"Honey, people will always talk. You can't help that. Just make sure you give them something worth talking about."

"That's just it. I don't want to give them anything to talk about."

"Well, then don't invite the preacher in for dinner anymore or share your lunch at school with him then. Try and keep him away, so there isn't anything to gossip about, and see what happens. That man has eyes only for you, and he isn't about to stop coming around as long as you let him."

Chapter 13

The next day was spent getting ready for Sunday. Catherine baked apple pies and let them cool on the window sill. She wanted to choose the best one for the dinner on the grounds.

She tested her skills at cooking fried chicken twice, once for lunch and then again for supper. She had trouble catching the chickens at first, since they were running all over the yard.

She soon had the knack of it, and two feisty hens later, she served large platters of fried chicken at each meal. Harl was beside himself.

"That is some of the best fried chicken you've ever fixed, Sis."

"You really think so?"

"'Course. I wouldn't say so if I didn't think it."

"It really is good. You should try your hand at chicken and dumplings sometime," her mother said.

"I could make chicken and niffles for you."

"Niffles? What are niffles?" her mother asked.

"They are long, fat noodles instead of dumplings. Dorothy Schumacher, a German woman in the logging camp, taught me how to make them."

"Sounds like more work than dumplings."

"It's not really. You just make the same dough for dumplings, only thicker, but then you roll it out and either cut it into strips and drop it into boiling water or you can roll it in your hand to make the noodles."

"So, why don't they call it chicken and noodles then?" Harl asked.

"I don't know. I never asked her."

"Well, this chicken sure is good."

"Think I'm ready for tomorrow?"

"I would say so," Harl said, taking another piece of chicken.

"Preacher will be sampling plenty of other people's fare. I wouldn't count on him eating a lot," her mother said.

"Oh. I didn't think of that. Still, we'll fix enough, so if he is hungry, there'll be plenty to eat for all of us."

Sunday morning dawned warm and bright.

"It's a perfect day for dinner on the grounds, and what a nice end to the summer," her mother commented.

Catherine hurried to fry two plump chickens. She mixed cornbread batter and placed it in the oven in a large cast iron skillet. As she fried the chicken on low heat, some of the grease splattered onto her black dress sleeve.

"We'll get that out, but it'll have to soak." her mother said, studying Catherine's face.

"I'll go change. Can you watch the chicken? I don't want it to burn."

"Sure will."

Catherine hurried upstairs to change, just as Clair was waking up. Grabbing her navy blue dress, she changed quickly and then helped Clair into her matching navy blue outfit. She combed and tied a blue ribbon in the child's hair. "There, now. Such a pretty girl."

"Thank you, Mama," Clair said.

Carrying the child downstairs, she hurried into the kitchen as her mother was turning the chicken in the skillet. Catherine stood Clair on the floor.

"Mmm, smells so good," Catherine said. "I'd love to have fried chicken for breakfast instead of eggs and ham."

Her mother laughed heartily. "We could have that sometime—just not today. Harl has his heart set on fried chicken for lunch, and we want to have enough for everyone to have seconds and thirds if they want."

"Looks like it's almost ready. I'll dish it up and put it in the oven to keep it hot until we leave."

Catherine pulled the cornbread from the oven to make room for the chicken.

Harl came in from outside sniffing the air. "Now, that's the way this house should always smell."

"What, like chicken?"

"Like fried chicken," he said. "Too bad that's not what's for breakfast."

"It's a lot of work to fry chicken this early," Hazel said. "Especially if you want it fresh."

"Nothing is too hard for you, Ma." Harl smiled, seating himself at the table.

Catherine stirred up scrambled eggs and cooked thick ham slices. She dished it up into a large bowl and onto a platter and positioned Clair and herself at the table.

Her mother sat down, folded her hands and nodded at Harl.

"Thank You, Lord, for this Thy bounty, and bless the hands that prepared it. In Jesus' name, amen."

Catherine scooped scrambled eggs and a small slice of ham onto Clair's plate and then onto her own. Cutting up the ham into bite-sized pieces on Clair's plate, Catherine said, "It looks to be a fine day to have dinner on the grounds."

"Should be," Harl agreed.

"I'd still bring a shawl, though," her mother mentioned.

"Papa sure loved his dinner on the grounds," Catherine said.

Harl laughed. "Remember that time when we were little that he ate so much of Mama's fried chicken and pickles that he had to stop the wagon and threw up over the side of it?"

Catherine laughed. "I had forgotten about that."

When breakfast ended, her mother washed the dishes while Catherine washed Clair's face with a wet rag as the child wiggled.

"Someone has a wiggle worm," Catherine said, tickling Clair's sides.

The child squealed with laughter.

Once the breakfast dishes were washed and put away, the women headed outside to the waiting wagon. Hazel climbed up next to Harl, and Catherine and Clair sat on quilts in the back with the large basket of fried chicken, cornbread, and apple pie.

They arrived at church, along with other families who came in from all over town. Catherine left the basket in the back of the wagon, carefully covering it with a quilt, and hurried inside the church with Clair.

Inside, they found an empty bench and sat down.

From behind her, Gladys Richardson tapped her on the shoulder. Catherine turned.

"My boys behaving in school?" she asked.

"Yes, they're doing fine, just fine."

"Good, 'cause they know if they weren't being good, their pa would skin them alive."

Margaret Fields waved at her from across the aisle and smiled. Hershel, Dorthea, and Easter sat beside her. Her husband, Ezzard, was not with them. Catherine wondered if he was outside with the men.

Penelope Harris stood and waved at Catherine from the boy's side of the school. "Look at where I'm sitting," she said and laughed. Her mother, Lucy Harris, pulled her back down onto the bench, hushing her as the child flailed her arms and knocked into her brother Jonathan, who sat next to her on the bench. Next to her were also her father, Caleb Harris, and her sister Elizabeth.

Mr. Elijah Grant and his wife, Tippy, sat in the front row. Behind him sat Henry Frazier chewing the inside of his cheek as he looked at Catherine. She felt her cheeks burn under his gaze. Catching his eye, she turned and faced forward, sitting stiffly until the service started.

Samuel walked up to the white podium at the front and opened the service in prayer.

"Bow your heads with me," he instructed. "Lord, thank You for this day and those that have come. Bless them, Lord, and our time together. In Jesus' name, amen." Several others echoed amen.

Opening a hymnal, Samuel called out, "Amazing grace, how sweet the sound." The crowd sang the lines of the hymn in response as Samuel called them out. When the singing ended, he preached on forgiveness and trust in God for all things. His eyes flicked to Catherine several times throughout the sermon.

Could he be preaching about me? Does he know the secret I hold deep inside?

Catherine shifted uncomfortably in her seat whenever their eyes met. Touching his finger tips to his lips, Samuel said, "Amen." Catherine sighed heavily and looked at the hem of her skirt. Was this sermon directed at her? Did she still need God's forgiveness? Hadn't He forgiven her already?

When the preaching ended, Samuel raised his arms and prayed, "Lord, we thank You for this day. Bless our gathering and dinner on the grounds now." Raising his head, he looked out at the congregation and said, "Amen." The church erupted out the door.

Her mother waved for Catherine and Clair to follow her, so they could get a good spot out under the shade of one of the trees. Catherine waved her ahead and carefully picked her way out of the schoolhouse holding Clair's hand.

"Fine day for a picnic, isn't it?" Tippy Grant asked, catching up to Catherine.

"Yes, it is." Catherine smiled at her friend.

"I made a roast chicken with potatoes and corn on the cob. What did you bring?"

"Fried chicken, cornbread, and apple pie."

"Mmm, that sounds good. See you at the store sometime?"

Catherine nodded.

By the time Catherine and Clair got outside, Hazel was under one of the big pine trees that surrounded the school. She was spreading a quilt under the branches of the tree. "Harl, bring the basket. We've got a good spot." Taking the basket, Hazel unpacked the contents.

Harl seated himself with his back to the tree. Catherine sat down and pulled Clair onto her lap. She scanned the crowd for Samuel and spotted him over at Dosha Clark's quilt talking with her and her girls.

"Dosha's a widow," her mother leaned over to whisper in Catherine's ear. "Her man fought for the South in the war. And got cut down in one of the skirmishes."

Catherine's brows pinched together. Was Samuel sweet on Dosha? She was an older woman with two older daughters. Catherine watched Samuel closely as he sampled some of Dosha's food. He refused to take a plate, patting his stomach instead. She watched as he made his way from quilt to quilt and spoke with the members of his congregation. Slowly, he made his way over to her quilt.

"Looks to be a fine day."

"Sure is," her mother agreed as Catherine placed the fried chicken on plates. Samuel sat down next to Harl.

"Mind if I join you?" he asked.

"Not at all. We'd be happy to have your company." Hazel looked sideways at her daughter.

Catherine looked at Samuel and said, "Unless there is someone else you'd rather eat with."

Samuel studied her before answering. "There's no one I'd rather eat with. Why? Did you think there was?"

Catherine gazed at him. "I wasn't sure."

Samuel smiled and laughed. "There's no one else that can make fried chicken taste like Hazel does, I'm sure."

"Catherine made it. She made it all," her mother explained, waving her arm over the food.

"Oh, well, then, this is a special treat." Samuel's eyes darted to Catherine, and the corners of his mouth twitched up into a grin.

Catherine heaped fried chicken and cornbread onto a plate, and then she handed it to him. She held her breath as he took a large bite of the chicken.

"Mmm. That's so good, it'll make you swallow your tongue," he said with a laugh.

Catherine exhaled and handed Harl a plate. When everyone had a plate of food, she placed a piece of chicken and a slice of cornbread on her plate and ate.

"Mmm, this *is* good," she agreed. It had been a while since she had made fried chicken—one of John's favorite meals. *If only he hadn't fallen between the logs on that river run, he'd be here enjoying my cooking, probably laughing and smiling at me.* Her shoulders sank at the thought.

When they ate their fill, Samuel excused himself to bid goodbye to those members of the congregation who were leaving.

Catherine placed the dirty dishes in a towel and set it in the large basket, along with the rest of the chicken and cornbread. She sliced pieces of apple pie and put it out on smaller plates.

"Well, it looks like you put on quite the feed," Henry Frazier observed, stepping over to Catherine.

Her head jerked upward toward his voice. "Yes, we had a good lunch."

"Looks like the preacher had a good time, too," he noted.

Catherine looked over her shoulder to where Samuel stood smiling and talking with one of the men of his congregation.

"I hope so."

"That apple pie sure looks inviting," Frazier said.

"Does it now?" her mother asked, flitting her eyes from Catherine's face to Frazier's.

Samuel saw Frazier standing over Catherine and limped over. "Came for the pie, did you, Frazier?" Samuel sat down next to Catherine.

Frazier turned his nose up. "Not especially fond of apple pie. I'm more of a blackberry cobbler man."

"We don't have any blackberry cobbler here," her mother said tightly.

Frazier turned on his heels and marched away.

Catherine exchanged glances with Samuel. "Thank you for coming when you did. Here, I thought I'd have to entertain Henry Frazier."

"No worries."

"Looks like Frazier just might be sweet on you," Harl observed as Catherine handed him a slice of apple pie.

"Now, Harl . . . " Hazel started.

"What? Can't a man have an opinion?"

"Leave it be," Hazel replied.

Catherine blushed as she handed Samuel his pie.

"Smells good."

Harl ate quickly and jumped up, chasing after Frazier. "Henry, wait up," he called.

Catherine and Hazel exchanged glances and stared after him.

"Well, let's finish our pie and get on home. I don't know about you, but I'm tuckered out," Hazel said. "I could use a nap."

Samuel handed Catherine his empty plate. "Thank you for such a lovely time and such good cooking. I better check and make sure everything is put back in order for school tomorrow."

Catherine smiled at him and nodded as he limped away back into the church.

"Well, go with him and help him," scolded her mother.

Catherine jumped up and rushed into the church. Except for the benches being unorganized, everything else was in place. The podium was gone, and the teacher's desk was back.

"Caleb and Benjamin moved the desk back in here after service let out. They put the podium in the back room. Here's your chair," Samuel said, dragging the cane-bottom chair out of the back room and standing it behind the desk.

"Everything looks to be in order."

"Let's hope Henry Frazier doesn't pay you a visit tomorrow. I don't think he would like having an adult learner in school."

"Why not?"

"If you haven't noticed, he's fussy."

Catherine and Samuel laughed at the absurdity of his statement.

"If he pays me a visit, I'm sure I can hold my own with him—board or no board."

"Good. Keep that attitude, and you should do fine."

He took a step closer to her. "Catherine, I . . . I really enjoyed that pie." His eyes bore into hers as if there was some unspoken something he wanted to say. Catherine looked briefly at the floor before returning his gaze. *Was there something more he wanted to say? What was on his heart?*

In his mind's eye, Samuel reached for her hand. He held it in both of his, rubbing the soft skin under the firmness of his. *If only I could tell this woman what is on my heart. Would she want a man that let his wife die alone and blamed and questioned God because of it? What would she think of me then?* Glancing down, Samuel was surprised to see their hands touching. *Had he moved that close to her while he was thinking?*

Catherine joined her hand with his. He gasped.

"You seem to be deep in thought. What is it?"

"I can't tell you, but I can tell you this feels right," he said, squeezing her hand.

"I know."

From the wagon, her mother called, "Catherine, shake a leg."

Their hands broke apart.

Samuel gestured for Catherine to exit the building ahead of him, which she did. He pulled the door shut and locked it.

"Well, until tomorrow." Samuel bowed slightly.

Catherine laughed and curtsied. "Until tomorrow."

Harl was just placing the basket of dishes and leftover food into the wagon as Catherine came out of the school.

"Hurry up, will you," he called. "I'd like to get home while it's still light out."

Catherine shook her head and hurried over to him.

"You know good and well that it's only the afternoon, Harl," she said.

She could have stood there with Samuel Harris holding his hand forever. She touched her hand to her cheek and closed her eyes. He had reached out to her. He had wanted her to take his hand. His hand was so warm and inviting. He had stepped closer to her. Was he wanting to kiss her?

When the quilts were loaded, Harl cupped his hands as a makeshift ladder for Catherine and Clair to get up into the back of the wagon. Seating himself on the bench behind the mules, he offered his hand to Hazel, who stepped onto the wheel hub and up onto the seat next to him. Harl spoke to the mules.

As they drove out of the churchyard, he smiled and nodded at Dosha Clark and her daughters, who were gathering remains of their meal into a large basket.

The trip home was a short one as Harl seemed to be in a rush to get there and so hurried the usual pace of the mules.

"It's such a nice day today and so warm. I really am going to lie down and take me a nap." Hazel yawned.

"Sounds good," Catherine said.

When they arrived home, Catherine took Clair upstairs and dressed her in her nightgown for a nap. She took off her navy blue dress and hung it on a peg in the wall and donned a nightgown.

Catherine slept for two hours and woke to the sound of Clair rustling in bed. She helped the girl dress. She put back on her navy blue dress and headed downstairs to the parlor, where Hazel sat darning some of Harl's socks.

Clair ran to the basket in the corner of the room and pulled out a small rag doll from among the other toys. Sitting at her mother's feet, she danced the doll on the floor.

"Where's Harl?"

"Where else?" Her mother nodded toward the kitchen.

"In the barn?"

"Yep. You want to help me with these?" Her mother offered Catherine a threaded needle, egg darner, and sock.

"Sure will." She took the items and sat opposite her mother on a black horse hair and walnut chair. Patting the place next to her, Clair walked over and sat down. She watched as her mother pushed the needle into the toe of the sock and pulled it out the other side of the hole.

"You can sit on the floor and play if you want," Catherine said.

"Or do you want your own sock to sew?" her grandmother asked.

"No." Clair shook her head and eased down onto the floor with her doll.

Catherine and her mother worked for several minutes silently until Mother spoke.

"We really should have offered Henry Frazier a piece of pie. For that matter, we should have invited him to join us—him being on the school board and a bachelor. Who knows how he has survived this long without a cook."

"What? And give him false hope? I don't think so. He can eat at the restaurant. I don't want Henry Frazier anywhere near me or my family. I don't like him."

"That's unjust and just plain ugly of you."

"Well, it's true. Why allow him to get his hopes up only to have them dashed?"

"He's a good, outstanding citizen like Samuel and his brothers. It wouldn't hurt to leave some room for kindness toward him."

"I don't want him to get the idea that I'm suddenly sweet on him and want him to come courting."

"Why not? Having two gentlemen callers is better than one."

"Samuel is not calling on me."

"Isn't he? Well, what are we feeding him so much for then?" Her mother laughed, peering slyly at her daughter. "I know he's sweet on you. And I think you're sweet on him."

Catherine felt her cheeks warm and jabbed the needle in and out of the sock before she answered. "I do like him very much, and he is a good man."

"Good enough to be the father of Clair and your husband?"

Catherine placed the sock on her lap. She gazed at a spot on the wall over her mother's head. She held her hands together and placed them near her heart.

Her mother stopped working and peered at Catherine. "That's an *awful* lot of thinking going on over there. What is it you're not telling me?"

Catherine returned her gaze to her mother's face. "He held my hand, Mama, in the church."

Her mother gasped and then smiled. "Well, that's a good sign."

"But other than that, he hasn't asked for anything more than a little of my time."

"You gotta watch them fellers that want only a little bit of your time. Soon, you'll be walking down the aisle with him."

"And what would be so wrong about that?"

"Absolutely nothing. I'd like to see you have a second chance at love and happiness and for Clair to have a good, decent man as her daddy."

Catherine grew quiet and focused on the sock on her lap. She finished darning it and handed it back to Hazel for inspection.

"A good job if ever I saw one."

"Were you *serious* about entertaining attentions from Henry Frazier?"

"No. I just wanted to see what your reaction would be, but I still think we should have asked him to join us out of the goodness of our hearts."

"I don't think he was suffering for food. He brought a big basket with him and ate under the shade of the pines off to himself."

"Oh, I didn't see that."

"Don't you give him a second thought, Mama. Here, hand me another sock."

"We're pretty much done."

"Any other chores you need me to do, Mama?"

"Not right now."

Turning her attention to Clair, she said, "Come on, honey. Let's go see what your uncle Harl is doing."

Catherine crossed the yard to the barn holding Clair on her hip. She spotted Harl standing in the doorway, picking his teeth with a twig.

"Hey, Harl," Catherine greeted him.

"Hey," he answered back. "Hey, Clair."

Clair held her doll out for Harl to see.

He nodded and smiled. "That's a good doll you got."

"Did you enjoy dinner on the grounds this afternoon?"

"You know I did. Didn't you see me take thirds of that fried chicken?"

Catherine laughed heartily and put Clair down.

"I saw you chase after Henry Frazier."

"Yeah, so."

"What did you say to him?"

"I apologized to him on account of my sister and mother having been so rude to him."

"You did not!"

"I did, too. Poor man went away without even so much as a slice of your apple pie."

"You know I don't want to encourage him?"

"Why not? He's as good a man as Samuel, maybe even better."

"You mean because he owns the livery in town that he's wealthier than a common preacher."

"Your words, not mine."

"And you'd want me to end up with someone that I don't love just so you could maybe afford to trade up to a couple of draft horses instead of these mules?"

"If it suits you, I don't have a problem if you don't end up with anyone. I just think that people should be neighborly to each other and act Christian-like."

"Did you know that Henry Frazier made an advance toward me in the schoolhouse?"

Harl dropped the twig. "What did he do?" he said, balling his fists at his sides.

"He invited me to dinner is all; but it was very uncomfortable, and I don't want to encourage him. Is that so wrong?"

"Ain't wrong at all if that's what you truly want."

"Yes, having Henry Frazier stay away from me and not make any more awkward advances is what I truly want."

"I'll speak to him if I get the chance."

"No, I can take care of myself in that area, and I'd rather that it came from me if he needs to hear it again."

"Light's fading. You best get inside."

Catherine turned and walked back to the house as twilight settled over the homestead.

From the front porch, Catherine pointed out the blinking lights of thousands of fireflies to Clair, who caught one in her tiny hands. Opening her hand and seeing the blinking light on her palm, the girl squealed, shook it off, and then laughed as the firefly flew away out into the night.

Hazel came out on the porch and sat next to her daughter on a cane-bottom chair. She rocked it back and forth as she sang a hymn. Catherine and Clair joined in the song as cicadas and crickets near the house serenaded them.

Chapter 14

In the morning, Catherine rose early. She dressed and kissed Clair's forehead, brushing her fingers through her hair as the child slept. She crept downstairs and found her mother and Harl seated at the table in the kitchen eating.

"You let me sleep in again."

"You needed your sleep; besides, it's only 5:30 in the morning," Hazel said. "The chickens aren't even up yet."

Catherine laughed and shook her head at the joke. "I'm getting a new student today."

"Really? Who?"

"Margaret Fields."

"Margaret Fields! You mean her no account husband is going to let her go to school while there's work to be done at home?"

"I guess so. At least that's her desire, to come to school and learn right along with the rest of the students."

"Ezzard Fields won't want his woman learnin' nothin'."

"How do you know, Harl?"

"I just do. Men like that don't cotton to their women learnin'. Might give them ideas. Ideas they can't control."

"Pish posh."

"I'd listen to your brother if I were you. You don't want to go startin' something that you can't finish."

Catherine frowned, looking from her mother to her brother. "I'll do the best I can. If she wants to learn, I'll make a way somehow."

Her mother smiled. "That's my girl."

As they watched, Catherine tucked a jar of apple butter into her lunch basket with a half loaf of bread. "You know, some butter would be nice with this."

"We've got plenty."

Catherine sliced off a hunk of butter and put it in a jar by itself and placed it in her lunch basket.

"Mama?" Clair called from the top of the stairs.

"Coming. Wait there."

Catherine went to get Clair and carried the small girl into the kitchen.

"Let's get you some breakfast, honey."

"I'll do that. You better hurry if you want to get the jump on your students," Hazel said.

Catherine gathered a few more morsels of food into her lunch basket and headed out the door.

It was a cool, fall morning. Dew lay heavy on the ground, wetting her shoes clear through to her stockings as she walked.

At the schoolhouse, she let herself in, lit a lamp, and started a low fire in the potbelly stove. She removed her wet shoes and stockings and placed them beside the stove to dry. Barefoot, she wrote lessons on the board for each grade, checked her work, and then went to see if her stockings and shoes were dry. As she put them back on, she heard a sound at the door.

"Ahem." Looking up, Catherine saw Margaret Fields, a short, hefty woman in a shabby dress, standing just inside the doorway. Her children looked around from behind her like chicks under a brooding hen.

"Come in, Mrs. Fields."

"You young 'uns stay out here and let me talk to Teacher in private."

Margaret Fields stepped into the classroom and said, "I didn't want to bother you none 'cause you was a puttin' on your shoes."

"That's all right. It's no bother at all." Catherine led the woman to the front bench and motioned for her to sit down. She sat next to the woman. Margaret looked at Catherine, at her hands, and then around the room. Her gaze finally settled back on her clasped hands in her lap.

"How can I be of help to you?"

Margaret chucked nervously. "Well, I asked my Easter to see if it would be all right if I joined the class for some learnin'. She said for me to come on, so I came."

"Well, you are most welcome to attend class with my other students."

"I ain't too old?"

"No, of course not."

"Or too ugly." She laughed a little at the joke.

"I don't think you are ugly at all."

"Why, thank ya. Ezzard always said if he didn't have me, the buzzards would. 'Cause of my ugly face."

Catherine clamped her mouth shut and studied the woman. It was a few moments before she spoke. "The students meet outside each morning, and we open with prayer."

"They say the preacher has been opening some days in prayer because he's here an awful lot," she said, eyeing Catherine suspiciously.

"Yes, well, he does live next door to the school and is on the board. He checks on me regularly to make sure I'm on task."

"You're on task all right."

"Shall we talk about what subjects you would like to cover?" Catherine asked, guiding Margaret's attention away from any more inappropriate comments about the preacher and what he had or had not been doing at the school.

"Reading and writing."

"Do you know the alphabet?"

"The what?"

"We'll start there; and when you have a good handle on the letters, we can turn to putting letters together to form words and then sentences."

"Sounds like a good plan."

"Can you sign your name?"

"Yeah, I can. Why? Did you have something you needed me to sign?"

"No. I just wanted to know if you make a mark or if you can actually sign your name."

"I can sign my name—the whole thing, including the Fields part."

"Good. Very good. Now, I think the best place for you to sit is in the back row. This will give us some privacy as I teach you the alphabet. It's far enough away from the other students so as not to interrupt their learning."

Outside, voices rose in greeting as more students arrived.

"Ah, my other students are arriving. Let's go out and line up."

Margaret followed Catherine out the door

"Boys on this side and girls on that, according to grade levels and age."

Margaret stood waiting at the back of the girls' line.

"Let us begin our day with prayer." Catherine bowed her head. "Our Father, thank You for these students You have brought to me to teach today. I pray You will guide each one and let their conduct be pleasing to You. In Jesus' name, amen."

Catherine ushered the students into the classroom and began the lessons for the day.

Peering out his parlor window, Samuel watched as Catherine began her day of teaching. He smiled to himself as he thought back to holding her hand. He had moved his hand close to hers, but it was she who reached out for it. She had worn a dark blue dress to church yesterday. Was she putting her time of mourning behind her? Was she ready to accept love again? Could he be a good husband to her and a father to Clair? Would he fail her as he had failed his wife? The thought stung.

He turned his attention back to the school. Catherine's greatest challenge in the form of Margaret Fields had arrived. Could she successfully teach Margaret to read and write? Time would tell.

As the morning waned, Catherine divided her time equally between her young learners and the older ones. She easily multitasked, encouraging one group of children to memorize lines of a poem, while others read from history books and answered questions written on the board.

She started slowly with Margaret Fields so as not to overwhelm her. She showed her a book with pictures associated with each letter of the alphabet and had her repeat the letter. By lunchtime, Margaret had made significant progress on each of the letters in the alphabet.

"You're doing well, Margaret; but we don't want to go too fast, or you may not retain what you are learning."

Margaret nodded her head.

"I think here is as good a place as any to stop for the lunch break," Catherine said.

She excused the class for recess and lunch. Margaret stayed seated on the bench looking over the book with the pictures and letters.

"Margaret? Don't you want to go home to fix lunch for you and your children?"

"Oh, yes. Yes," she answered absently.

"You can take the book with you if you like."

"I can? Thank you, Teacher. I would like that." Margaret rose and scurried out the door. She found her children kicking a rock around a tree nearby. "Come on; we're going home for lunch." Her children ran to her side. Dorthea held her hand, and Easter walked along beside her while Hershel continued to kick the rock as they walked.

"Looks like you are making progress. I see you have a new student," Samuel said from the doorway of the school. Catherine stepped up beside him.

"Yes, she's doing quite well learning the alphabet. Are you ready for lunch? I packed us a picnic." She retrieved her basket of food from the shelf in the backroom, where she had placed it in the morning when she arrived. Samuel hauled a chair out of the room and set it on the opposite side of the teacher's desk.

"Sounds good. I'm hungry. Did you bring some of Hazel's apple butter?"

"Sure did," she said, unpacking the contents. "Here, have a slice of bread to try it on." Catherine spread some apple butter on a slice of bread and handed it to him. He took a bite.

"Mmm. That sure *is* good."

"Here, try some with fresh butter on it."

He took the offered bread. "That is good. Tell Hazel thank you from me."

"Why? Aren't you going to be helping with the harvest again tonight?"

"I thought I was wearing out my welcome."

"Not at all. You are always welcome at the farm."

Samuel studied her for a moment. He liked the way her lips moved when she spoke and chewed. She had lovely, kissable lips. *What kind of a thought was that?* he scolded himself. He looked at the bread in his hand, drawing his gaze away from Catherine's lips. They had held hands yesterday. What would today bring? He longed to touch her hand again. Absently, he touched the back of her hand briefly over the desk before pulling his hand away.

"Catherine . . . I . . . "

"I really enjoyed dinner on the grounds yesterday. Ma thinks I should cook dinner all the time and invite you so you can get a taste of my cooking, so you know that I actually can cook," she said cutting him off.

What was Samuel thinking touching her hand with the children so near? One of them could have seen them.

He let the subject of holding her hand fall.

"I know you can cook. That chicken was out of this world. Besides, you were married, after all, and you wouldn't have been for long if you couldn't cook," he teased.

She smiled at him but swallowed the lump forming in her throat. Her husband, John, enjoyed eating as much as any man. Even though he had been dead for months, the pain of loss was surprisingly still fresh. Catherine looked away to the pitch pine trees just outside the window and changed the subject. Now was not the time to let her fresh grief rattle her.

"It's a pretty day out there."

"Better enjoy it while you can. There won't be too many more days like this. Soon, that little stove is going to be going all day long just to keep the students warm."

"I'm sure we'll manage."

From outside came voices of students returning from lunch. Catherine wrapped up the rest of the bread and snapped the glass jar lids back on the apple butter and regular butter and tucked them away in her basket. She placed the basket back in the backroom.

"Well, we'd better say goodbye for now. Don't want students carrying tales to their folks as much as we can possibly help it."

"Goodbye then. Until later," Samuel called, limping out the door.

Chapter 15

Margaret and her children returned for the afternoon session, along with the rest of the class. Catherine directed Margaret to keep working with the picture book on her own as she helped various students with their assignments. Late in the afternoon, Catherine dismissed the class for the day.

"You can have the book and take it home with you if you want, Margaret, so you can study tonight if you have time."

Margaret's face spread into a wide smile.

"Thank you. This is the first book I ever owned. Thank you. You're a good teacher."

Catherine watched as the woman and her children walked away from the school. When they were out of sight, she turned and busily set things back to right in the schoolhouse. After she finished, she met Samuel in his wagon out in front of the school. Grasping her hand, he helped her up onto the seat beside him. An electric charge coursed through her arm. She gasped. Did he feel it, too? If so, he didn't let on.

"How was school?"

"Fine, just fine," she said, smoothing her skirt as she settled beside him.

"All your students behaving?" He looked at her inquisitively and then spoke to the horses.

"If you mean to ask about Margaret Fields, yes, she did just fine."

He cast a glance at her as the horses plodded along out of the schoolyard.

"She's not disturbing the other students, is she?"

"No, not at all. Why would you think that she would?" She looked at him quizzically.

He shrugged. "Just wondering is all."

They stole glances at each other as they rode out to the orchard. Samuel smiled at her.

"What I wanted to say to you this afternoon is I . . . think . . . I . . . think . . . I'm . . . I . . . might . . . be . . . falling . . . in love with you."

Catherine sat bolt upright and stared off into the fields on the right. What was it she felt for this man beside her? Could she open her heart to love again?

"Well?" he asked. "Do you have feelings for me?"

When she didn't answer right away, he held his hand out, "I'm not asking you to marry me. I don't even know if I'd make you a good husband, but I sure would try. Not that I'm asking you to marry me," he added quickly.

"Well, yes, I have feelings for you. I don't deny it, but I don't know that I would make you a good wife."

How could she not? She was tender with Clair and a good daughter and sister from what he had seen. She was the one he wanted to be his wife.

He started to say more, but her mother met them in the yard.

"So, what did you think of my apple butter?"

"Some of the best I've tasted," Samuel said, avoiding Catherine's eyes as he helped her out of the wagon. The conversation would have to be put on hold for a while longer.

"Ha," her mother said and laughed. "Wait 'til you taste Catherine's apple butter. She beats me all to pieces."

"Mother!" Catherine exclaimed. "I do not. You're the best cook around these parts."

"Where's Harl?" Samuel asked, changing the subject.

"He's tending to one of the mules in the barn."

Without another word, Samuel climbed down and hurried over to the barn. He opened the door and disappeared inside.

A group of men picked up crate after crate of the heavy apples and set them in the back of Samuel's wagon. As the men worked, several small children and Clair ran around playing tag among the apple crates waiting to be loaded.

"Whose are all these children?" Catherine asked.

"Them's mine," said a tall, dark man wearing a tan, felt hat. When he spoke to Catherine, he removed the hat from his head and turned the brim around in his hand.

"Yours?" She turned to face the big man.

"Yessum. Them all mine. I hope it was all right to bring 'em." He licked his lips nervously.

"These children are school-age. They should be in school."

"I didn't know the school would allow them to attend."

Catherine's eye brows shot up. "I don't see why not. What is your name, sir?"

"Ezra Williams." The work halted as his comrades looked from him to Catherine.

Ezra called to the children. "Y'all come on over and meet the teacher."

Clair and the three children ran over to him.

"My name is Mrs. Reed."

"Ms. Reed," he repeated for them. Three children stood beside him. Placing his hand on each one's head as he introduced them. "This is my oldest son, Jonah; he's ten. And here's little Zillah. She's five, and Micah's seven. And this one is your little one," he laughed standing behind Clair. Catherine joined in the laughter and held her hand out to her daughter.

"Hi, Mama," Clair said sweetly.

"Well, it's very nice to meet you." The child skipped over to her mother and wrapped her tiny arms around her mother's skirt. Catherine stroked the child's hair.

"Would you like to go to school and learn how to read and write?"

The children nodded their heads vigorously, including Clair.

"No, Clair, you're still too young," Catherine reminded her.

Turning back to the other children, Catherine continued, "We can get them started tomorrow morning. School usually starts around 7:00 a.m."

"They'll be there." Ezra smiled, showing large teeth.

Another worker stepped forward and said, "I got children, too. Can they come to school and get some learnin'?"

"I don't see why not. As long as we have room for everyone, anyone is welcome to come and learn."

The workers looked at each other and smiled.

"Thank ya, Ms. Reed, thank ya," Ezra said, stepping back into the line of workers.

"Come on; let's get a move on," Harl called, stepping from the barn, followed by Samuel. "We ain't got all afternoon to load and get this bunch to market."

The group of men hurried to load the last of the apple crates into Samuel's wagon and then climbed up onto it.

"Mr. Adams, sir, I'm gonna take my young'uns home with me, if that's all right with you. You've got some good hands right here." He nodded toward the back of the wagon. "You won't miss me if I ain't there."

"Go on home then, Ezra. Here's your pay for today." Harl reached into his pocket and pulled out several coins. "You'll come back tomorrow?"

"Yes, sir, if I'm still welcome."

"Why wouldn't you be? Of course, you're welcome to come on."

"I'd have to bring my little ones again. Their ma is over caring for a sick neighbor. Children ain't got no business around sickness."

"Bring 'em with you then. I'm sure my niece is enjoying having playmates around," he said, looking at Clair as she ran off with the other children.

Catherine listened as the men talked and then hurried into the house to help her mother by setting the table for the evening meal. Clair followed her mother.

"Did you have a good day?"

"Yes," Clair said.

"Show your ma what we made," her grandmother said, handing the child a paper doll cutout.

Clair held it up for her mother to see.

"You made this?"

"Uh-huh," Clair proclaimed, smiling.

"Look at that! And when you unfold it, they are all holding hands in a line," Catherine said, picking the girl up.

"I'll be right back," Hazel said, stepping out onto the porch. In a moment, she returned.

"Samuel said he's coming back for dinner. You've just got enough time to stir together a blackberry cobbler."

Catherine put Clair down.

"We picked the berries this morning." Clair hopped up onto a chair and held up a fat blackberry from a large bowl in the center of the table.

"You did? Well, look at all these fine berries you picked," Catherine said, popping one into her mouth. "Mmm . . . and so plump and juicy."

"Do you want to help your mama make a cobbler?" Catherine asked Clair, who nodded her head enthusiastically. "I'll get the flour and butter so we can make the dough for the top. Here's the berries for the bottom, and we'll add some sugar and let them cook down so they'll be good and sweet under the crust."

Clair added ingredients to the mix as Catherine instructed. They rolled out the dough for the top and cut it into long, thick strips. Catherine added the cooked, sugary berries to the bottom of the gray enameled pan and laid dough strips over the top. She placed the cobbler into the hot oven and finished setting the table.

"Hot cobbler will be just the thing with some cold, fresh milk when the men get back."

"It'll be a nice treat," Catherine agreed.

Hazel took the cobbler out of the oven when they heard the jingling of tack and the sound of hoofs.

Catherine wiped her hands on her apron. She fidgeted with the edges of it until her mother asked, "Aren't you going to take it off?"

"I'm not sure. I want Samuel to know who made the cobbler."

"Oh, honey, he'll know; and if he doesn't, I'll make sure to tell him it was all your doing. I don't think you need to wear the apron in order to impress him with your cooking skills."

Catherine pulled the apron off and hung it on a peg beside the door leading into the hallway. She smoothed back her hair and smiled at her mother.

"How do I look?"

"You look fine, real fine, but you might want to change out of that mourning dress sooner than not. It's been months since John died. I think it's time you gave yourself permission to live a little."

Catherine gaped at her mother. It had been months since John's untimely death, but did she have a right to wear something other than black? Was it time to halt her grieving and allow herself to live? What would the school board think if she were to change into her navy blue dress permanently? What would Samuel think? Would it be proper? She bit her lower lip as she pondered these questions.

Catherine helped set the food on the table as the men came in the door.

"Smells good." Samuel grinned at Catherine.

"And Catherine made a fresh blackberry cobbler for dessert," her mother piped up, placing the last dish on the table.

"Did she?" Samuel licked his lips. "Well, I'll have to leave room for a piece of that."

Catherine smiled at him.

When the meal ended, her mother brought the piping hot cobbler to the table with a quart of fresh, cold milk. She turned the stack of bowls and the serving spoon over to Catherine, who dished out healthy portions and passed them around the table to each person. "Here," she said, pouring fresh milk onto Samuel's cobbler. "Try it like this. It's so much better with milk than just plain."

He took a bite. "Mmm, I do believe you are right. I think this is the best cobbler I've ever had the pleasure of eating."

She laughed. "Thank you. I'm glad you like it."

Catherine glanced at her mother, who smiled at her.

After the cobbler was eaten and the dishes washed, Samuel and Catherine retreated to the front porch. Samuel patted his belly. "I do believe if I ate anymore, I'd be popping out of my britches." He chuckled.

Catherine laughed. Surely, the Lord was one for second chances. Was Samuel her second chance at love?

Clair bounded out onto the porch holding the cutout and climbed up onto her mother's lap. How could he be the answer to her prayers for a second chance when there was Clair? The child was ever the reminder of her and John's mistake. Even so, Clair was the light of her mother's life.

Catherine buried her face in the child's curly blonde locks and breathed in the sweet scent. "Your mama loves you, honey."

"I love you, Mama." Clair turned and threw her little arms around her mother's neck. She planted a wet kiss on her cheek. Scooting off her mother's lap, she held the cutout for Samuel to see.

"Did you make that?"

Clair nodded.

"Let's see."

She handed it over. He unfolded the cutout so each person was holding the hand of the one next to them. "Well, would you look at that?"

Clair stepped closer to him and leaned against his knee.

"You want to come up and see me?"

The child nodded. Samuel looked at Catherine.

"It's all right," she agreed.

Samuel pulled Clair onto his knee and wrapped his arm around her. "What did you do today?"

"Played."

"What did you play?"

Clair shrugged. "I don't know."

"You played with this," Samuel said, handing her the cutout.

"And you were running around with the other children," Catherine said.

"Uh-huh . . . we played tag," Clair said.

"Whose idea was that?" Samuel asked.

Clair shrugged.

"The game was already going when I let Clair go out and see if they would let her join," her mother said, stepping out onto the porch.

"We runned around and hid so the boys couldn't find us," the child said, leaning against Samuel's chest. She folded and unfolded the cutout, showing it to him each time she unfolded it. He hugged her close.

"Well, would you look at that," her mother said. "I think you are working your way into that child's heart."

The crickets chirped merrily off the side of the porch, and the cicadas buzzed up in the trees. Long streaks of pale pink edged fluffy clouds.

"It's a fine evening," Samuel observed.

"Yes," Catherine agreed. She breathed deeply. "Oh, I love the smell of the earth at twilight. What a sweet, fresh smell."

Clair yawned. "Oh, it looks like someone is getting sleepy," Hazel said, stepping back into the kitchen.

"You wanna go see your mama?" Samuel asked the child.

She nodded and slid off his knee.

Catherine pulled the child up onto her lap and rocked her.

"Well, I better be heading home. It's been a fine night. Thank you for dinner."

"You're welcome; anytime you want a good meal, you just stop on by."

"I think I'll hold you to that."

"I hope you will."

Catherine waved goodbye as Samuel climbed up onto his wagon. Whispering to Clair, she said, "Come on, honey; let's get you in bed."

Clair rubbed her eyes and yawned again in response.

In their room, Catherine helped the child dress in her nightgown and brushed the ringlets in her hair.

"Now, let's say your prayers."

Clair climbed into bed and folded her hands and closed her eyes. "God bless Mama and Grandma and Uncle Harl and Preacher."

"That's good. Now, you get some sleep." Catherine placed the covers under the child's chin and kissed her daughter on the forehead.

Back downstairs, Catherine stopped outside her brother's room and knocked lightly.

Harl opened the door. "It's mighty late for you to be up. What do you need?"

"I was just wondering how many more trips into town you'll be making."

"Plenty. Why?"

"Just wanted to know how much longer Samuel will be coming for dinner, so I can plan accordingly."

"Don't you worry, Sis. You just say the word, and he'll come running." He laughed.

"What do you mean?"

"I see the way he looks at you, the way he is with you and Clair. He's sweet on you. Has been ever since we were kids. He only went for Isabella once he decided he'd lost you to John."

Catherine folded her arms in front of her. "Oh."

"Don't you worry. We'll be seeing a lot more of the preacher, even after harvest time."

In spite of herself, she smiled. "That's good to know."

"Anything else?"

"No, that about does it."

"Got your menu planned for the next dinner on the grounds—whenever that is?" he teased.

"I'm working on it."

"Better be. I'm looking forward to more of that chicken," Harl said, snapping the door shut.

Catherine met her mother in the kitchen scooping tea leaves into a teapot. She set two china cups covered in tiny rose buds and saucers on the table. She poured boiling water into the pot and placed it on the table. Catherine sank into a chair opposite her mother. She drummed a thumb on the table and looked over at her mother, who was studying her.

"It's awful nice of the preacher to be helping Harl the way he is," her mother said.

"I think Harl should pay him."

"Oh, honey, he's getting paid with plates of food, and don't you worry none. He'd come around, even if we didn't offer him anything to eat or anything to do."

Catherine grinned and folded her hands on the table.

Her mother was right. Samuel would come over, even if there wasn't an offer of food. The thought sent warmth throughout her body.

Being a widower, his heart was probably still tender toward his wife. That wasn't something that would ever go away, but just how deep did that hurt run? People said he left her on her deathbed to go comfort a sick parishioner and when he returned home, he had found her dead. What a horrible thing to have happen to him. How he must punish himself with what might have been if he only would have stayed by her bedside.

There was nothing to be done, much like her husband's death. There was no way for her to prevent it. He chose the job he did because of the money. And it was good money. When he slipped and fell, it ended their dream of a home away from the logging camp. Now, she was back home rekindling a lost love. *How would it all go? Could their like for each other grow into something more? Could it be a second chance at love?* He said he was falling in love with her. She wondered at her own feelings. The sparks between them were telltale signs that maybe she, too, was falling in love with him.

Her mother poured Catherine a cup of tea and slid the sugar bowl toward her.

"Got a mighty lot going on in there," she observed.

"Yes. I was just wondering if Samuel is far enough along after his wife's death to consider someone else."

"That someone else being you?"

"Yes."

"I don't see why not you. I haven't heard of him spending nights eating at some other woman's home."

"I'm serious. Do you think enough time has passed for both of us?"

"For it to be proper for you to court? I think so. The question is, do you think so?"

Catherine studied the question. Would it be proper for her to change out of her mourning dress into something more colorful to show that her time of mourning was ended? Was she ready for a relationship? She must consider Clair in all of this, too. The girl was conceived out of wedlock. John and she married when Catherine discovered she was pregnant, but Clair would always be an illegitimate child. That was something no amount of time could cover up.

Catherine loved Clair more than the air she breathed. But could Samuel love her like his own, or would he be weighed down by the stigma of an illegitimate child? Maybe he didn't have to know. Could she hide such a secret from him? Would that be fair to him? Catherine's head ached as she sipped her tea. Bed was what she needed. She wanted to stop thinking and drift off into sleep and gentle dreams.

"My head aches, Mama. I'm going to head up."

She washed her cup and kissed her mother on the cheek. She held her head with one hand on her forehead and retreated to her bedroom. Clair slept soundly. She dressed in her nightgown and slipped between the covers of her bed. Lying in the darkened room, she prayed, "Lord, Your will be done in Samuel's and my lives. If he isn't meant to be in my life, please take him away."

Chapter 16

In the morning, Catherine rose early, donned her navy blue dress, kissed Clair's sleeping face, and proceeded to the kitchen, where she found her mother hard at work over the hot stove.

"How does biscuits and gravy sound to you this morning?"

"Sounds wonderful." Looking around, she asked, "Harl already out?"

"Sure is."

Catherine set the table and poured herself a glass of milk. Leaning against the cupboard beside the stove, she said, "Today's the day that Harl's workers bring their children to school."

"Humph. Henry Frazier will have something to say about that."

"Not if he doesn't know."

"That man knows everything there is to know in this town. Ain't no use trying to keep secrets from him."

"I'm not trying to keep a secret. I just don't think it is any of his business whom I teach. Everyone should have the opportunity to learn."

"I agree, but Henry Frazier may not. His people sided with the South during the war."

Her mother set the piping hot biscuits and sausage gravy on the table. Catherine and Hazel sat at the table and bowed their heads.

"Would you do the honors?" her mother asked without raising her head. Catherine folded her hands under her chin.

"Lord, thank You for this day and all it brings and thank You for this Your fare and bless the hands that prepared it. In Jesus' name, amen."

"Amen," her mother said, passing the plate of biscuits to her daughter.

Catherine studied her mother.

"Ma, promise me you won't tell Henry Frazier anything about what's going on at the school."

"I promise, but there might not be anything to tell him. Maybe it'll be too hard, and your new students won't want to learn and will skedaddle."

"I hope not," Catherine said, finishing her meal.

She washed her dishes and put them away, then turned her attention to packing her lunch. She packed extra bread, apple butter, and ham in her basket. With her basket packed, she headed out through the orchard, picking apples as she strolled and placing them in her knapsack until it was almost too heavy. She adjusted the shoulder strap on the bag and hurried through the orchard. She wanted to arrive at the school before her students.

The early morning sun was streaking the sky a rosy color as she rounded a bend in the road; up ahead, standing near the schoolhouse, were several men and women with their children. The boys wore overalls and buttoned-up white shirts. The girls shone like angels in the growing morning light in freshly pressed white dresses.

Ezra and a short woman, whom Catherine determined must be his wife and the mother of his children, stood beside Jonah, Micah, and Zillah. Ezra smiled brightly when he saw Catherine and waved his hat at her. When she was close enough to hear, he spoke. "Good morning, Ms. Reed."

"Good morning, Mr. Williams," she said.

"You know my children, and this is my wife, Wilda."

"Pleased to meet you." Catherine held out her hand.

The woman hesitated and then smiled and shook the offered hand.

Ezra guided Catherine over to the other families with their children and introduced them. "Here's Hezekiah Williams and his wife, Esther. They got two of school age. This is Aaron; he's fifteen. And Ruthie's five."

"Oh, you're a Williams, too. Are you related?" Catherine asked.

"No, we are of no relation," Ezra said quietly. "We belonged to the same master."

"Oh," Catherine said awkwardly and took a step backward. "I'm so sorry."

"That's all right. Some people say we look alike." Ezra chuckled.

Moving on to the next family, Ezra introduced Clyde Haskell and his wife, Lucy, and their three daughters. "These girls are Nancy, age twelve; Rachel, age eleven; and Rebecca, who's ten," Ezra said. "Well, that's all that wanted to come today."

"There's more?" Catherine asked.

"Why, sure, there's more, but this ought to keep you busy for a while." He laughed heartily. The other adults joined him in laughter. "I don't think your schoolhouse could hold all the ones that need an education, but we'll start with these. Them are the ones that want to learn."

Catherine nodded her head and turned toward the schoolhouse. "Come in, won't you, and rest while I start the fire."

"Don't seem right for a woman to be doing man's work. I'll get the fire going for you," Ezra offered.

"Thank you, Mr. Williams, I would like that." Catherine unlocked the door and stepped inside the cold room. She lit a lamp and set it back on her desk while Ezra piled wood into the potbelly stove. In moments, there was a nice blaze.

"There, now." He rubbed his hands together over the top of the stove. "That should warm things up in here nicely." Turning to the students milling about the room, he asked, "Where do you want them to sit?"

"The girls sit on the right, and the boys sit on the left. Aaron, you'll sit in the back row about here with the Richardson boys." Catherine pointed.

Catherine noticed Ezra and Hezekiah exchanged glances.

"Nancy, Rachel, and Rebecca, you'll sit in this row with Penelope Harris. And Ruthie and Zillah, you'll sit here . . . " She pointed to the front row. " . . . with Dorthea Fields. Micah, you'll be over here with Hershel Fields."

"Did any of you bring books or a slate?"

"No, ma'am," Ezra apologized. "They didn't know what they needed, but we'll get it for them."

"I'll give each family a list at the end of the day as to what they need to bring with them to class." Looking around, she asked, "Did you bring lunches?"

"No, ma'am, they didn't. Their mamas will bring them at lunchtime if that's all right with you."

"We usually take our lunch at noon." She nodded. "Some of the students run home for the lunch hour."

Ezra chuckled. "Naw, that wouldn't work for our children. They'd just get home and have to turn around and come on back."

"Oh, I see. The other students should be arriving soon. Let's go outside and meet them."

The parents and children filed out of the schoolhouse and stood on the lawn as the sun was just peaking over the horizon.

The first students to arrive were Penelope, Jonathan, and Elizabeth Harris. When they saw all the people milling about, they stopped. "Is there something wrong, Mrs. Reed?" Penelope asked, trepidation in her voice.

"No, not at all. These are your new classmates and their parents. Come say hello."

Penelope, Jonathan, and Elizabeth hesitated before stepping over to where their teacher stood.

"This is Nancy, Rachel, and Rebecca Haskell and their parents Mr. and Mrs. Haskell. Rachel and Rebecca will be in your grade, Penelope."

"Oh. Nice to meet you." She stuck out her hand. Rachel and Rebecca looked at their parents, who nodded their approval. The girls shook hands with Penelope, who quickly stepped back with her brother and sister.

"Jonathan, this is Aaron Williams. He'll be in your grade." Jonathan nodded and looked away.

"Elizabeth, this is Ruthie and Zillah; they'll be with you in your class with Dorthea."

"Who will be?" chimed the small voice of Dorthea Fields from the shadows.

Catherine looked up as the Fields children and their mother walked toward her. "These are your new classmates. Ruthie and Zillah Williams."

"New classmates!" Dorthea exclaimed excitedly, hurrying over to the girls. "I'm Dorthea. We live on Liver Mountain, up near you."

"Liver Mountain? That's the first I've heard of that." Catherine laughed. "Why Liver Mountain?"

"'Cause there's a rock hanging out that looks like a liver," Easter said. The adults nodded their heads, and some chuckled.

Last to arrive were the Richardson boys, Frank and James. They scowled when they saw the new students but didn't say anything.

"Boys, you have some new classmates," Catherine explained. "This is Aaron Williams. He'll be in your class."

The Richardson boys exchanged looks. Aaron stood perfectly still next to his parents and eyed them, his brows pinched together.

"Well, it looks like everyone is here now. Get into your lines," Catherine said. The children obeyed, and the new students followed suit—the boys on one side and the girls on the other. When everyone was in a line, Catherine asked, "Ezra, would you do the honor of opening us in prayer?"

"Pleased to." He and the other men removed their hats, and everyone bowed their heads. "Father God, we thank You for giving our children the opportunity to learn from this here teacher, who will watch over them and keep them out of harm's way. Thank You for her and all these children. We pray a blessing upon them and their day. In Jesus' name, amen."

"Now, we'll go inside. Ladies first." Catherine ushered the girls into the room. The new girls waved goodbye to their parents, who waved back. The boys did the same.

"Your mamas and me'll be here with vittles at noontime," Wilda called.

The children quickly took seats in the rows they were shown. Dorthea and Elizabeth sat close to Ruthie and Zillah and shared their books and slates with them. "See how I can write." Dorthea spelled F-R-O-G on her slate. Zillah laughed.

"Look at my book," Elizabeth instructed, not wanting to be outdone. "I can read, 'The cat ran. The dog ran.'" Ruthie nodded.

Penelope sat in the middle of Nancy and Rachel like a queen bee. "You'll get the hang of this school. It's fun to learn, and the teacher is really nice."

On the other side of the room, the boys weren't faring so well. Frank and James Richardson sat at the opposite end of their bench as if a rattlesnake were on the other side. Aaron sat up straight and looked ahead. His cheeks and mouth were puffed out, and his brows were pinched together.

Catherine wondered if the Richardson boys had said something to him when they were coming inside.

Margaret Fields sat in the back row and surveyed the classroom. She raised her hand.

"Yes, Mrs. Fields."

Margaret waved Catherine to her. When she was close enough, she leaned forward and said, "I don't think this is a good idea."

"Why ever not?"

"Shhh, them Richardson boys ain't gonna stand for this, and neither will their pa."

"Well, let me worry about them. You just concentrate on learning your letters in your book."

Catherine went around the room to each group of students and instructed them on the lessons of the day. Since none of the new students brought slates or books, she wrote out their lessons on the board and asked the new children to memorize them. Catherine was surprised at how quickly the new students learned their lessons. They were able to recite the lessons without looking at the board and knew their ABCs as well as some poems.

"Who taught you all of this?" Catherine asked.

The answer was the same—a neighbor by the name of Jeremiah Watkins had instructed the children on the basics of reading, writing, and even math until he moved away. Catherine was impressed with the determination of her new pupils to learn.

By lunchtime, the new students had attempted to recite their lessons to her along with the rest of the class. Catherine dismissed the school for lunch; the mothers of the new children had arrived with baskets of food. They each brought a gift of food for the teacher. Wilda brought a jar of blackberries freshly canned. Lucy brought sweet honey, and Esther brought a loaf of bread.

"I know you've got bread; but it was what I was making today, and I made you a loaf," Esther explained.

Catherine thanked them for thinking of her and sat in the shade of one of the big pine trees and ate with them.

Samuel limped out of his house and over to where Catherine sat eating with the women and their children. "Smells good."

"Can we tempt you, Preacher, to eat with us?" Wilda Williams asked.

"I might have a piece of that chicken," he agreed.

Using a clean napkin, Wilda Williams picked up a large breast and handed it to him. He stood surveying the rest of the students with their lunches under the shade of other trees.

"The Richardson boys go home for lunch today?"

"Yes."

"Hmm."

"But they always go home for lunch."

"Uh-huh." He nodded.

"Sure is a fine day for an outdoor picnic," Esther acknowledged.

"That it is," Samuel agreed, looking warily off in the distance.

"You waitin' for something, Preacher?" Lucy Haskell asked, looking sharply at him.

"Just making sure that everyone is behaving themselves. Think I'll go see what the Fields are up to." He limped over to where Mrs. Fields and her three children sat under the shade of a large oak tree.

"Seems like he's expecting trouble to come by the way he's acting," Wilda observed.

"Hush now," Esther scolded her friend. "There's no call to be pointing out what isn't there."

"Mama, I'm finished," Aaron Williams said. "Can I go play with the others?"

"Sure."

Aaron joined Jonah and Hershel in a game of "Kick the Rock" nearby.

"What's the object of the game?" Aaron asked, as Catherine listened in.

"We're supposed to try and kick it past the other guy and get it into that dirt patch. First one that does it wins," Hershel said.

"What does he win?"

"Nothing. He just wins." Hershel kicked at the rock.

Catherine watched as Aaron was the first one to successfully kick the rock into the dirt patch and so won the game.

About that time, the Richardson boys, followed by their father, came hurrying through the fields on the south end of the school.

"Uh-oh, looks like troubles a'comin'," Wilda said and whistled. The women hurriedly packed up the rest of their lunch baskets and the contents and stood up.

"So, it is true." Paul Richardson marched over to where Catherine stood. She noticed he scowled at all the dark faces in the crowd. "I just about tore the hide off of these two thinking they was telling lies that you are allowing *these people* to attend school with *our* children."

Catherine brushed crumbs off her skirt and stood to her full height, which was still a head shorter than that of Paul Richardson. "They have every right to be here—same as your boys do."

"Have you lost your senses, woman?" Paul Richardson yelled. "Don't you know you can't teach them together? They'll slow down my boys' progress." Frank and James, who now stood behind their father, nodded their heads in unison.

"Come now. My lessons are such that each child gets individual attention suited to their level and needs and learns at their own pace. From what I saw this morning, their learning is up to speed."

From the corner of her eye, Catherine saw Samuel limping over toward her. She shook her head and returned her steady gaze to Paul Richardson.

"You are welcome to sit in and observe the happenings in my class if you promise not to interrupt."

"Ha! You know who *does* need to do some observing of your class is Henry Frazier. He's on the board. Does he know what you've done? He ought to know. Think I'll walk over to the livery and tell him myself."

"I'm on the school board, too, Mr. Richardson," Samuel chimed in, stepping around beside Catherine. "I wouldn't mind observing Mrs. Reed's teaching style."

"Ha!" Paul Richardson mockingly laughed again. "Lot of good that would do. You're sweet on the teacher. Everybody knows that, so you ain't no help. No, this is a job for Frazier. We'll just see how long he lets these *people* attend school with our children."

"Mr. Richardson, you are making such a fuss over such a small matter. Don't you believe that getting an education should be a freedom that everyone is entitled to?"

"No, I don't. Let them educate their own. There are schools for black people. Let them go there."

"But there aren't any schools like that around these parts. The children would have to travel many miles before finding such a school, and it just isn't practical for them to go so far from home for an education."

"I hear ya, Missy. But you ain't hearing me. Maybe Henry Frazier can listen better than you can," he yelled over his shoulder, huffing off in the direction of the livery.

Frank and James stood awkwardly, staring after their father.

"That's enough now, Class. Let's get back to work." Catherine clapped her hands for attention.

"You mind your teacher now, Jonah, Zillah, and Micah," Wilda said, her eyebrows furrowed with worry.

"You hear? Mind." Esther Williams said to Aaron and Ruthie.

Lucy hugged and kissed her three girls. Catherine watched as she whispered in each one's ear.

Catherine managed to shift the students into two lines—one for boys and one for girls. She let the girls go in first, followed by

Margaret Fields. Then the boys followed after once the girls were seated. Frank and James lagged behind the boys and took up the rear, implored by Samuel, who guided them into the room and to their seats like a shepherd herding sheep.

Samuel sat in the back of the room and watched as Catherine taught the various levels of students, helped them solve problems, and praised them for correct answers. *She was a natural at teaching. She was a natural at motherhood, too.* It was too bad that Isabella had died carrying their baby. He would have liked to have had a child—someone to remind him of his love for his deceased wife.

Catherine worked diligently with each of her classes, knowing that at any moment Henry Frazier could burst into the room. After an hour of class, she decided to dismiss it early when she heard a commotion outside. The children quickly scattered out the door as she came to see what was the matter. Just outside the door stood Paul Richardson and Henry Frazier staring after the dark children on their way home as they gave the two men a wide berth.

"I wouldn't believe it if I didn't see it with my own two eyes." Frazier looked from the departing children to Catherine, who still stood inside the door of the school.

"See, I told you, but you didn't believe me. Had to see it yourself. Ha! That's what," Paul Richardson said.

Frazier shook his head. "Mrs. Reed, why would you defile us like this?" he asked.

"Everyone is entitled to an education. Same as these children, no matter what color they are," she answered, stepping out onto the porch.

"It's a defilement and a waste of resources," Henry Frazier snapped.

"Now, wait a minute." Samuel stepped around Catherine. "Mrs. Reed hasn't done anything wrong. She's just trying to do her job is all."

"And you think this is part of her job?" Frazier asked caustically.

"Yes, I do."

"Educating black children along with our children ain't part of her job," Richardson spit.

"Yes, it is. I wasn't told anything about not educating anyone who decided to step over the school threshold, so I educate anyone."

"Well, now, that is something we'll need to discuss tonight at your ma's place," Frazier said with a nod at Samuel.

"Very well. I'll let her know."

"I suppose just because we didn't tell you not to take the children up a mountain and then spend the night out in the wilderness with them that we are at fault for that, too."

"That was a mistake and oversight, for which I am very sorry." Catherine straightened her shoulders and narrowed her eyes.

"I suppose we are going to have to be very clear with you as to what is and is not expected of you from now on, or else you'll come up with some other cockamamie adventure to put us all through," Frazier said, rubbing his face.

Catherine bit her lip and sucked in air through her nose. "What time tonight should I be at Mrs. Harris' place?"

"Better not make it too late," Frazier said. "You *might* have school tomorrow. Let's say 7:00 p.m."

"I'll be there."

Frazier tipped his cap to her and hurried away, flanked by Paul Richardson, who—from his wild gestures—was giving him an earful.

Catherine turned to Samuel and shook her head. "What now?"

"This is a conundrum. It may be the board will vote down allowing black students to attend the school, but if they vote that down, they should vote down allowing adult learners in the class, too."

Catherine chewed the inside of her lip. "I don't see a way out of it. I think everyone deserves an education. Wouldn't an education help them to become better citizens, better employees and clients?"

"That's not how Frazier sees it."

Catherine turned back toward her classroom and bustled around the room straightening the benches and picking up dropped books and slates as Samuel talked.

"He sees that now you have double the students on which to spend your time, which takes away from the original students. He doesn't like that. He thinks all your energy should go toward making the original children outstanding citizens, and that job doesn't leave room for anyone else."

Catherine wiped stray hairs from her face with the back of her hand. "That doesn't give him the right to stop some students from learning in a classroom."

"He's part of the board—and a big part of it. You may not be able to recover from this blow."

"So, you see it as negative, too?"

"No, I didn't say that. You've already had one strike against you and now this. The others on the board may side with Henry Frazier to bar these new students from learning here."

"I wish I could just teach without the interruption of the board," she said with a huff.

"If you did that, it wouldn't be the board paying your salary. It probably wouldn't be anyone paying your salary, and how would you live if you weren't with your mother?"

"I'd find a way."

"Well, let's cross that road when we get to it. What time should I pick you up tonight?"

"Why don't you come home for dinner? I'm sure Ma and Harl would like to see you."

"I'll get the wagon in case Harl still needs it for the harvest."

Catherine waited at the school while Samuel went to hitch the horses to the wagon. As she waited, she wrote the lessons for the next day on the board. When she finished, she heard the sound of hoofs and jingle of tack and knew Samuel was back. She hurried outside and found Samuel in the wagon waiting for her. He stretched out a hand, helping her up onto the wagon seat beside him. Their eyes met, and they smiled at each other.

"This is getting to be a habit. I think your mother should start charging me for how much I eat at your place."

"Well, you aren't charging Harl for the use of your wagon, so I don't see the harm in a good home-cooked meal every so often."

"It's more like every day almost."

"Really, we don't mind, and we enjoy the company, and so does Clair from the looks of it."

"We?"

"Yes, *we* do."

"No I enjoy the company?" Samuel jiggled the reins to hurry the horses, looking at her.

Catherine felt her cheeks warm and turned away to look out at the fields on the right side of the wagon before answering. "I enjoy your company, too," she said quietly.

Samuel smiled to himself and jiggled the reins again. The horses picked up the pace.

"Was that so hard to admit?"

"Yes, it was, but I don't see much coming from that acknowledgment."

"Really? Why is that?"

"There are things in my past that even you couldn't forgive."

"Try me."

"No, I can't. I won't. Please don't ask me again."

"All right, but you're not the only one with an unforgiveable secret."

"Really?"

"Yes, really." He bowed his head briefly, and then he softly continued. "I left my wife on what I didn't know was her deathbed to go tend a sick parishioner. I knew she was having complications with her pregnancy, but I didn't think . . . When I came home, she was dead."

"I remember. Mama wrote to me about it."

"You know, I've never forgiven God for what I thought He was going to do. I thought He'd heal her if I stepped out in faith that day."

"Oh, Samuel. I had no idea," she said.

"No, I don't think anyone knows that."

"How will you make it right?"

He gazed at her and shook his head. "I'm not ready is all I know."

When the orchard came into view, he slowed the horses to a walk and enjoyed the sweet scent of ripe apples. *What secret could Catherine possibly hold that I wouldn't be able to forgive?* He wanted to question her more about it; but he agreed not to, so he didn't.

"Looks like Harl has everything under control," he said.

Catherine gazed at the faces of the men standing around Harl's wagon. The faces were grim with worry and even some with fear.

"What's going on?" Catherine asked Samuel as he slowed the wagon and parked it in front of the porch.

Samuel looked over at the men and scowled. "I don't know. Maybe Harl will know." He helped Catherine down and followed her. "Harl?" he called.

Harl came around the side of the wagon and met Samuel—his face grim. Catherine caught up with Samuel.

"You just couldn't mind your own business, could you?" Harl threw a rag under the seat of his wagon.

"What do you mean? What's wrong?" Catherine asked, looking at the faces before her.

"You go and invite all their children to come to school." He gestured widely to the men standing around the wagon.

"Yes, so? Everyone deserves an education."

"Not if that education is going to scare the daylights out of them."

"What's happened?" Samuel asked.

"'Bout two o'clock, their young'uns come running through the orchard like they were being chased by the devil. They tell their papas that there is trouble up at the school and that they aren't welcome. Didn't you think to check with the school board first before going and inviting people?"

"I didn't think it would be a problem."

"Well, it is—they all ran home now, and who knows what disturbing tales they're telling their mas. You gotta think past your nose," Harl scolded.

"There's a board meeting called for tonight."

"Better put on your red dress then 'cause this may be the end of your teaching career."

"Harl!" Catherine yelled. Tears began to course down her face. She wiped at them, but they only flowed faster. "Oh, Harl." Turning, Catherine lifted her skirts and hurried into the house, shutting the door behind her and leaving Samuel to deal with Harl and the other men.

"Henry Frazier called a board meeting tonight. I'm sorry if he scared your children," Samuel apologized to the group of men.

"From what our children told us, seems that the teacher might lose her job over it. We don't want to give no cause for that," Ezra said, stepping forward.

"If I have any say in it, she won't lose her job. We are an open-minded family and never owned slaves, unlike Frazier. If he could still have slaves, he would."

"We don't want to stir up no trouble, Reverend Harris," Hezekiah Williams said.

"We'll just have to see what comes about tonight during that meeting. You all plan on sending your students to class tomorrow, unless you hear differently. I'll ride out to Ezra's place and let you all know. Will you spread the word, Ezra, to the other families?"

"Yessuh," he agreed.

"Good. Now, Harl, you need a hand with the rest of these crates?"

"No, I think I'm good with just one load tonight," he said, climbing on board his wagon.

Ezra, Hezekiah, and Clyde climbed up over the sides and onto the bed with the crates of apples.

"We'll be seeing you, Preacher." With that, Harl slapped the reins on the mules' backs and set them off into the orchard at a fast trot.

Samuel turned and headed to the house. He knocked on the door, which was opened by Clair.

"Oh, hello there." He stooped to her level. "Where's your mama?"

Clair pointed to the ceiling. "Upstairs."

"She'll be down in a bit," Hazel said, striding into the kitchen.

"Is it all right that I stay for dinner?"

"Of course. Why wouldn't it be?"

"Catherine was mighty upset. I didn't want to set her off again."

"As I heard it told, you weren't the one who set her off. Sounded to me like that Paul Richardson and Henry Frazier were the troublemakers."

"They do have a way of doing that."

"Come on and have a seat. Dinner's almost ready, and Catherine is getting freshened up. She'll be down shortly."

"Thank you, Mrs. Adams. You've always been so good to me."

"Call me Hazel if you like."

Hazel bustled about the kitchen stirring pots, turning slabs of meat in skillets on the hot stove, and making sure everything was just right.

"Clair, go call your mama to come eat."

Clair ran down the hallway. At the bottom of the stairs, she shouted, "Come on, Mama. Time to eat."

She didn't wait for her mother but ran back down the hall to the kitchen. A few minutes later, Catherine entered the room. Her face was pinker than normal, Samuel observed. Her mother dished up and set the food onto the table. Catherine set the table, keeping her eyes on her task.

Her mother sat down and bowed her head, followed by her daughter. "Preacher Harris, would you do the honors please?"

"With pleasure." He bowed his head. "Dear Lord, thank You once again for the hands that prepared such a fine meal. I pray for guidance for tonight and Your blessing on Catherine as she stands before the board. In Jesus' name, amen."

Catherine met his gaze and whispered, "Thank you."

"Can't nothing change what's going to happen tonight. You've got the Lord on your side, but the damage has been done. Henry Frazier may not see reason," her mother said, passing a plate of steaming potatoes.

"There's no one who knows the outcome of the meeting tonight other than the Lord, so it's best not to dwell on it too much," Samuel said, stabbing his fork into a pork steak.

Catherine ate slowly, methodically, as if she prolonged her meal, she could delay the outcome of the board's decision.

Catherine noticed her mother looking from her to Samuel. She did not say anything to either one. It was a quiet meal. When it ended, Catherine helped her mother with the dishes. Afterward, she walked out onto the front porch, where Samuel sat looking out over the fields in the distance beyond the barn. Catherine sat on one of the cane-bottom chairs and sighed.

She opened her mouth to say something but then shut it just as fast. After a few moments of silence, she tried again. "It just isn't fair. I'm trying to do the proper thing and believe I'm doing the right thing, and all I get is the promise of trouble for it."

"You only have the promise of trouble from Henry Frazier, not from the rest of us. Though I'm not sure what the rest of us will decide once Frazier has his say."

"But you know what you'll do, right?"

"Yes."

"And what is that?"

Samuel propped his arms on his knees and leaned forward. "I'll do whatever I can to help save your job and keep those kids in school."

"You think you can do that, even with Henry Frazier's leanings?"

"I hope so. I know the others don't share Frazier's ideals concerning slavery, but I have no idea what they will think about sharing the school with ex-slaves' children. If it were up to Frazier alone, he'd have you run out of town, riding a rail, after the Johnson's Point fiasco."

"I don't understand why anyone wouldn't want them educated. Don't they know the educated make better citizens, workers, and clients?"

"Fear of the unknown makes people do strange things, makes them assume the worst in others when the worst is staring them in the face every morning when they look in the mirror. If there was any call for alarm, your brother never would have hired Ezra or the rest of them. He's quiet, but a good judge of character, that Harl."

In the distance, Catherine heard the methodical clomping of hoofs and the jingle of tack as Harl returned to the farm. Turning, she watched for his coming. Harl nodded his head when he came into view. Turning the mules toward the barn, he hopped down and unhitched them.

"Think I'll go help him," Samuel said, limping down the stairs.

Catherine remained on the porch and watched as Harl and Samuel slid the harnesses and yokes off the mules' necks and backs. Harl led them into the barn.

Her mother came out onto the porch, followed by Clair, holding a cookie. Hazel sat in the chair that had been occupied by Samuel and looked toward the barn.

"Samuel's out helping Harl," Catherine said in answer to her mother's unasked question.

"He's good for Harl. It's nice to have him here so often." Her mother looked sideways at Catherine. "He's good for you, too."

"Ma," Catherine said quietly.

"I think it's about time that you come around and see what's going on here."

"And what is that?"

"The preacher's sweet on you."

Catherine's cheeks burned as she sat looking at her hands. "I know," she said finally.

"I know you're friends and all, but what do you think about him as more than a friend?"

It was a few minutes before Catherine answered the question as Clair ate the cookie and played with her doll at her mother's feet. "It feels wonderful to have someone like that pay attention to me again."

Hazel nodded her head. "That's just what I thought about it. A man don't come to this many meals unless he has serious thoughts about the one he's eating with."

"Ma!" Catherine said, softly scolding her.

"Well, now, I'm just telling it like it is. Nothing wrong with that, is there? No law against telling the truth, right?"

"No, but . . . " Her voice trailed away.

"No, but it's not something you want to think about. You want to remain friends for as long as you can. A man gets tired of just being friends and might like a little something more—say, a wife."

"But you know we can't be anything other than friends."

"And why not?"

"It's because of . . . " Catherine pointed toward Clair.

"What's that child have to do with anything?"

"Oh, Ma. She . . . she was conceived out of wedlock," Catherine said quietly.

Hazel sat back, her eyes filling with tears. She took a breath before responding. "You know, people make mistakes. Don't mean that they are bad people. And the sooner someone sees and knows about it, the sooner someone can start forgiving someone else about it. John was a good man. Doesn't mean everything he did was good, but he was a good man. He stood by you. There are other men like that out there. You just have to give them a chance to know what happened and give them the space to make up their own minds as to what they're going to do with that information."

"It's not something I want to think about right now."

"Fine. Don't think about it, but don't come crying to me if Dosha Clark gets her hooks in him."

"What does Dosha Clark have to do with anything?"

"Didn't you see the way the preacher and her were carrying on at dinner on the grounds?"

"I didn't think anything about it."

"Didn't you? You turned three shades of beet red when you thought the preacher enjoyed her company over yours. Or don't you remember that?"

"I choose not to remember."

"Well, remember. There are more widows in this town than just you. You don't want one of them snagging him, do you?"

"No."

"Well, then, don't you think it's time to make your intentions known and let him see how much he means to you?"

"There's no way to do that without being improper."

"Improper! Ha! Do you think Dosha Clark and the rest of the widows in this town are thinking they're being improper when they're hiding behind their fans at church, all the while scheming how they're gonna get them a preacher?"

"I don't think he'd give them the time of day. Shhh, here he comes."

The preacher limped across the lawn and came up onto the porch.

"Well, I'll go fix us some sweet tea. Would you like that, Preacher Harris?" her mother asked.

"Sweet tea sounds just fine."

"You know, Catherine makes a good sweet tea, too. Maybe she should make it this time, so we can sit out here and talk. It'll take time to cool."

Catherine rose and went into the kitchen. The water was already hot on the stove. She took down a gray enamel pitcher from a high shelf over the cupboards and scooped out two cups of sugar into the bottom of the pitcher. She added tea leaves and then stirred in the hot water. She kept stirring until all the sugar dissolved.

As she stirred, she listened to snippets of conversation on the porch.

"Do you really think the board will fire Catherine over letting black children learn right along with white children?" her mother asked.

"I know the majority would probably want to keep her, but if Frazier had his way, she'd be gone."

"It's a shame that he feels that way. There's no difference in them from us 'cept the color God made them."

"You're right there."

Once the tea cooled enough, Catherine poured it into three glasses and took them out onto the porch. Samuel sipped his slowly. "Turned out to be a pretty day."

"Sure did," her mother agreed.

"I hope the tea's not too hot for you. I let it cool for a while, but it's still warm."

"Suits the day," Samuel responded.

They all sat together quietly, lost in their own thoughts of what was to come.

Chapter 11

Samuel stayed at the house until 6:30 p.m., the time he agreed to take Catherine with him to the school board meeting.

Catherine changed into her black mourning dress and climbed up into the wagon with Samuel, while her mother stood on the porch watching with Clair at her side.

"Don't you worry about what you cannot change. Leave it in the Lord's hands," she called as they drove away.

As they rode, Catherine mulled over what she would say to the members of the board to convince them to let her keep the job. She prayed a quick prayer. *Help me know what to say, Lord.* She thought over her reasons for wanting the teaching job. She wanted to teach children—all children—to read and write and learn arithmetic. She felt it was her God-given talent, her love of learning, which was something she could share with others. *How can I convince the board of this?* Attending one semester at Millersburg worked in her favor, too. She had studied teaching courses. That was something not every small-town teacher could boast. *No, I shouldn't boast.*

She didn't do anything wrong except allow young, former slaves the right to learn at a proper school. *I was being progressive.* And wasn't that what education should be about? Including everyone by giving them a free education, so they could become better citizens and clients for the businesses in town? Isn't that something that Henry Frazier would agree with? Shouldn't he agree with that?

As she thought through her answers to the questions that may arise, Catherine chewed on the inside of her bottom lip. She let out a gasp of air and shook her head. Samuel sat silently beside her, guiding his horses to his mother's home, where the meeting would take place.

"Aren't you going to say something? Offer up some words of encouragement?"

"I already said all I had to say. There isn't anything more to tell you, other than to wait and see what the board has to say and what they decide. I know where they stand on the issue of slavery. They're against it. But on the issue of inclusion, I'm not sure. My mother and brothers shouldn't give you any problem on it, but Frazier sure will."

"Ugh! Frazier! Why is he even on the board?"

"He's on the board because he is a financial supporter of the school and an outstanding member of the community. He's one of the wealthiest business owners in the town—besides my family," Samuel explained.

"Then why isn't Garlin Moore, the owner of Moore Hotel and Restaurant, on the board? He's an outstanding citizen and wealthy, I'm sure."

"He was asked but turned down the job. I'm not sure why. I don't think he wanted the responsibility for the youth in the community and the time commitment."

"And you did?"

"Yes. I knew with the responsibility of the job came the chance to see the growth of our young people, who would become the future citizens and business owners in our town. I wanted to have a hand in creating good citizens from the start, and you do that with education."

"I'm glad you see it my way."

Catherine smoothed her hand over her dress and looked out at the fields.

"It'll be getting dark soon," Samuel observed.

"Hopefully, the meeting won't last too long."

Samuel cast a glance at her. "I would think you would want the meeting to go longer than shorter, seeing how we are fighting for your job."

The pair rode in silence the rest of the way to his mother's home. When they arrived, they saw lights burning brightly in the parlor windows. Three horses and two buggies stood sentry to the entrance of the home.

"Looks like everyone's here." Samuel helped Catherine down out of the wagon.

"Oh, dear," she exclaimed, looking at Samuel. "What if this is the end?"

"Shh, don't let them hear you talk like that. You must be brave. Stand tall and keep your chin up."

Catherine took a deep breath, squared her shoulders, and walked toward the door.

Samuel held the front door open for her, and she walked past him into the empty foyer. Sliding the enormous parlor doors open, he stepped inside and waved her in. He shut the doors behind her. She sighed heavily as he shut the door.

Mrs. Maude Harris was seated on the couch while Henry Frazier paced around the room chomping on an unlit cigar. Benjamin and

Caleb talked with Elijah Grant about the price of various grains. Caleb asked Elijah to order him a new sickle when he turned his gaze to Catherine. She noticed that Doctor Johnson was not among them.

Elijah Grant took a seat near the couch when he saw Samuel and Catherine walk in.

"Good evening," Mrs. Harris greeted Catherine warmly.

"Good evening," Catherine returned.

Maude Harris gestured to a chair across from her—the same chair Catherine had sat in to get the job. The same chair she sat in when being reprimanded for her lack of judgment in taking a wagonload of students up the side of the mountain to Johnson's Point. It was now the chair she would sit in to hear Henry Frazier rant and rave at her concerning her choice of students. She sat down and placed her feet squarely on the rug under her feet. Samuel pulled a chair up beside Catherine and sat down.

"Doctor Johnson should be joining us momentarily. Now, we are here to discuss the situation at the school." Maude introduced the topic.

"Ha!" Henry Frazier laughed spitefully.

"We are not here to accuse anyone of wrongdoing." Maude shot an icy look at Frazier.

"You may not be, but I will," Frazier groused.

Maude scowled and sat up straighter. "As this is my house, you'll do no such thing. You'll keep a civil tongue in your head and remember who allowed you on this board."

Frazier looked as if someone had given him a lemon instead of a cigar on which to chew.

The sound of someone knocking on the front door reached Catherine's ears. Caleb raised his hand as Samuel stood.

"It's probably the doctor," Caleb said, opening the sliding doors. Voices rose in greeting in the corridor. Doctor Johnson walked through the open parlor doors, followed by Caleb, who shut the doors behind them.

"Sorry I'm late, had a sick patient up at the hotel," the doctor said, taking a seat.

"Better late than never," Benjamin said.

"Now, then." Maude began. "I understand you wish to teach ex-slaves to read and write. Is that correct?"

"Yes." Catherine sat up straight and met the other woman's gaze.

Frazier pulled at what little hair still remained on his balding head and yelled, "No, no. We can't have that. Tell her we can't have that."

"And why not?" Maude asked, craning her neck to look at the man pacing behind the couch.

"We don't want any black children learning around these parts. They'll start reading and writing. There's no telling what they would do if they learned to read and write," he screamed as the veins in his neck pulsed. His cheeks were bright red, and sweat beads broke out on his forehead.

"You just don't like progress is all." Benjamin Harris turned to look at Frazier. "Never have. Never will."

"So, what if I don't? I'm not wrong," Frazier yelled.

"I said there was to be no yelling in my house." Maude turned a shade of crimson. Her mouth was set in a firm line. "If you cannot contain yourself, you'll need to leave my property." She cocked her head to the side and stared Frazier down with a steely gaze.

He raked his hand over his balding head. "All I'm saying is we can't allow these children to go to school with our students because they'll be using up the resources reserved for them."

"Every child deserves an education, no matter what color they may be," Caleb Harris chimed in.

Frazier twisted the cigar in his mouth and sputtered, "Are you listening to yourselves talk? We have limited resources and can't be using them on everyone who decides to come to that school."

"Limited, my foot!" Maude scoffed. "We have more than enough to share. It seems to me you want these children to be as dumb and lifeless as the men who tend your stock at the livery."

At this pronouncement, Henry Frazier stopped pacing. His mouth hung open as he stared at Maude. It was as if the woman could read minds from the look on his face.

Turning away, he said, "Do whatever you want, woman. Goodness knows you will, anyway—no matter whether it is right or wrong."

"And what's so wrong with allowing these children to learn to read and write?" Maude repeated.

"Let them learn on their own time with their own people. I don't want them near our children."

"Why not?"

"I don't want them mingling with our children is all."

"If I might be permitted to speak," Catherine interjected.

Maude gestured to her with an open hand. Frazier stuffed his hands into his waistcoat pockets and stood rolling the cigar around in his mouth with his tongue.

"I think having these children in with your students would be good for them. The children of Ezra—Hezikiah and Clyde—are intelligent. They learn their lessons quickly; they don't cause any trouble; and I like having them in school. I want to teach them if they want to learn."

"I agree," Doctor Johnson said. "There's no reason not to let these children learn in school."

"I believe, if what you say is true, that having the two groups of students studying together would be good for all," Elijah Grant said.

"What about Paul Richardson and his boys? They won't stand for something like this."

"What *about* them?" Catherine cast her eyes at Henry. "Mr. Richardson is welcome to remove his sons from my classroom if having black children among the rest will upset him as much as you say."

"Now, just wait a minute. Don't go shoving words in my mouth."

"But if he won't stand for it, he has every right to seek an education elsewhere."

"Elsewhere?"

"At home, perhaps. The boys have their books and slates. They could learn at home."

"Their ma is too sickly to allow them to learn at home."

"So, it's decided then?" Maude asked, waving her hand. "The new students will stay."

"Appears like it." Henry shoved his hands in his pants pockets.

"Good. So, it's settled," Maude offered with a smile.

"I don't know why I'm on this stupid board if I never get a say in anything."

"You keep a civil tongue in that head of yours in my home. Besides, you had a say, Henry."

"When?"

"When we decided to hire the teacher. Just because your opinions aren't the opinions of the majority doesn't mean you are any less important to us," Maude said.

"Son, you take care of our teacher," his mother said.

Samuel nodded. "I will, Mama." He walked over to his mother and placed a gentle kiss on her upturned cheek.

Returning to Catherine, he took her elbow and helped her stand. Catherine straightened. Maude peered over her glasses at her son and the elbow he held and grinned. Catherine removed her elbow from Samuel's grip.

"Thank you very much." She nodded to each of the board members.

Samuel again grasped her elbow and guided her toward the large sliding doors. He opened them; she stepped through; and he followed. Catherine waited until he had shut the doors and then whirled around to face him. She wanted to throw her arms around his broad shoulders and kiss him on the cheek, but that wouldn't be proper. Instead, she clasped her hands under her chin and smiled at him.

"Oh, my goodness!" she exclaimed. "Thank goodness that's over."

"Over or just beginning?"

"What do you mean?"

"Frazier's friends with the Richardsons. He knows how to stir up trouble. I'd keep a sharp eye on the Richardsons if I were you."

"Even so, there isn't anything that can deter my thankfulness now that the meeting is over."

"Well, let's get you home, then, so you can prepare your lessons for tomorrow."

Catherine stepped out into the cool night air. A breeze blew little wisps of hair around her face and rustled fallen leaves on the ground. The moon shone full and bright in the cloudless sky. It was a perfect night—a perfect night for new beginnings.

Chapter 18

At home, Catherine hurried into the house to relay all the evening's doings to Harl and her mother.

"Henry Frazier was as mad as a wet cat. There for a while, I thought he was going to bust a vein; the ones in his neck throbbed so."

Her mother sat with needle and thread mending one of Harl's shirts while Catherine continued to relay the events to them.

"The Harrises, Doc Johnson, and Mr. Grant are for including Ezra, Hezekiah, and Clyde's children in the school. I was so surprised that they didn't back off of Frazier, but they took my side of things, saying those children should be included and get an education."

Catherine paced around the room as she spoke. She clasped her hands under her chin and smiled. "Now that I have the board's approval, maybe there will be other children who will come to the school from that community."

"Other children? Or adults?" Harl asked. "What's to keep the adults from infiltrating the school once they see you'll let anyone learn there."

"And what exactly is so wrong with more adult learners? The children seem to behave themselves much better with Margaret Fields in the classroom."

"I just think you're getting in over your head," Harl said. "Just because the board agreed to allowing ex-slaves in the classroom doesn't mean your fight is over."

"What do you mean?"

"Not everyone in the community shares your sentiment of educating those who are willing to learn. Some would rather see you run out of town on a rail like Paul Richardson and his boys."

"If they cause trouble, I'll just have to deal with it when it comes."

"Maybe comin' quicker than you think."

"All right, Harl. That's enough. Let Catherine have her dream and see it through. It's time we all went to bed. Catherine, you've got a big day ahead of you. Best get to bed now."

"Yes, Ma." She kissed the older woman on the cheek and then hurried around the table to her brother and kissed him on the cheek, too.

In bed, Catherine tossed and turned, giddy with the possibilities of teaching new students and doing her part in the community to turn out fine citizens in them all. She slept fitfully and woke groggy the next morning before the sun came up.

Low, heavy fog clung to the fields and moved like a snake among the apple trees as she made her way to school. At times, she found herself trotting out of the fog into a clearing, only to be met with more fog.

At the school, she made a fire in the potbelly stove to ward off the chill of the morning. She wrote the lessons for the day on the blackboard. Stepping back, she surveyed her work. Satisfied, she went about straightening the benches. The first students to arrive were Ezra's children—Jonah, Micah, and Zillah—along with Aaron and Ruthie. Next came Clyde's children—Nancy, Rachel, and Rebecca—followed by Penelope, Jonathan, and Elizabeth Harris. Catherine watched as child after child walked out of the fog surrounding the fields and roads around the schoolhouse. The last to arrive were the Richardson boys. When all the students were assembled, she divided them into lines and prayed for their day.

"Oh, Lord, bless this day and these students who have traveled so far to learn at my hand. Help us have a good day of learning. In Jesus' name, amen."

The girls went in first, followed by the boys. Catherine waited outside the school for Margaret Fields and her children but did not see them. Not wishing to keep the students waiting, she hurried into the school and closed the door.

By lunchtime, Margaret Fields and her children still were not there.

"Where's your neighbor Mrs. Fields and her children?" Catherine asked Wilda Williams, who was unfolding a patchwork quilt near her lunch basket.

The woman shrugged.

"Maybe she don't cotton to our kind at the school," Esther Williams said.

Catherine swallowed. How many more of the parents felt this way but continued to send their children? How long would the children be allowed to attend school? Is this how the entire town felt?

Catherine walked around the lawn until she found the new children seated with their mothers a good distance from the school under the shade of a tree. She sat down with her lunch basket and spread some apple butter on a slice of bread and nibbled on it. She scowled at the sky, which was a shade of blue behind fluffy clouds.

"What's wrong, Teacher?" Ruthie Williams asked.

Catherine did not answer. She only shook her head.

Samuel limped over to where she sat. She laid her bread on the cloth napkin beside her and then spread apple butter on another piece of bread and offered it to him. He took it. "I see Margaret Fields and her children aren't here today."

Catherine cleared her throat and shook her head.

"Think I'll hitch up the buggy and pay her and her family a pastoral visit."

Catherine dusted off her hands and stood. She walked with Samuel a fair way out of earshot of the children and their mothers. "I think she's not here because of these other children being allowed into the school."

"That's something you definitely have to consider—that you may lose some students because of it. Are you willing to lose pupils over it?"

Catherine looked to where the Richardson boys stood with their hands in their pockets kicking a small stone around the lawn. "Yes, there are some I'm willing to part with if it comes down to that."

"Every student deserves an education, you said. How can you provide that to them if they aren't here?"

"Maybe I need to take the school to them then."

Samuel locked his eyes on Catherine's face. She had such a delicate face for a woman with so much responsibility and determination. Could she stand in the mounting face of opposition? Would she be able to continue teaching if there was no one left to teach? Time would tell.

"Well, I'd better be going if I'm going to get in that pastoral visit. Do you think Harl would mind if I swung by and picked up some apples for them?"

"Not at all. See if he has some milk and butter to send, too. We usually try to get up there once a week, but we were so busy this past Saturday that we didn't go. See what Ma can send as well."

"Thank you. I know they'll be grateful for anything they can get."

Class that afternoon whisked by quickly. Catherine dismissed the class early and hurried home to Ma and Clair. She was greeted by Clair, who ran to meet her as she came up the road through the orchard. She scooped the girl up into her arms and covered her small face with kisses.

"Did you have a good day with Grandma?"

Clair nodded.

"What did you do?" she asked, walking up onto the porch to where her mother stood.

"What did we do? We played house. I got her to scrubbing the kitchen floor with me. We sang songs and had a good time cleaning. Didn't we, darling?"

Clair laughed. "Uh-huh."

"Did she do a good job?" Catherine asked.

"She did. Just come look and see how pretty our floor is."

Catherine walked into the house with Clair on her hip.

"Show your mama what we did."

Clair climbed down and went to a spot on the floor and pointed.

"Is that where you scrubbed?"

"Uh-huh," Clair answered.

"We scrubbed the table and put down new newspaper in all the cupboards. We did a lot, didn't we, Clair?"

Clair nodded her head.

"Are you hungry? I've got dinner cooking., and it smells like it's almost done."

"Yes, I could eat. I'll just go freshen up a bit."

Catherine carried Clair up the stairs to their room, where she ran a wet rag over her face and washed her hands in the basin and then went back downstairs. By the time she walked into the kitchen, her mother had dished everything up, and it was sitting on the table. Harl met his sister as he came in the back door.

"Preacher was here today asking for charity for the Fields," he said, seating himself at the table.

"Well, what did you give him?"

"He got a crate of apples, a bucket of milk, a dozen eggs, and a pound of butter. I think Ma might have given him something as well."

Her mother looked up from serving the food. "I sent two loaves of bread and a large jar of apple butter. You know they need all the help they can get, seeing how that man of hers don't work."

"He gets odd jobs here and there," Harl said, sticking his fork into a thick pork steak.

"When he's not drinking," their mother added.

"Shh, now, this kind of talk isn't good for little ears to hear," Catherine said, nodding toward Clair.

The rest of the evening meal was spent with Harl bemoaning the price of seed and worrying over his apple crop.

Chapter 19

The next day, Catherine ate quickly and left for school early. A cold mist hung in the air. She pulled her shawl about her shoulders tighter and hurried on her way. At the school, she lit a fire. She wrote lessons on the blackboard and hoped to get a glimpse of Samuel to hear his news of Margaret Fields and her children.

It wasn't until lunchtime when Samuel made an appearance. Catherine sat at her desk eating lunch and looking out the window watching the Richardson boys play "Kick the Rock" when she heard footsteps on the plank flooring. Looking toward the door, she smiled when she saw Samuel. He smiled back. She studied his broad shoulders and thick, dark hair—such a good-looking man.

"What did you find out about Margaret and her children?" she asked, gesturing toward a bench. Samuel sat down and leaned forward.

"She's not ill, as I had supposed. Never seen a sick woman cart in all the goods I brought her from your brother and mother quick as a lick. It was actually comical watching how fast she could go. She and her children beat me all to pieces—that's how fast they unloaded the buggy. When it was all said and done, all I had to do was carry in the basket of eggs. Though she did have a slight cough when I asked about her condition and if I could pray for healing for her," he said and laughed.

"Did you find any indication as to why she and her children were not in school?"

"Dorthea asked her ma if they could go with me back to school. Her mother hushed her. Dorthea blurted out that her ma didn't want them to associate with the new students. 'It ain't right' is how Mrs. Fields put it."

"Oh, I thought as much. I had such high hopes that your visit would bring them back here."

"Well, if Dorthea has anything to say about it, you'll see them again."

"Why? What did she say?"

"She begged her ma to let them return to school. Said she would be good and not even talk to Ruthie. She told her ma that she liked learning to read and that she should let them go back."

"And?"

"Her ma said she would think about it."

Catherine shook her head. "It was so good of you to make the trip up to see her. Are you always so generous with your time?" Though after the hours he had spent with her, she knew the answer to the question.

"Yes, I like to think so," he said softly, his sharp, blue eyes gazing at her.

She turned to look outside. "I need to call the children in from lunch," she said, rising.

When she stepped out onto the lawn, the mothers were gone. She called the class over to her, but Aaron stood to her right by a tree, his hand pressed upon it. His sister Ruthie danced around him shouting something at him.

"What's all this?" Catherine asked, hurrying across the lawn toward Aaron. When she reached him, she took two steps backward, for blood was running down his face and onto his clean, white shirt and overalls.

"What happened, Aaron?" Catherine breathed.

Aaron shook his head.

"Tell her," Ruthie shouted.

Catherine scanned the crowd of students, who gathered around Aaron—all except the Richardson boys, who stood by the door to the school, their backs turned toward her.

"Did they do this to you?" Catherine asked, pointing toward Frank and James.

Aaron stood stock still. With his hand on the tree, his head drooped, and tears ran down his face.

"Yes, yes, they did, Teacher," Ruthie cried. "I seen the whole thing. They asked him if he wanted to play 'Kick the Rock' with them. And he said yes, so they picked up the rock and chucked it at him; and it hit him in the head."

Catherine listened to the little girl and then asked, "Did they do that on purpose, or were they just tossing it to him?"

Still, Aaron kept his head down as Ruthie answered, dancing on her tiptoes. "They meant to do it. Them's bad boys," she said as she glared in their direction.

Catherine held her hand over her stomach. She called to the boys, "Frank and James, come here."

They walked over with their hands in their pants pockets and their heads down.

"Did you do this?" Catherine asked, pointing to Aaron's head.

Frank shrugged and rolled his eyes. James met her gaze and sniffed.

"I want an answer. Did you do this?"

"I already told you, Teacher, that them bad boys done it. Don't you believe me?" Ruthie asked from behind Catherine.

Catherine stooped down to Ruthie. "Yes, I believe you, but I want them to tell me they did it."

Ruthie stopped dancing and looked pained. "They won't tell you it was them."

"What's all this?" Samuel limped across the lawn to where the crowd of students stood. "What's happened?"

"Ruthie says Frank and James hit her brother with a rock," Catherine explained.

"It wasn't both of us. Just one of us did it." James balled his fists at his sides.

"Which one then?" Catherine snapped.

James shook his head, while Frank dropped his gaze and kicked a blade of grass.

"Well, if neither one of you will admit fault, then I'll have to suspend you from classes until I have a chance to speak to your father about this. Get your things and go on home now."

The boys slowly made their way into the schoolhouse. As soon as she saw Frank and James start down the road toward home, Catherine called her class together.

"Now, then, class, let's go in." She shepherded the students into the school.

Samuel stood beside Aaron and Ruthie. "I'll take care of this; you go on in with the rest of the students," he said to Ruthie. She ran to catch up with the others.

Once the students were seated inside and working on the afternoon lessons, Catherine came out to check on Aaron, who still stood at the tree. Samuel dabbed his handkerchief over the boy's bloody face, while Aaron wiped tears on his sleeves.

"I'm so sorry this happened to you, Aaron," Catherine said.

"It weren't your fault. I asked for it," Aaron mumbled.

"How do you mean you asked for it?" Catherine questioned.

"They asked if I wanted to play, and I said yes, so they threw the rock at me. I never should have said yes."

Catherine and Samuel exchanged looks.

"It was a dirty trick they played on you," Samuel said.

"Do you feel good enough to join the others?"

"Yes, ma'am, I do."

Catherine and Samuel walked with Aaron into the school. They paused just inside the doorway, their voices low.

"I'll have a talk with Paul Richardson as soon as I can about his boys' behavior. In the meantime, they're out of school until I give the say to let them back in." Catherine's eyes gleamed with fire.

"Once Paul hears about it, he may go to Frazier, who could force the issue to let the boys back in."

"He can't do that."

"He could." Samuel held her gaze so intensely, Catherine felt the color rising to her cheeks.

"I'd like to go see the boys' father tonight after school. Will you go with me?" she asked, her lips pressed into a thin line.

"Of course, I'll go with you. I'll have the buggy ready once school lets out."

"Thank you so much. I'll see you then."

When the class was dismissed for the afternoon, Catherine quickly gathered her books and stuffed them into her knapsack as the clomp, clomp, clomp of hoofbeats played on her ears. Samuel was here. She hurried out to meet him. At the door of the school, she stopped; for it wasn't Samuel's buggy that she heard, but Henry Frazier's, and in the seat next to him sat Paul Richardson with his arms crossed over his chest. His face was bright red.

"If you don't beat all," Frazier exclaimed, climbing out of the buggy. "Paul here's been filling my head with quite a story."

Catherine took several steps backward into the shelter of the school doorway. "He said his boys got suspended for playing 'Kick the Rock' with one of the black children. Now, I can hardly believe that. Will you be so good as to tell me what's going on at this school?" He pushed his hat back on his balding head and placed his hands on his hips.

Catherine squared her shoulders and stood up tall. For a moment, she wasn't sure what to say, but then it all flooded out of her.

"Frank threw a rock at Aaron Williams and hit him in the head on purpose."

"No, he didn't," Paul argued. "Frank said they were throwing it *to* him to catch, and it hit him in the head. He told me you made them leave school because of it."

"That isn't what happened." Catherine inhaled sharply.

"How do you know? You seen what happened?" Paul questioned, pulling his handkerchief out of his back pocket and blowing his nose.

"Ruthie Williams saw it. She told me Frank threw the rock *at* him, not *to* him."

"Oh, and you'd take her word over that of my boys?" Paul spit out. "Teacher, you taking sides?" He hooked his thumbs in his pants pockets.

Catherine looked from Paul to Frazier and back. "There's no reason for me to not believe the word of a five-year-old."

"I'm starting to wonder if we shouldn't send out another advertisement for a new teacher if you can't keep your students from lying and carrying on as such."

"There'll be none of that." A familiar voice thundered just out of Catherine's view. Samuel limped over to them. He gestured for Catherine to come to him. She pressed forward and closed the door behind her. Stepping over to where Samuel stood, she rose to her full height, which was still a head shorter than Samuel's. "We aren't going to have a need for another teacher when this one is doing a fine job of educating our youth."

"And I say she's not." Frazier chomped on his unlit cigar.

"What makes you say that?" Samuel asked, puzzled.

"She teaches everyone the same and then when a misunderstanding takes place, she blames our children and makes them leave school, that's what," Frazier accused.

"Yeah," Richardson pointed at her with a gnarled finger. "Maybe you'd rather teach blacks, and we should get a real teacher to teach ours."

"If you don't stop teaching their children, I'll withdraw my sizable support from the school and you." Frazier's gaze was caustic. Catherine felt a burning sensation in the pit of her stomach.

"You're not the only one in this town who supports the school and teacher," Samuel said.

"If you're talking about the board . . . " Frazier said.

"No, I'm talking about the townsfolk. I've heard people talk about what a good thing it is to have a teacher like her here."

"Ha, what people? Name one that isn't on the schoolboard," Frazier challenged.

"Yeah, name them," Paul said.

"Well, there's Garlin Moore."

"The owner of Moore Restaurant and Hotel?" Frazier spat.

"Yes, one and the same. I ran into him in the street, and he said he was glad the town finally had a teacher with progressive ideas here. Then there's Anton Franklin."

"The sheriff? I don't believe it," Frazier said. "He's a friend of mine."

"Don't believe that your friends can have a different opinion than you? That's just two, but there are others."

"Really? Let's find out just who is and isn't for including them then," Frazier said.

"How do you plan on doing that?" Samuel asked.

"Call a town meeting after church on Sunday. Most of the town attends church anyway, so it would be easy to discuss this issue since they're all in one spot."

"Frazier's right. We should have a town meeting to decide the outcome," Samuel said, turning to Catherine.

"What's that? I didn't quite catch it." Frazier smiled, placing his fingers behind his ears.

"You're right. We'll call a meeting for this Sunday."

"But that only gives us a few days to get the word out," Catherine said.

"If you don't think this thing is going to spread like wildfire, you got another thing coming," Frazier said.

"I'm sure we can expect Frazier and Mr. Richardson to do their part to spread the word," Samuel said.

"See you in church on Sunday then, Preacher," Frazier said.

Paul Richardson grinned as Frazier climbed back into the buggy and set off back toward town.

"You all right?" Samuel asked when the men were out of earshot.

"Yes. A bit shaken, but all right. What do you suppose the town will decide?"

"I'm not sure. We won't know until the meeting."

"I think we should go up to Liver Mountain and let the Williams and the Haskells and everyone know what is going on," Catherine said.

The drive was a bumpy one, full of ruts and rocks in the road. Samuel did his best to avoid them, but to little avail. "It's quite a drive out here," he said.

Catherine sat up straight. "Well, if the meeting doesn't go well on Sunday and if the town decides to keep these children away, what's stopping me from teaching them in their own homes?"

"About five miles one way." He chuckled.

"No, I'm serious. Harl's getting the last of the crops in and won't need the wagon much longer. I could drive it out here and set up a school for them in one of their homes or barns."

"It would have to be a home. A barn would be too cold in the winter and too dangerous to heat it."

"What do you think?"

"Well, when would you have time to teach school at the schoolhouse and drive out here and teach again?"

"I'll make time."

"You'll be exhausted, and neither Harl nor I will allow you to drive out to Liver Mountain by yourself. You don't know what you'd meet all this way out here."

"Then maybe I could have school at our place. That would save me time. I'd just be repeating the lessons from the day at home."

"But would Hazel and Harl cotton to something like that? Your house would be full of people wanting to learn."

"That's all right. That's just the kind of people I want—the ones who want to learn."

Samuel nodded his head toward a weathered shack that leaned slightly on its foundation in the distance. "This is where they live."

As they drew closer, Hezekiah Williams, his wife, Esther, and Aaron and Ruthie came out and stood on the hard-packed dirt that was their front yard. They watched silently as Samuel drove the buggy up to the house. He stopped in front of Hezekiah and greeted him and his wife. Hezekiah's neighbors came out of their homes, equally as weathered, to watch the approaching buggy.

"Aaron told us what happened today at school. I guess that's why you're here," Hezekiah said.

"Yes. Aaron, how is your head?" Catherine asked the boy.

"Fine, Teacher."

"You drove all this way just to check on my boy?"

"Well, there's been some . . . developments," Catherine said. "I'm so sorry, Mr. Williams, but it might be best, for now, if your children do not return to school."

Hezekiah took a slight step backward as if punched.

"But they can go back eventually?"

Catherine shook her head. "No, I'm afraid not. They can't come back to school for now. We'll have a town meeting about it on Sunday after church."

Esther and Hezekiah exchanged pained looks. Aaron stood staring out at the bare fields in front of him. Ruthie's eyes grew large. "I can't come back to school to get more learnin'?" she asked.

"No, I'm so sorry," Catherine whispered.

"I understand why Aaron can't come back, but Ruthie? She's just a child," Esther said.

"Henry Frazier is on the school board, and he is threatening to pull his sizeable contribution if I continue to allow . . . " Her voice trailed away.

"Our children to come to school," Hezekiah finished the sentence for her.

"But the others can come?" Esther asked.

Catherine shook her head. "No, no, they can't either."

Hezekiah's mouth dropped open. "You mean, all of our children can't come back to school just because some boys had a disagreement with my Aaron?"

"Yes and no." Catherine said. "Your children and that of your neighbors may not return, but it's not over the disagreement. It goes a lot deeper than that."

Hezekiah's head drooped. He shoved his hands into his pants pockets. "I understand. You don't want blacks at the school no more."

Catherine bit her lip, and her brows pinched tightly together. She sighed heavily. "No, if it were up to me, I'd allow everyone who wanted to learn. But it's not up to me."

"It's Frazier. He's going to withdraw his contribution to the school, which we need, and he's threatened to get rid of Catherine, too, if she doesn't stop your children and all others like them from attending." Samuel waved his hand toward the homes of the neighbors in the distance.

Taking their cue from his gesture, the neighbors rushed over.

"Afternoon, Preacher Harris," Ezra Williams greeted Samuel. He was followed by his wife, Wilda, and their three children—Jonah, Micah, and Zillah.

Clyde and Lucy Haskell walked over with their three girls—Nancy, Rachel, and Rebecca. Clyde nodded his head in greeting at Samuel as Ezra asked, "What's all this about? Why'd you come all this way out here?"

Samuel relayed the message that their children were not to return to school as Catherine nodded miserably.

"This true, Ms. Reed?" Clyde asked.

She nodded vigorously. "I'm so sorry," she said.

"How are our children supposed to get an education?" Hezekiah asked. "Their ma and me can only go so far with them. Jeremiah Watkins taught them some, but not enough."

Catherine's voice came out strangled. "I don't know."

Esther stepped forward and put out her hand. Catherine took it, held it. "Now, don't you worry none, honey. You did the best you could. You don't worry about us now, you hear?"

"We'll know more after church on Sunday," Catherine said. "Don't give up hope."

"Well, we better be getting back." Samuel took up the reins. "I'm sorry it was such bad news."

Catherine squeezed Esther's hand and looked out at all the faces surrounding them. "I'm so sorry," she whispered. "I'm so, so sorry."

With that, the preacher slapped the reins on the horse's back, and it started trotting away from the small, weathered house and its occupants.

Catherine looked back and choked back a sob. Samuel tossed the reins into his left hand and put his arm around her shoulders. He rubbed her arm. "I'll let the board know about the meeting Sunday so they can prepare," Samuel said.

Catherine stared straight ahead, her lip quivering.

When they reached the farm, Catherine thanked Samuel for the ride and excused herself. "I have a headache," she complained. "Or I'd invite you in for dinner."

"I don't feel much like eating tonight."

"Me neither. I just keep thinking about their faces when I told them they couldn't come back to school. They're devastated."

"Yeah, I'm so sorry about this."

Turning, Catherine hurried inside the house. In the kitchen, she picked up Clair and held her in her arms.

"Well, I was starting to wonder about you," her mother said.

"Henry Frazier threatened to withdraw his support from the school if I didn't . . . quit . . . teaching . . . the other . . . students."

"Oh, no." Her mother held a wooden stirring spoon. "You didn't tell the others they weren't welcome at the school anymore?"

Catherine nodded, and a sob erupted as tears streamed down her face.

"Why is Mama crying?" Clair asked.

"Because some people were treated unfairly today, and your mama has such a kind heart that it's broken for them."

Catherine plopped into a chair at the table placing Clair back on the floor.

"I have such a headache, Mother. I'd like to go straight to bed. Could you tuck Clair in for me after she's eaten?"

"Of course. Now, you run along."

Catherine headed for her room, rubbing the back of her neck with one hand.

In her room, she dressed in her white, cotton nightgown and climbed into bed, throwing the covers over her head; she sobbed into the pillow until she fell asleep.

Chapter 10

In the morning, Catherine woke refreshed. When she remembered the previous day and its events, she sighed heavily and shook her head. There was not anything else she could do but wait until after church on Sunday when she would make her plea to the community.

At school, she wrote the lessons on the board. At the door, she broke the students into two lines and let the girls in first after morning prayer. The boys followed. The two Richardson boys, Frank and James, walked by her with smirks on their faces. If only they hadn't thrown the rock that hit Aaron. If only they had behaved, she never would have expelled them from class, and Aaron and his neighbors would still be attending school. There must be some way to get them back into the school without upsetting the delicate balance. It was something that deserved considerable thought.

At lunchtime, Catherine didn't eat her lunch. Instead, she gave it away to the Fields children, who had returned. They readily accepted and ate it heartily. Samuel came over for a visit, knocking at the door before entering. He caught her eye as she sat at her desk alone in the room. "Mind if I come in?"

"Come on." She gestured him into the room.

"I just want to say again how sorry I am about what happened yesterday."

"Why? It wasn't your fault."

"I spoke to the members of the board this morning."

"And?"

"And they want to see you teaching anyone who wants to learn. Whether that's Margaret Fields or anyone. They said they'd stand behind you come Sunday."

"That's good to know."

"You know, Frazier said they just couldn't come to *this* school. He didn't say anything about going to school somewhere else. What if we provided a school for them in someone's home?" Samuel asked.

"We already thought about that, and our parlor isn't large enough for them. And I'm not sure Mama would want a lot of people traipsing through her house."

"There's a place that they could go that Frazier won't have any jurisdiction over."

Catherine sat up, her senses tingling. "Where's that?"

"My house."

"You have a parlor that can fit all those students in it and their parents?"

"I do. It's just sitting empty; and since I rarely have time to entertain, it would be the perfect setting for a new kind of school, don't you think?"

Catherine's eyes brightened as she thought about the possibilities of a new school next door, where she could teach the other students in peace without any interference from Frazier.

"But isn't Frazier on the church board?"

"No, he isn't. And I'll make sure he never gets on it. I'm supported mostly by contributions from the Harris clan—my brothers and mother—Garlin Moore, Sheriff Franklin, and others. They don't have a problem with you teaching black people. So, there is no problem. My house is my own, paid for in full, and Frazier isn't welcome there."

Catherine smiled brightly. The thought of finishing a day at regular school and then starting again next door in Samuel's parlor excited her.

"I can't believe it. The Lord answered my unspoken prayers. Thank the Lord and thank you. I would hug you, but it wouldn't be proper."

"But we still need to see if the community would let them back into the school or not."

"Yes, we do. You've given me hope."

Chapter 21

Sunday dawned bright and warm. Catherine wore her navy blue dress and put Clair in her matching outfit.

At church, many more wagons were lined up that Catherine didn't recognize. Hurrying into the building, she saw it was standing room only. There were faces in the crowd that she recognized and many she didn't. Standing in the back of the room, she scanned the benches for a seat.

Benjamin Harris and his brother Caleb stood and motioned her down to the front row. With her mother behind her, Catherine walked down the aisle and greeted the brothers.

"Were you saving this for us?"

"Yes, I knew it was going to be busy today, and I wanted you to have first choice of seats," Benjamin said.

"Thank you. I appreciate it," Catherine said, seating herself and Clair. Her mother sat next to Clair.

"Would you look at this turn out," her mother said, craning her neck. "Never seen so many people in church before."

In a few minutes, Samuel stepped out of the backroom and over to the podium. Surveying the crowd, he said, "We have a fine turnout today. Would the brothers around the room open the windows please?"

When the service ended, instead of filing out the door, everyone remained seated or standing against the wall.

"Let's have the children go outside and play while we have our discussion," Samuel said.

After the children and students had gone outside, Samuel addressed the adults. "As all of you have already heard, the schoolboard has called a special meeting of our community members to discuss whether or not to allow black children to continue learning in our school."

"You mean, they've been learning right here in this school?" a voice in the crowd called out. Many people gasped.

Catherine craned her neck around to see who had spoken. A short, thin man with beady eyes stood next to Paul Richardson, who folded his arms over his chest and nodded toward the man next to him. Catherine frowned.

"That's Cletus Tooth. Paul Richardson's neighbor," her mother whispered in her ear.

Samuel raised his hand. "Let's not shout out our questions," he said. "We want to keep this meeting orderly, and yes, they were learning in this school."

Near the front row, Dosha Clark raised her hand.

"Yes, Dosha?"

"They was here?" she asked.

"Yes," Samuel said.

"And we didn't have a say before they came?"

Samuel gazed at her and sighed.

Catherine stood, turning toward the woman and the rest of those gathered. "I didn't think it would be a problem. There were only a handful of students, anyway."

"Not a problem?" Dosha said. "My man died in the war fighting for the South."

Catherine swallowed.

"So did my brothers," Margaret Fields said.

Many heads nodded, and a murmur cut through the crowd.

"Even so, we've entered a new era. They are no longer slaves, but free men and women, and they deserve an education."

"Yeah, but not if they are in with our children," Archibald Grey said from the back of the room. Many heads nodded.

"What's so wrong with giving everyone the same opportunities?" Catherine asked.

The room grew quiet.

She looked at Henry Frazier standing near the door. He grinned and looked around him. Paul Richardson stood nearby. He rubbed his scruffy chin and folded his hands in front of him.

"Wouldn't they make better citizens and customers?"

"No business owner would doubt they would make better customers," Garlin Moore said from the back of the room. "I think we should let them come to school."

"So do I," Sheriff Anton Franklin agreed.

"Well, I don't," Paul Richardson said, stepping forward. "Let them teach their own."

"There's only so far that their parents can go with them," Catherine said. "They need a proper education."

Paul rubbed his chin again and then stepped back to his place. Turning to the short man standing near him, he whispered something.

"Let's put it to a vote," Samuel said. "How many are for letting the black children continue at the school?" Only a few hands went up. "How many are against?"

Many hands went up around the room. Catherine turned toward Samuel.

"The no's have it," he said.

Catherine sat down as a whoop from Paul Richardson sounded by the backdoor. Looking up, she met Samuel's gaze. He shook his head. "I'm so sorry," he said as the townspeople filed out of the room.

Garlin Moore extended his hand to her. "I'm sorry, too," he said.

"There were just too many of them and not enough of us," Sheriff Franklin added.

Catherine remained seated until everyone had left the room. "Well, we do have Plan B," she said and smiled.

"I'll drive you home, and we can go over the details of setting up class in two places. And maybe it's time we had a little talk about some other things as well. I'll go get the buggy ready."

"I look forward to it." Catherine stood. Samuel bowed slightly, then limped from the room. When he was gone, his brothers brought out the desk and chair and put the podium in the back room.

"I sure am sorry you won't be allowed to teach the Williams and the rest of those children," Benjamin said.

Catherine only smiled and followed them out the door.

Samuel arrived in his buggy. Catherine hopped in, smiling at him.

"I've been thinking about our plan and think it's a good one. I know Harl still has Ezra, Hezekiah, and Clyde working for him, so I can tell them about our plans at the farm tomorrow. Then they can let their families know, and we can start school Tuesday afternoon."

"Sounds like you have this all worked out." Samuel laughed.

"I do have it all worked out, and Frazier won't be able to touch it," she said with a giggle and sat back into the leather buggy seat folding her arms across her chest.

Samuel didn't want to tell Catherine the real reason he wanted the school at his place. It would give him more time to spend with her. She turned out to have a heart of gold—one that could forgive him leaving his wife on her deathbed while he comforted another family during their time of illness. Oh, that he could take back what her final moments were and stay with her. But there was nothing he could do. What was done was done.

"Lord, forgive me for blaming You for her death for so long," Samuel muttered.

"What's that?" Catherine asked. Samuel hooked his arm through hers and sighed.

"It's just something I should have done a long time ago."

Samuel smiled and sat up straight. He breathed deeply.

Catherine studied his face. "You're not going to tell me, are you?"

"Not right now," he said.

Catherine bit her lip and turned her head away.

"All right. I'll tell you. It's just that I blamed the Lord for allowing Isabella to die while I was comforting another parishioner. I believed that he would heal her completely; and so I stepped out in faith and went to see that parishioner, and she died. Just like that. Without me by her side." Samuel swiped his thumb under his eye and looked out at the fields on his left.

"Oh, dear. I had no idea. I'm so sorry. But what could you have done if you would have been there with her?" Catherine said, placing her hand on his arm.

Samuel cleared his throat. "Not much of anything, but it would have eased my conscious to have been with her 'til the end," he said, turning back to Catherine. "I just wish . . . "

"I don't believe it was God's will for her to die alone. I was disobedient without even knowing it."

Catherine slid closer to Samuel, wrapped her arm around his and leaned her head on his shoulder. "The Lord can and will forgive you."

"Yes, I believe He has already."

The next day after school, Harl was just finishing up the chores with Ezra, Hezekiah, and Clyde when Catherine and Samuel drove up. Catherine leaned out of the buggy, smiling.

She waved at Harl, flagging him down. "Gather the men around. We have something important to tell them." She gestured toward Samuel.

Harl waved for the men to come over to the buggy. When they were gathered around it, Harl asked, "What's the news?"

"I've come to tell you that your children can go to school after all." Gesturing toward Samuel, she said, "We came up with a plan. Tell them, Reverend Harris."

She scooted back into the buggy seat with her hands folded in her lap, smiling and watching the men's faces as Samuel leaned forward and explained the new school in his parlor.

Ezra tilted his hat back on his head and asked, "Won't that be against Mr. Frazier's plans for us to have school at all?"

"He didn't say you couldn't be educated." Catherine smiled. "He just said you couldn't go to school at the schoolhouse."

The men exchanged glances. Catherine waited, holding her breath. Their faces were blank and did not give away their emotions. "Well, aren't you happy about this news?" she asked.

"Yes, ma'am, we are." Clyde stepped forward. "It's just that we ain't used to getting good news, and we don't want to be overly greedy with it."

"But your children will be able to continue to read and write and all sorts of things."

Hezekiah smiled sheepishly. "She's right, and ain't that what we want for our young'uns?" Turning toward her, he took his hat off. "Don't you worry none, Ms. Reed. We'll have our young'uns at the preacher's tomorrow with their books and slates ready to learn."

Catherine's face burst into a wide smile. "That's all I can ask. School will commence after the first one lets out around 2:00 p.m. Everyone should be gathered at the preacher's home beforehand, so no one sees your children go in. We'll have a shorter day packed full of learning and get those children home by dinnertime. How does that sound?"

The three men nodded their heads. "Sounds good," Ezra said, putting his hat back on his head.

"They'll be pleased. Wait 'til I tell Lucy and the children they can go to school again." Clyde clapped his hands.

"I'll believe it when I see it," Hezekiah said.

Catherine nodded slightly to each man and hopped down from the buggy. She burst into the kitchen, where her mother was pulling pans of hot bread from the oven. Catherine couldn't contain herself and poured out the plan to hold school at Reverend Harris' home to her mother.

"Isn't he afeared that he'll get into trouble?" her mother asked. "Seems to me Henry Frazier has a hold on his position with the church."

"No, he doesn't. I asked. He's supported by donations from the community and his mother and brothers mostly, he said."

"That don't mean Frazier hasn't got his hand in the till somewheres."

"He might have it in there, but according to Reverend Harris, it isn't very deep."

Catherine was so excited by the news of a new school that she whirled about. Swooping down, she picked up Clair and whirled her around the kitchen with her while humming. Clair laughed.

"We're going to have a school, where everyone can learn," she sang to Clair.

"Me, too?" Clair squealed in delight.

"No, little one, not just yet. You're still too young. Next year, I promise," said Catherine, gently setting her daughter back down.

"Dinner will be ready shortly. You should go freshen up," her mother suggested.

Catherine danced Clair up the stairs to their room, where she washed her hands and face in the basin of water.

"Your mama's going to teach two schools," she said gleefully to Clair, who giggled, sitting on her bed holding her doll and watching her mother dance around the room.

The next day, the hours in the classroom at the schoolhouse dragged by. Catherine checked the small locket watch pinned to her dress just above her heart. Two o'clock seemed like it would never come.

"You all right, Teacher?" Frank Richardson asked, scrutinizing her.

"Yes, I'm fine. Thank you. Finish your lesson now, Frank."

"I done did five minutes ago."

"Well, why didn't you say something?" Catherine asked, walking over to his bench. "Let's see it."

He handed her his slate. She quickly looked over the assignment and deemed it correct.

"You seem mighty preoccupied, Teacher. Is there anything wrong?" James asked.

"No, there isn't anything wrong." Catherine smiled.

The time couldn't go fast enough. Finally, the moment came to dismiss the schoolhouse students and go to the preacher's house for school in his parlor.

Catherine waited until all of her students left the building. She hurried to shut and lock the door and walked over to the preacher's home.

Samuel greeted her at the door with a wide smile. "We have a parlor full, and there's some adults with them, too."

"Adult learners? Good. You're never too young or old to begin learning," Catherine said. Rounding the corner into the parlor, she was surprised by the number of young students sitting on chairs, the couch, and the floor. She noted that there were three older men sitting on chairs in the room—*the adult learners.*

She positioned herself in front of the fireplace—in the most direct sight of all the students. Looking around the room, she saw many familiar faces, including all of her former students. "I'm afraid

I don't know all of you. Would you mind introducing yourselves?" she asked, looking at the men.

A tall, lanky man stood up and said, "Lowel Edwards, ma'am."

A short, stout man stood and waved at her. "Seth Howard."

A broad-chested man with powerful muscles stood; he bowed his head and said, "Isaiah Wright."

"If you came to learn, you are all welcome here."

Catherine quickly assessed each child's and adult's learning skills and placed them into groups of the same skill set. The adult learners she placed together. She worked effortlessly with each group to make sure they were learning the correct lessons and not having any difficulty with the courses she set before them.

Looking over at Samuel, who leaned against the doorframe, she smiled contentedly. He matched and returned her smile. She moved from group to group, instructing each individual to keep them on task.

The lessons flew by quickly. Soon, it was dinner time. Catherine dismissed the students with plenty of homework for the week. She said goodbye and waved from the side door of Samuel's house.

"Whew!" she said, turning to face Samuel. She swiped little stray hairs off her hot face. "More days like this and I'll need a long rest. That was intense." She laughed. "But a good intense."

Samuel smoothed his hand over his hair. He stepped over to her and caught a strand of hair between his fingers and smoothed it back behind her ear.

"Catherine," he said, his voice growing husky. "I know we haven't talked much about this, but I love you, and I think you have feelings for me as well."

"Yes, I do," she said, holding his gaze.

He pressed his hand to the side of her face. She leaned her head into his hand.

They stood for a moment staring into each other's eyes.

"I've loved you for so long," he said stepping forward.

"I know. I've felt it."

"And I know you care for me the same. At least, I think you do."

He reached his other hand out, but Catherine pulled away. "Wait. Let's not speak like this here. Now."

"What is it?"

"There's something about me . . . you don't know." A sob caught in her throat.

"What thing? Nothing could be so bad to change my love for you."

"No, don't ask me."

"All right," he said, taking a step back. "But we have to talk about it sometime." Then changing the subject, he said, "Think you'll be able to do it all again tomorrow?"

"Why, sure."

"You're not unhappy with your daytime students, are you?"

Catherine wiped her eyes and took a shaky breath. "No. They are coming along fine. Having these students and the adult learners who really need me makes me feel warm inside. I like being needed." Then she added, "If I wasn't teaching the daytime students, the board would find someone else to teach them, and they would go on learning. But what person would agree to teach this lot? Not any that I know of."

"You have a point there." Samuel rubbed his arm. "Come on. I'll drive you home."

When Saturday rolled around, Catherine prepared to head into town with her brother.

"You've got the list?" her mother asked.

"Right here," Catherine said, holding it up. "Flour, sugar, molasses . . . "

"Good. And don't forget the baking powder."

"Nope, it's right here on the list."

"Well, you two have fun," their mother said.

"We'll be back as soon as we can," Catherine said, stepping onto the wagon wheel hub and taking Harl's offered hand. "Thank you, Harl. Bye, Mama."

Harl jiggled the reins, and the mules set off toward town.

"I was sorry about what everybody said on Sunday about them not wanting you to teach . . . well, you know."

"Thank you, Harl. I know you chose to fight for the North. Why did you?"

"'Cause I didn't think slavery was right, and I wanted to do my duty."

"Oh, I never knew. And it wasn't everyone who was against it."

"We should get those that were for you teaching both together and see if we can't persuade the town to be in favor of it."

"I tried Sunday."

"Yeah, but I don't think you tried hard enough. People would listen to reason, I'm sure."

"It's a little late notice, dontcha think?"

"No, no, I don't. If it's that important to you to teach them by going behind the town's back, then you need to say something to the assembly tomorrow at church."

"But not everyone who opposes will be there."

"Well, there will be enough of them there to make a dent in what happens at your school."

It was a few minutes before she spoke. "All right. I'll just need to tell Samuel what I plan to do."

"I can drop you off after we're done in town."

"No, no, wait for me. I don't want Mama to watch Clair longer than she has to, seeing how she watches her all day when I'm at school."

"All right."

Harl jiggled the reins again, and the mules picked up the pace.

When they arrived in town, it was bustling with activity.

"Look, there's Archibald Grey," Harl said, pointing. "You can start with him. See if you can get him to change his mind."

"You want me to do that now instead of at church?"

"Yes, why not? Start now. And there goes Dosha Clark and her girls, and we'll see Margaret Fields this afternoon when we take them some food. So, there you go," Harl said, hopping down. He walked around and helped his sister out of the wagon.

"Go to it," he said.

"But what about . . . ?" Catherine said, holding up the list. Harl snatched it from her hand.

"I'll take care of this. You go start talking to people, see if you can change their minds." Then he added, "Good luck, Sis."

Catherine looked both ways. When there was an opening between wagons, she threaded her way across the street to where Archibald sat reading the newspaper outside of the *American Bugle*, the town's weekly newspaper.

"Mr. Grey," Catherine called. "Mr. Grey," she said waving as he scanned the crowd to see who was calling his name.

She stepped up onto the boardwalk. "Hello, Mr. Grey. Fine morning, isn't it?"

He folded the newspaper and leaned forward, his elbows resting on the chair arms.

"Yes, very fine. It's my favorite time of the year when the leaves are falling," he said.

"Yes, it's my favorite time, too," she said rocking on her heels.

"Well, what can I do for you?"

"I wanted to talk with you about your decision to not let the black children into the school."

He sat back, his eyes widening. "That's not something I care to discuss."

Catherine sighed. "But I think it is something that we need to discuss for the sake of all our children."

"All our children?"

"Yes, these men and women and their children are free now. There's no reason to lock them out of a good education with our children. Is there?"

"Well, I . . . I don't think they belong together."

"Why not?"

"I don't rightly know. It's just the way I was raised."

"And that's probably the way that most of the community who is against putting them together was raised, too."

He swallowed and looked up and down the street, rubbing his brow with one hand.

"I don't know about the entire community."

"Don't you think the sooner we put them together, the sooner we will heal as a nation, as a town?"

"Excuse me," he said, standing. He hurried up the plank walkway to a horse waiting outside of the saloon, put his foot in the stirrup, and boosted himself up. He turned the horse and rushed it away deeper into the town's clogged street.

"Well, hello, Teacher," someone said. "I thought that was you."

Catherine turned to see Dosha Clark and her daughters standing near her.

"Mrs. Clark."

"Call me Dosha," she said, wiping sweat from her forehead. She held her stomach with her other hand.

"All right, Dosha. It's good to see you and your daughters . . . Are you all right?"

"Yes, yes, go on," Dosha said with a wave of her hand.

Catherine wasn't so sure, but she continued, "I wanted to talk to you."

"Oh? What about? My girls behaving in school?"

"Oh, yes. They are doing really well. The school is just the thing that I wanted to talk to you about."

"Girls, here's a penny each. Go buy yourselves some penny candy over at Mr. Grant's store and let the teacher and me talk in private."

Her daughters turned and ran across the street to Mr. Grant's Mercantile. Dosha watched them until they were safely inside the store, then turned her attention back to Catherine.

"Now, what's on your mind?"

"Well, you remember our discussion on Sunday after church?"

GRETA PICKLESIMER   275

Dosha nodded. "What about it?"

"I think it's important for the community for both sets of children to be educated together."

Dosha leaned back. "I thought that was settled."

"No, it's not settled, and we need to talk about it as a community again."

Dosha pulled a handkerchief out of her sleeve, mopped her forehead, and then wiped her nose. "You know how I stand on the subject. My husband was killed fighting for the South."

"I understand. But don't you think it's time to put it all behind us and do what's right?"

"You're not going to let this subject drop, are you?"

"No, no, I'm not. Not until the community sees reason."

"Oh, do what you want then. I can't stop you."

"So, I have your vote for including them in our school?"

"Yes," Dosha said reluctantly. "You have my vote."

"Thank you. That means a lot."

Dosha turned toward the mercantile. "Come on, girls," she called, waving them over. "Teacher," she said crisply before heading up the plank walkway to Moore's Restaurant.

Chapter 11

Catherine worked her way through the town on both sides of the street talking to everyone she could about including both sets of students in the school. Many changed their opinion; some did not.

Looking up the street toward the livery stable, she saw Paul Richardson, followed by Cletus Tooth, staggering out of the saloon. She frowned and huffed a sigh as she watched. Clenching her hands at her sides, she marched up the boardwalk toward the men, who now stood laughing in the street.

"Gentlemen," she said when she reached them. Cletus turned and laughed harder when he saw her. "What's so funny?" she asked, turning her nose up at the smell of alcohol that permeated the air around them.

Cletus shook his head and looked at the taller man beside him. "Nothin'," Cletus said, sobering.

"I'm glad to find you both."

"Oh? Why's that?" Paul asked.

"I wanted to speak to you about changing your decisions about allowing all students to attend school at the schoolhouse."

Cletus doubled over holding his sides and burst out in uproarious laughter. Paul slapped him on the back and bent over laughing, too.

"I don't see anything funny about the situation," Catherine said, her checks burning.

"Lady, give it a rest," Cletus said, straightening. "You can't change our minds."

"Yes, but won't you see reason?"

"No," Cletus said, doubling back over in laughter. A crowd was forming around them. In the street, people driving wagons and carriages stopped to gawk.

Catherine's frown deepened. Turning from the men, she hurried away back toward the mercantile.

Mrs. Tippy Grant was sweeping off the boardwalk in front of the store. She greeted Catherine.

"Nice day, isn't it?" Tippy said.

"Yes, very nice."

"I see you're working hard to change people's minds about having black children in the school. How's that going?" Tippy asked, leaning on her broom.

"A bit rough, I'm afraid."

"Harl's still in the store. Care to come in and have some tea? The water's hot."

"That sounds wonderful."

The two women turned into the mercantile. They passed Harl, who was seated on top of a barrel at the counter talking with Elijah Grant, who was turning pages of a catalog. He stood up when he saw his sister.

"You ready to go already?"

"No, Mrs. Grant invited me to tea."

"Oh, well, take your time. There's no rush," he said.

Catherine nodded.

Mrs. Grant placed the broom in a corner behind the counter and waved Catherine to follow her through the door into the stockroom.

She led the way to another door in back of the room that led out into a cream-colored kitchen. Windows in front of her and to the left illuminated the room with cheerful light. Half curtains of white muslin with tiny, embroidered, pink roses hung at the windows.

"Oh, how lovely," Catherine exclaimed.

"Yes, being the wife of a store merchant does have its perks. Here, sit down," Tippy said, pulling out a chair from the oak table in the middle of the room. A white, muslin runner with pink roses at the edges spanned the length of the table.

Catherine sat down as Tippy took a white tea pot with pink roses off the shelf near the stove. "You certainly do like your pink roses."

Tippy laughed. "Yes, and Elijah doesn't seem to mind at all."

Tippy placed tea leaves into a strainer at the top of the tea pot and poured hot water over them. "How do you take your tea? Strong or weak?"

"Strong."

Tippy bobbed the strainer up and down in the neck of the pot. She brought two delicate-looking teacups and saucers to the table. Returning to the stove, she pulled out the strainer, set it aside on a plate by the stove, and placed the lid on the teapot.

"Here we go." She placed the teapot on the table and brought over the sugar bowl. "Do you take cream?"

"No, thank you."

Tippy poured tea into Catherine's cup and then into her own and sat down next to her friend.

"Now, tell me the news. Are you having any luck changing the minds of the townspeople?"

"Some."

"I'm not surprised. This town was split during the war. Most of those fighting for the South didn't come home, and many of the families still haven't gotten over it. My first husband fought for the North. Thought that blacks had the right to be free. I agree. He was right, but he didn't come home.

"Oh, I made some delicious molasses cookies. Do you want some? What am I thinking? Of course, you'd like some. Give you the chance to sample some of my cooking."

Tippy bounced up and over to the counter by the stove. She uncovered a platter of dark brown cookies and placed it before Catherine.

"Try one," Tippy said, seating herself again.

Catherine picked one up, smiled at her host and bit into it. "Mmm, that's good and perfect with the tea."

Tippy smiled widely. "Now, what can I do to help you?"

"I don't know. Maybe if you could spread the word among your customers we are going to have another meeting? That would be helpful."

"That I can do." Her smile faded. She stretched out her hand and squeezed Catherine's. "How are you doing?"

"Quite well, actually, if I could just get the town to see reason," Catherine said, finishing the cookie.

"No, I meant with the passing of your husband."

"Oh, well. It still hurts," Catherine said, lowering her head.

"I'm sure. When my first husband died in the war, I wasn't sure I could go on without him, but I found a way. It took time, though." She pulled back her hand and picked up the teapot. "More tea?"

"No, no, thank you. I better get back to Harl."

"It was nice chatting with you," Tippy said.

Catherine's smile was warm. "Yes, thank you."

In the front of the store, Catherine met George Wayright, the owner and proprietor of *The American Bugle,* the weekly newspaper.

"Mr. Wayright," Catherine said in greeting as she passed him.

"Mrs. Reed, how nice to see you," he returned.

Spinning on her heels, she asked, "Mr. Wayright, would be willing to run an article in your paper about why we should allow black children to be educated with our own?"

He took a step backward. "That's a hotbed issue."

"Yes, but would you?"

He smiled. "That's just the thing to waken this sleepy town. Of course, I'll do it. It could go in next week's paper?"

"Any chance it could go in sooner?"

"The paper only comes out on Wednesdays. But I could put together a handbill—kind of a special to the paper—and distribute it here in town. Better come over to my office and I'll jot down what you want it to say."

Catherine's smile deepened. She waved at Harl as she left the mercantile.

At the newspaper, Mr. Wayright offered her a chair beside his messy desk. "Now, what would you want it to say?"

"Put in there that these freed slaves have every right to an education as our children. That with an education, they will make better citizens, workers, and customers. Every opportunity should be offered to them, for they are free men and women and should have the same rights as free men and women no matter the color of their skin. We'll meet to discuss the matter Sunday after church at the school."

Mr. Wayright chuckled.

"What's funny about that?"

"Nothing. I was just thinking you should be a politician instead of a school teacher."

She smiled. "What do I owe you?"

He shook his head. "Nothing. I'll post this all over town and hand out a few to those I can catch. You should have a humdinger of a meeting tomorrow."

By the time she returned to Harl, he had loaded the wagon, and she was dizzy with excitement.

"Oh, Harl," she cried, taking his hand as he helped her into the wagon. "Most of the people I spoke with have changed their opinion and say that we should have both sets of students in the classroom. Mr. Wayright will be printing and posting handbills around town."

Harl smiled. "That's great, Sis."

Catherine returned his smile as he jiggled the reins for the mules to walk on. Near the outskirts of town, Henry Frazier stepped out in front of the wagon. Harl pulled the reins back hard to keep from hitting him.

"What are you doing, Henry? I could have run you over!" Harl shouted.

"You're a better driver than that," he said. Looking at Catherine, he smirked. "Think you've got me beat, do you?"

"Whatever do you mean?" Catherine asked.

"You talking to the town about including the black children in school, that's what."

"Yes, I am. I think what is happening to them is outrageous. They should be included in not only school, but also community life as well."

Frazier narrowed his eyes. "Well, I'll be there at service tomorrow, and we'll just see who wins."

Catherine sat up straighter. "This is not a competition."

"We'll still see," Frazier said, moving out of the path of the wagon.

Harl jingled the reins, and the mules started off again. He tipped his hat to the man as they passed him.

"That's going to some meeting tomorrow. You trying to turn the rudder that sails the ship. Think you can do it?"

"I'm sure I can if what people said when I approached them was any indication."

When they arrived at Samuel's home, Catherine knocked on the front door. He opened it and smiled.

"Catherine, what a pleasant surprise."

"We need to have another meeting after church tomorrow."

"Oh, do you think the town will change its mind?"

"Yes, I do. If what I've been hearing from people is any indication."

"Talked to the entire town, have you?"

"No, not everyone, but enough. I think most of them are willing to stand with me."

"Against Frazier and Paul Richardson?"

"Yes."

"Okay, then. We'll have another meeting after church tomorrow."

When they arrived home, Clair ran to meet them, followed by her grandmother.

"Hello, honey," Catherine said, climbing down from the wagon. "Were you good for Grandma?

Clair nodded, "Uh-huh."

"Tell her what we did, Clair," her grandmother prompted.

"We made cookies," the child shouted, jumping up and down.

"Mmm. What kind?"

Clair turned to her grandmother.

"We made gingerbread cookies."

"Oh, yeah," Clair said.

"I thought it might be nice to take something sweet up to the Fields as well as everything else."

"I'll get the milk. Ma, could you bring the eggs? Catherine, get some of those cookies," Harl instructed.

When everything was loaded in the wagon, everyone climbed aboard, and they set off for Liver Mountain.

When they arrived at the Fields' place, Margaret and her children came out of their weathered shack and stood on their packed-dirt front yard.

"I was wondering if you all were coming up today," Margaret said.

"We have lots of goodies for you," her mother said, climbing down.

Harl jumped down and helped his niece out of the back of the wagon. When her feet touched the ground, she ran to Dorthea. "Let's go play," Clair said, pulling Dorthea by the hand.

"Yes, you all go on and play," Catherine said, as her brother helped her out of the wagon. "There's something I need to talk to your mama about."

The three children obeyed and ran around the side of the shack.

Catherine turned and swiped at the stray hairs hanging around her face.

"There's going to be another meeting tomorrow after church."

"Is there now?" Margaret said.

"Yes, and I want you to be there."

"Why?"

"I think we've made a grave mistake in not allowing the black students into the school."

"Oh?" Margaret touched her face.

"Yes. I know your man fought for the South, but that doesn't mean you have to. The war's over. Let's get on with our lives. They are free, and they should live like it with all the advantages of a free people."

"Well, I was just siding with the majority."

"And if that majority has changed their minds?"

"Then I'll still side with the majority."

Catherine's smile was like daybreak. She stepped over to Margaret and hugged her. "Thank you," Catherine whispered.

"We put everything in on the table," Harl said, climbing back up onto the wagon.

"Oh, I almost forgot. We brought you some cookies, too," Catherine said, pulling a little basket covered with a dishtowel out of the back.

"Cookies!" Dorthea shouted. Her siblings and Clair came running around the house to Catherine.

"Can I see?" Dorthea asked.

Catherine uncovered the cookies and held the basket down.

"Mmm, my favorite."

"What kind are they?" Hershel asked.

"Gingerbread," Catherine said.

"I helped make them," Clair said.

"Can I have one now, Mama?" Dorthea asked.

"Why, sure."

Dorthea grabbed two, one in each hand.

"Don't be so greedy," Easter whined.

"I'm getting one for me and one for Mama," Dorthea explained.

"Oh." Easter smiled.

"So, we'll see you tomorrow?" Catherine asked, handing over the basket. Harl helped her and Clair into the back of the wagon.

"Yes," Margaret said, taking a bit of cookie. "Mmm, that's a good cookie. Thank you."

"Glad you like it," Hazel said, climbing aboard.

Harl tipped his hat to Margaret and her children and turned the mules around.

When they arrived home, Harl tended the mules while Catherine and her mother started dinner. When it was ready, Harl came in.

"Harl, would you say grace?" his mother asked him.

He nodded and bowed his head. "Dear Lord, we thank You for this meal set before us. We thank You and pray a blessing on the hands that prepared it. We also pray for Catherine tomorrow that You would give her the right words to say. In Jesus' name, amen."

"Amen," Catherine and her mother said in chorus.

Chapter 23

The next day dawned cool and bright.

Catherine dressed her and Clair in their matching blue dresses and headed into the kitchen for breakfast. Her mother was kneading dough on the counter.

"Here, Mama, let me do that. Or do you want me to make the gravy?"

"You can make the gravy. I'm almost done here."

Catherine tied on an apron. She shaped and fried sausage patties in a cast iron skillet. Once the sausage was cooked, she took it out and put it onto a plate, added flour into the skillet, and stirred. When the flour was brown, she added milk to the mixture and stirred until it bubbled. Then she spooned it out into a bowl. She set the bowl and plate of sausage on the table.

"I'll just pop this in the oven while you go call your brother."

Catherine walked out onto the porch and found Harl walking toward her.

"Time for breakfast," she said.

"Be right there."

He stopped at the well and washed his hands in a small dishpan used for that purpose.

"Harl's coming," Catherine said, walking into the kitchen.

When breakfast ended, Harl left to hitch the team for the drive into church. He helped his mother up onto the wagon seat and went to help his sister and niece into the back.

"You ready for today?" he asked.

"Yes, I've prayed about it and know the Lord will help me with what to say to the community."

"I'll be praying for you," Harl said.

"Me, too," their mother offered.

Catherine smiled and scrambled up onto the bed of quilts.

When they arrived at church, there was quite a crowd waiting for them. Catherine hurried to a bench at the front where men's coats had been draped.

"Were you saving me a seat?" she asked Benjamin Harris, who stood nearby.

"Yes, of course," he said, removing his coat from the bench. He picked up the other one and tossed it back to his brother.

"You've got this," Caleb said. "Me and Ben have been talking your idea up around town with favorable results. Those handbills that George Wayright put up helped, I'm sure."

"Thank you. I knew I could count on the Harrises to help."

When the service ended, Samuel nodded at Catherine, who stood and turned to face the crowd.

"I see many faces that I was able to speak to yesterday about our meeting today. I want you to know that a great wrong has been done to a people that didn't deserve it. Their only fault was being born a different color than you and me; but there is no difference in them, and their children deserve to attend school with your children."

A murmur went through the crowd with many nodding their heads.

"Has Harrisville changed their mind about properly educating them?" she asked.

"Now, wait just a minute," Henry Frazier said from the back of the room. "Have you people lost your heads? Don't you see what she is doing?"

"She's trying to be fair is all," Archibald Grey said.

"Yeah," Dosha Clark agreed.

"I don't think this war we just came out of was fighting for fair . . ."

"Oh, Henry, sit down and listen to reason for once in your life," George Wayright said.

"All I want is to—"

"All you want is to keep doing things the old way," Catherine cut him off. "The old way isn't our way. It's not this town's way."

"That's right," Benjamin Harris said.

"We need to embrace change, starting with allowing these freed children into school. Once they are educated, they will have better opportunities. And as they grow, they will get better jobs, have more money, become better customers and citizens of our town."

"But won't they take our jobs?" a man's voice asked from the back of the room.

"Not if you or your children are properly educated. There should be plenty of work for us all."

"Yeah, but what about those that don't get an education?" Margaret Fields asked.

"Then their opportunities will be fewer than those who do?"

"Won't they be bad citizens then?" she asked.

Catherine placed her hands on her hips. "Not necessarily. You live out by them. Have they been bad neighbors to you?"

Margaret's face turned a deep shade of pink as the eyes of the congregation fell on her. "No," she said quietly. "They helped me get the crops in this year and last when my man . . . when he was a bit slow in doing it."

"You see? Aren't those the type of citizens that deserve inclusion, that deserve to have their children educated right along with yours?"

A murmur coursed through the crowd, and many nodded.

"Oh, have it your way," Henry Frazier said, waving his hand. Turning on his heels, he fled from the building.

Several people chuckled; a few applauded.

"Yeah, well, Frazier's not the only one who wants to see them kept out," Paul Richardson said.

Catherine ignored him. "How many of you are for allowing them into the school?"

Many hands shot up.

Catherine counted. "Twenty-three. And opposed?"

A few hands tentatively went up.

"Come on, come on. Don't let this woman and her wiles get to you," Richardson said, holding his hand high.

"That is six. The yesses have it," Catherine exclaimed.

"Dagnabbit!" Turning on his heels, Paul marched out of the church after Frazier with Cletus Tooth not far behind.

Following his lead, the church rose. Several chuckled and thumped each other on the back. Tippy Grant approached Catherine, smiling.

"Thank goodness that's over," she said, reaching out her hand to take Catherine's. "After our chat yesterday, I spoke to our customers about coming out to the meeting and supporting the cause. I'm so glad it turned out so well. I think those handbills George Wayright posted all over town helped."

"I think so, too," George Wayright said, stepping up to the ladies. "Until I caught Frazier tearing them down. Made me so mad, I went and told the sheriff. He put a stop to it right then and there." And then sticking out his hand, he shook Catherine's. "Congratulations."

"Thank you. I'm so excited."

"Looks like you singlehandedly took care of both Frazier and Richardson," Samuel said, approaching Catherine.

She smiled.

"Care to go tell them the good news this afternoon?" Samuel asked.

"I'd love to."

While Samuel went to hitch the buggy, Catherine sat waiting on his front porch enjoying the cool day when Paul Richardson rode up on his horse. He shook his head.

"This isn't over," he said, his eyes narrowing. "There's going to be trouble if you allow so much as their toe in that schoolhouse. Mark my words." He pursed his lips and dug his heels into the sides of the horse's flank. The horse shot off down the road.

Catherine's mouth dropped open, and her brows pinched together as she watched the retreating form of Paul Richardson until he was out of sight around a bend in the road.

The jingle of tack to her right caused Catherine to turn her head. Samuel sat in the buggy smiling at her. His face dropped when he noticed her expression.

"What's wrong?"

"Paul Richardson. He said there was going to be trouble if I allowed them in the school."

Samuel reached out a hand to help her into the buggy. He scowled. "I'll let the sheriff know there may be trouble. All we can do is to be vigilant and pray for the best."

When they reached Liver Mountain, the Williamses came out on their yard.

"Hello," Catherine called, waving.

"I hope it's good news this time," Hezekiah said.

"Yes, it is. You can't believe what's happened this morning."

"I'll believe anything."

Samuel helped her out of the buggy.

"Your children can go to school starting tomorrow."

Hezekiah placed his hand over his heart and gasped.

"What's this?"

"Mrs. Reed's been talking to the townspeople. She called a meeting today after church and singlehandedly corralled the lot of them. Well, a lot of them, anyway."

"You mean my Aaron and Ruthie are going back to school? In the schoolhouse?" Esther Williams said.

"Yes." Catherine's smile widened.

"What's this we hear, Teacher?" Ezra Williams said, walking over with his wife and children. "Is our young'uns going back to school?"

"Yes, isn't that wonderful?"

"I thought the town was against it," he said.

"Not anymore . . . well, most aren't thanks to a little persuasion," Samuel said, beaming at Catherine.

Ezra and his wife, Wilda, smiled. Ezra turned to Clyde and Lucy Haskell, who were standing on their yard, and yelled, "Our children are going back to school."

"What?" Clyde called, cupping his hands behind his ears.

"Going . . . back . . . to . . . school," Ezra shouted.

"What's that about the school?" Clyde called.

"Oh, get over here," Ezra said, motioning to him.

Clyde and his wife ran over to them, followed by their daughters.

"What's wrong at the school?" he asked.

"Nothing is wrong," Ezra explained. "Our children are going back tomorrow."

Clyde did a jig, then stopped. "I thought the town was against it."

"Not anymore," Hezekiah said.

"Won't you come in for a bite to eat?" Esther offered.

"No, no, thank you. I've got lessons to plan, and you need to get ready for the children's first day back."

"Thank you for coming all this way out to tell us. That means a lot, Teacher," Hezekiah said.

Catherine climbed up into the buggy and smiled at Samuel. She waved as they drove away.

Hooking her arm in his, she sighed. He looked at their hooked arms and smiled.

"Want to come get a bite to eat?"

"No, you've got a lot of planning to do for your classes tomorrow."

"Yes, I do."

At home, Catherine raced up the steps, taking them two at a time. Her mother sat on the porch breaking beans.

"Land's sakes! What's after you?" her mother asked.

"We just came from telling the Williamses and Haskells that they can attend school tomorrow. I'm dizzy with excitement."

"What about your adult learners?" Samuel asked.

"Oh." Catherine spun around. "I didn't think of them. Well, I guess if they show up, I can teach them, too. It will certainly make my life easier to instruct everyone all together."

In the morning, both sets of students arrived around the same time. Everyone was gathered, except for Frank and James Richardson. Not wanting to wait, Catherine began the day with prayer and let the children into the school.

Sometime later, there was a ruckus outside as the students learned their times tables. Everyone hopped up from their seats and ran to the windows. Paul Richardson stood over his boys with his belt loop, ready to strike. Catherine ran out the door as he laid the first blows on his boys' upraised arms.

"Mr. Richardson," Catherine screamed. Pausing, he glared at her.

"How dare you come here causing a ruckus," she said clapping her hands. "You frightened my students."

"Yeah, well, here's a few other ones that can be frightened of me, too," he said raising the belt high over his head.

"We do not punish. We correct," she said. "Why are you doing this, anyway?"

"Tell her," he said, raising the belt higher.

"Pa caught us sneaking off to school and didn't want us going."

Their father lunged at them, holding the belt high. He brought it down with a crack on Frank's back.

"There'll be none of that please," Catherine said, clapping her hands.

Paul Richardson stood to his full height and glared at her. He moved his mouth into a menacing smile. When Catherine didn't budge, he rolled his eyes and put the arm holding the belt down. "Fine. Boys, get on home."

"Yes, sir," both boys said as they stood up.

"Now, git." He lunged at them, and they ran off back down the road toward home.

Paul peered around Catherine. She turned toward the schoolhouse to see what he was looking at. Several dark faces stared out at them.

"Tsk, I see you did let them children in."

When she turned back to him, she saw he had his hands on his hips and his hat pushed back on his forehead.

He shook his head and laughed coldly. Turning, he called over his shoulder, "I'll be seeing you, Teacher."

Catherine shook as she walked back to the schoolhouse. Paul Richardson was planning something. She felt it in her bones. She was so distracted that she let the students leave for the day at lunchtime.

As she tidied up the empty room, she heard a tentative knock on the door. Gazing up, she saw Samuel standing in the doorway.

"Where are all your students?"

"I sent them home."

"Why?" he said, stepping into the room.

"I couldn't . . . Paul Richardson caught his boys sneaking off to school and was whipping them. When I stopped him, he saw the black students and said there would be trouble." She let the words pour out of her as she sank onto a bench. Samuel sat down across the aisle from her.

He let the air whoosh out of his lungs. He shook his head.

"I'll let the sheriff know," he said.

"But what can he do?" Catherine wailed.

"He could have a talk with him, let him know he's being watched and not to do anything."

"But then there's Frazier."

"What about Frazier? Has he made threats, too?"

"Not yet."

"Well, let's keep it that way. You want a ride home?"

"Yes, please," she said, putting her head in her hands.

"I'll be right back." Samuel rose and limped from the room.

Catherine sat with her head in her hands and elbows on her knees until she heard the jingle of a harness. Rising, she gathered her things, locked the schoolhouse door, and stepped into his buggy.

Chapter 14

The next morning, Catherine drank only tea for breakfast.

"It's as much as I can stomach right now," she explained to her mother.

"Well, take some biscuits with you, anyway."

Catherine agreed and set off for the schoolhouse through the bare orchard. She hurried along, wanting to make sure she arrived long before her students. As she walked, she wrapped her shawl about her tightly. Above her, in the trees, birds chirped merrily. Along her path, cold fog crept like an unwelcome visitor. As she neared the schoolhouse, the whisper of early morning dawn streaked the sky in the east. The school stood out eerily against the darkness of the trees surrounding it. Tiny hairs raised on the back of her neck as she felt someone's eyes on her. She hurried her steps, but then stopped.

Several of the windows in the school had been broken out. She rushed forward, holding her key at the ready; she pushed it into the lock, but the door swung open before she had a chance to turn it. Looking more closely at the doorframe, it showed splintered wood where the latch went in.

With eyes wide, she stumbled forward and almost fell over a bench that was turned over in her path. Looking about her, she noticed all the benches were overturned and in a jumbled mess. Gazing up at the board, she saw written in large, white letters that dripped down the board: GO BACK TO LIVER MOUNTAIN. Catherine stumbled backward and dropped her knapsack and lunch basket.

She rushed out the door and over to Samuel's dark home. Banging on the door, she shouted, "Samuel!"

It was several moments before a light illuminated the dark front-room window and the door was opened by a groggy-looking Samuel in his nightshirt.

"Catherine? What is it?"

"Someone's vandalized the school."

"What?"

"Please get dressed and come."

"Wait here." He turned, leaving the door open behind him and ran from the room. In a moment, he was back fully clothed, oil lamp still clutched in his hand. He closed the door behind them and dashed toward the school. He groaned when he saw the overturned benches and the writing on the board. Placing the oil lamp on top of the cold potbellied stove, he set about righting the benches as Catherine walked to the board. Taking the cleaning rag in hand, she tried to erase the lettering to no avail.

"It's painted on," she said over her shoulder, hiccupping back a sob.

Once all the benches had been righted, Samuel joined her at the board. Taking the rag from her, he scrubbed at the letters. Placing his hand on the board, he stared at her.

"You'll have to call off school today. We can't have the children see this."

Catherine nodded. "It seems Paul Richardson got his revenge."

"It could have been any number of dissenters."

"Yes, but he was the most outspoken and made a threat."

"You go greet your students at the door. I'm going to fetch some turpentine from my house and see if I can't take this off."

Catherine obeyed and stood at the ready at the closed school door. As her students arrived, she told them the bad news that school was canceled for that day.

"What's wrong, Teacher?" Dorthea Fields asked.

"It's just that we aren't having school today."

"Why?" she insisted. "Is it 'cause of them broken out winders that we can't come in?"

"Yes, that's part of it," Catherine said.

When she turned away all of her students, she rushed back into the school. Samuel was just finishing wiping down the entire, now clean, board with the turpentine.

"I'll hitch the buggy, and we can go into town and get Elijah Grant to come see about replacing the windows that were broken."

Catherine nodded as she looked at the broken glass on the floor on both sides of the room. "I'll get the broom and dustpan from the backroom," she said, moving forward stiffly.

By the time Samuel arrived back with the buggy, Catherine had swept up all the debris and placed it in the trash bucket in the backroom.

"I don't understand who would want to do such a thing," Samuel said.

"You didn't see Paul whipping his boys because they had gone off to join black children at school."

Samuel gasped and turned toward her. "I didn't know."

"You also didn't hear his threats that day."

"Maybe we should swing by the sheriff's office first."

"I think that would be best."

Samuel gazed at Catherine a moment before saying, "I'm so sorry this happened."

"So am I," she responded curtly.

"You're not mad at me over this, are you?"

Her shoulders relaxed. "No, I'm not. It's just . . . how did you not hear the glass breaking?"

He thought a moment and then answered, "I sleep pretty soundly, but I didn't hear anything until you were banging on my door yelling."

In town, Samuel guided his horse over to the jailhouse at the edge of town where the sheriff's office was housed.

Sheriff Anton Franklin strode out of the jailhouse onto the boardwalk in front of his office. His silver spurs jingled as he walked. Catherine stared at the badge in the shape of a star on his coat.

"Mighty early for you two to be in town," he said, chewing the last of a part of a biscuit he held.

"There's been trouble at the school," Catherine blurted.

The sheriff swallowed hard, his eyes widening. "What's happened?"

"Someone smashed several windows, broke in, over-turned the benches and wrote, 'GO BACK TO LIVER MOUNTAIN' in paint on the blackboard."

The sheriff shook his head. "I'm sorry about that. I wondered if there might be trouble after Frazier stormed out of the meeting Sunday."

"Yes, but I think it was Paul Richardson who did the damage," she said.

The sheriff cocked his head to one side. "Why? I know he and Frazier are friends, but I don't think he'd be caught up in something like this."

"He threatened the school after the meeting Sunday, saying there'd be trouble, and then again when he caught his sons trying to attend."

"Why didn't you come to me straightaway? I could have spoken to him, maybe averted his temper."

"Because I didn't think there would be trouble. Could you go have a look at the schoolhouse and then go talk to Mr. Richardson? Maybe arrest him for destruction of public property?"

"We don't know he did it," Samuel said.

"But once the sheriff talks to him, we might get a confession out of him."

"That we might," the sheriff agreed. "At least I can see what he knows about the break in. Who else knows about this?"

"No one."

"Let's keep it that way."

"We're on our way to the mercantile to try and get the windows and door fixed," Samuel said.

"Let Elijah and Tippy Grant know not to breathe a word to anyone about what has happened. The culprit, or culprits, just might be itching to let the cat out of the bag, so to speak, and will incriminate themselves by asking questions about the break-in."

Catherine nodded.

"Thank you, Sheriff. Are you heading out to the Richardsons' place, anyway?" Samuel asked

"Sure will. Just let me grab my things from the office and get my horse over at the livery, and I'll be on my way."

"Thank you," Catherine said as Samuel turned the horse toward the center of town. The sun cast long shadows into the street as they drove. The town had very few inhabitants going about their morning business when they pulled up to the mercantile, where Tippy Grant was sweeping the boardwalk in front of the store as Elijah carried heavy-looking barrels out onto it.

"Well, good morning," Tippy said.

"Morning," Samuel said.

"What brings you here so early this morning?" she asked.

Catherine's chin began to quiver, and tears rushed out of the corners of her eyes. "Oh, Tippy, something awful has happened."

Tippy leaned her broom against the store and stretched out her hands to Catherine, just as Elijah was returning with another barrel. Catherine staggered down from the buggy and fell into her friend's arms.

"What's this?" Elijah asked. "What's happened?" he asked, looking from Catherine to Samuel and back again.

"The school . . . was . . . broken . . . into," Catherine sobbed against her friend's chest.

"Oh dear, oh dear," Tippy soothed. "Better come in."

"Yes," Elijah said. "Let's go inside, so we can have privacy." He extended his hand in gesture to Samuel, who limped out of the buggy and tied his horse to the hitching post in front of the store.

Catherine walked with her friend into the store, followed by Elijah and Samuel.

When they reached the back counter, Elijah asked, "The school was broken into?"

"More like vandalized," Samuel explained. "Several windows were broken; the room was ransacked; and 'GO BACK TO LIVER MOUNTAIN' was written on the board in white paint. I'm sure we know who the culprits were directing their message to."

Elijah and Tippy's mouths stood open, their eyes wide.

"Goodness gracious," Tippy said, pulling Catherine close to her again.

"We were hoping that you could fix the lock and the broken windows," Samuel said.

"Yes, I should be able to. I have new lock mechanisms and glass I can cut to size. Tippy, can you run the store? Maybe keep Catherine with you until we get back?" Elijah said.

Tippy nodded and rubbed Catherine's arm. "Get Catherine a stool out of the stockroom. I'll go pour us some tea."

When Elijah and Tippy left the room, Samuel stepped over to Catherine, who was bracing her hands on the counter. "Will you be all right until we can get back?" he asked.

She looked up at him, her eyes full of worry. She pulled a handkerchief from her sleeve and dabbed at her moist eyes. "I think so. Hurry back, please."

Elijah brought a stool out of the stockroom and placed it beside Catherine. She sat. Tippy returned momentarily, carrying a large tea-service tray with the fine china rosebud teapot, cups, and saucers and an assortment of cookies on a matching plate.

"We'll be back as soon as we can," Elijah said, as Tippy poured the tea.

"We will be fine, won't we, Catherine?" she asked.

"Yes," Catherine answered shakily.

As the men walked toward the door, Samuel suddenly spun around. Holding out his hand he said, "It's important that no one know about the damage to the school. So, you must not tell anyone what has happened."

"All right. You can trust me to keep a secret," Tippy replied.

Samuel looked at Catherine. "It might be better to have tea in private than at the counter. It'll start getting busy here soon, I'm sure."

Tippy picked up their teacups and saucers, returned them to the tray, and motioned for Catherine to follow her through the stockroom and into their private quarters.

"I'll have to leave you here, dear. I need to be out front in the store for when a customer comes in. Will you be all right?"

"Yes," Catherine said. "I'll be fine."

"Make yourself at home then. It might be better for you to stay out of sight back here. People will wonder why the teacher isn't in school, and I don't want you to have to explain yourself half a dozen times."

"Thank you. You are right. It's best I stay back here."

Tippy patted her friend's arm and shut the door behind her.

Catherine drank her tea slowly and waited.

Chapter 15

At the schoolhouse, Elijah Grant and Samuel surveyed the damage more closely.

"The lock isn't broken; just the wood around the frame of the door is. That's an easy fix. Now let's have a look at those windows," Elijah said, pulling a tape measure from his pocket.

After measuring the glass panes with the help of Samuel, he rolled the linen tape back into the brass compartment of the tape measure. "That does it," Elijah said. "No other things out of sorts inside, are there?"

"I don't think so, but let's go in and check anyway."

Just inside the door, Samuel found Catherine's knapsack and lunch basket turned on its side. He picked these up. The benches they had righted still stood in straight lines. Samuel opened the door at the front of the room. There didn't seem to be anything amiss in the small room. The pulpit stood in one corner, a wastebasket by the door. Peering into the wastebasket, Samuel saw shards of glass. He picked it up and tucked it under his arm. Shutting the door, he limped toward Elijah, who stood waiting outside by the buggy.

"I'll just be a moment," Samuel said. "I'll take this around to the back door."

"What is it?"

"Glass shards. Here," he said, handing Elijah Catherine's knapsack and lunch basket. "Put these in the buggy, if you don't mind."

"All right."

When Samuel returned, Elijah was sitting in the buggy with Catherine's things at his feet.

Samuel stepped up and in. Taking the reins, he jiggled them and spoke to the horse to "walk on."

"Let's swing over to the lumber mill and pick up some wood to replace the door jam," Elijah said.

"Yes, thank you."

Once that was done, they returned to the store.

Tippy brought Samuel into the kitchen, where Catherine sat over her empty tea cup and a half-eaten cookie.

"Elijah bought some wood to repair the door jam with," Samuel said, seating himself next to Catherine. "He said the lock isn't broken; just the wood around the lock was damaged."

Catherine looked at him and swallowed the lump that was forming once again in her throat.

"He's going to cut the glass and bring it over this afternoon, but first he's going to fix the door," he explained.

"There, you see. My husband will make it just like new again, and you can hold classes with no one the wiser."

"We still don't know who did this," Samuel said.

"I have a pretty good idea," Catherine said.

"Let's go wait for Elijah at my house," Samuel said.

Catherine nodded and stood. "Thank you for your hospitality. I appreciate it," she said, turning to extend her hand to Tippy.

"My pleasure. Glad to do it."

At Samuel's home, Catherine sat outside on a chair on the porch while Samuel busied himself inside. "I'll just be a minute," he called through the open front door.

Paul Richardson, followed by Sheriff Anton Franklin, rode up.

"Sittin' high on the hog?" Richardson asked.

"No, why would you think that?"

"I see your boyfriend isn't around. You've got a lot of nerve sending the sheriff after me. Anybody could have busted up the school, and it wasn't me."

Catherine turned her eyes to the sheriff and back again to Paul.

"How did you know the school was busted up?"

"I . . . well . . . I . . . the . . . sheriff . . . asked me about it . . . I got this neighbor, see, and we was talking, just talking. He was at the first meeting. I didn't think he'd do anything, but he did."

"You were the only one who made threats. Threats that were realized."

"Now, don't go putting words in my mouth," Paul said.

"And who is that neighbor?"

"Cletus Tooth. I mean, it weren't me. He said he was going to, but I never dreamed he would." Paul shifted on his saddle.

The sheriff looked at Catherine and shook his head. "Why didn't you say anything when we were up at your place?"

"Didn't want him to hear me."

"Uh-huh, let's go talk to Cletus."

"Oh, you leave me out of this. I'll wait in town until you come back with the right man who done this."

"Fine, but if I hear anything to the contrary, I'm coming back to look for you."

Catherine watched the two men on horseback. One went toward town, the other away from it. Her gaze followed them until they were out of sight and earshot.

Samuel walked over to her and sat down in the chair opposite her.

"You missed seeing Paul Richardson and the sheriff."

Samuel gasped. "He caught him?"

"Seems that Mr. Richardson confessed that he was talking to Cletus Tooth about busting up the school and Cletus did it. Mr. Richardson said he didn't do anything. The sheriff rode out to Tooth's place to talk to him, and Richardson went into town to hide."

Samuel laughed.

The jingle of a harness caught Catherine's ears. She looked over her shoulder and saw Elijah Grant coming on with his wagon. He raised his hand in greeting.

"Won't take me but a couple of hours to get these windows in and the door jam fixed. Why, you'll be able to have school tomorrow if you want."

Samuel helped Elijah remove the broken windows and place in the new ones. By the time Elijah had replaced the wood around the door jam, it was time for lunch.

"What do I owe you, Mr. Grant?" Catherine asked.

"Not a thing. Just doing my civic duty as a member of the board. Besides, I'm happy to help the school."

Catherine sighed. "Thank you."

"Glad you're on the board, Elijah. I wouldn't have known how to do those things," Samuel said.

"I better be getting back to Tippy. She'll have lunch ready for me and will wonder what's taking so long. Care to join us?"

Catherine looked at Samuel before replying, "No, thank you. I think we'll go back to the orchard for our lunch. I'm sure Mama will have something cooked."

Elijah smiled and climbed up onto his wagon. "I hope you don't mind, but I'm taking the broken glass with me. Not all of it is bad. If it's cut right, it might just fit some smaller window panes."

"Not at all." Catherine waved until he turned the wagon around and headed back toward town. Turning to Samuel, she said, "Care to drive me home?"

"Love to." Samuel smiled.

At home, her mother and Clair stepped out onto the porch. Hazel's mouth hung open when she saw her daughter and Samuel approaching in the buggy.

"Everything all right up at the schoolhouse?" her mother asked.

Catherine looked around her. "No," she said. "I'll explain inside."

Samuel helped her down and then hopped down and tied the reins to a pillar near the stairs.

Catherine turned back to Samuel, waiting for him. Harl walked out of the barn and rushed toward them. "What's wrong? Why are you here this time of day?" he asked.

"She's going to tell us inside," his mother said, motioning everyone into the house.

Her mother shut the door and gestured for everyone to take a seat at the kitchen table.

"Go get me a pretty apple from one of your uncle's trees in the orchard," Catherine said to Clair. The child skipped out the door and down the steps.

"Now. What's happened?" her mother asked.

"Someone broke into the school and ransacked it. They wrote 'GO BACK TO LIVER MOUNTAIN' on the board in white paint and turned over all the benches and broke several of the windows," Catherine said.

"Oh, dear!" her mother exclaimed.

"You all right? Did you catch them in the act?" Harl asked.

"No," said Samuel. "We thought Paul Richardson had done it, but he confessed that it was his neighbor Cletus Tooth who did it."

"We went to the sheriff right away and told him what we thought we knew. He set out after Richardson and brought him over to the school this morning. He said his neighbor had done it. So, the sheriff set off for the neighbor's place while Mr. Richardson went into town to hide."

"So, the sheriff's going after Tooth?"

"Yes. That's what it looks like."

"What do you think the sheriff will do?"

"There's probably not much that he can do," Samuel interjected. "Hold him for destruction of property, make him pay a fine. I'm not sure."

"That's it?" Catherine said.

"Well, I'm not a lawyer—and I don't know for sure—but he wouldn't stand trial for something like this."

Catherine's brows pinched together, and the corners of her mouth turned down.

"Don't you worry about it," her mother said. "How soon 'til the schoolhouse is back in order?"

"It's back in order now as long as someone else doesn't do something to it."

Catherine shook her head as Clair burst into the kitchen carrying a shriveled apple. "It's the only one I could find," the child said. Catherine smiled.

"That's good, honey. Give it to Mama and go play while we set the table for lunch."

After lunch, Samuel, Catherine, and Clair retreated to the front porch to sit, while Harl went out to work in the barn. Clair hopped up onto Samuel's lap with her doll.

"Clair, let Mr. Harris alone," Catherine said. "Maybe he doesn't want you sitting on his lap."

Clair and Samuel looked at each other and laughed. "It's fine. I don't mind. I actually like having her up here with me," he said, putting his arms around her middle. "Is that Mary?"

"Uh-huh."

"As soon as our lunch settles in, you want to take a drive up to town?" Catherine asked.

"Can I go?" Clair asked.

"No, honey. We need to go see the sheriff," Catherine said.

"Oh."

Her mother came out on the porch carrying three glasses of sweet tea. She handed one to each person. "Did I overhear you that you'll be going into town to see the sheriff?"

"Yes, Mama," Catherine said, taking a sip of the tea.

Her mother nodded and went back into the kitchen. In a moment, she returned with a chair. Placing it beside Catherine, she sat down and watched Clair playing with her doll in Samuel's arms.

"What do you think'll happen to Tooth?"

"Probably get a jail sentence, serve time, maybe get fined, and if he can't pay it, more jail time," Samuel said.

"See he gets a whopper jail sentence and fine," her mother said. "We don't want the sheriff going too easy on him, or he might do something again."

They sat in silence for several minutes. Catherine enjoyed the cool, fall day, listening to the birds chittering among the apple trees in the orchard.

Catherine finished her glass of tea, reached over and took Samuel's empty glass from him. Clair had barely touched hers.

"You going to drink yours, honey?" Catherine asked Clair.

The child shook her head. "Go pour it out over there," Catherine instructed, pointing to the end of the porch. "Make sure you don't get it on Grandma's rosebushes."

Clair obeyed and brought her empty glass to her mother.

"I'll take them," Hazel said. "You two better skedaddle if you want to catch the sheriff in his office. He might have plans for the afternoon."

"Thank you, Mama," Catherine said. She opened her arms to Clair and hugged the child. Clair bounded over to Samuel and hugged him, too. He hugged her back and chuckled.

They climbed back into his buggy and set off for town.

Samuel guided the buggy up to the hitching post in front of the jail and helped Catherine down. He eased out of the buggy and tied the reins to the hitching post.

Inside the jailhouse, they found the sheriff looking over a stack of "Wanted" handbills and posters. He looked up and smiled when they entered.

His office was sparsely furnished with three chairs standing against the wall opposite the door, a row of rifles in a case against the wall behind his desk to the right of the door, and a wall of "Wanted" handbills and posters along the left side of the room. The room had been painted a drab color of gray.

"Come to visit me or the prisoner?"

"Both," Catherine and Samuel said simultaneously. They laughed and exchanged smiles.

Samuel gestured for Catherine to begin.

"Did you get a full confession?" she asked.

"Pretty much. When I tracked him down at his mother's place up on Dog Trot Fork, he was hiding in the barn up in the hayloft. Asked me if there had been trouble at the school and that he didn't know who would do such a thing. I pulled him out of there and arrested him on the spot."

"Will he be housed here or in the county jail? Or sent further in?"

"He'll be housed here probably for a week or so. Put the fear of God in him, so he doesn't pull a stunt like this again."

"And that will serve as his punishment."

"And I fined him fifty dollars. Said he can't pay. If he can't, then he can stay in jail for a while longer."

"It's just that I don't want any more surprises up at the schoolhouse."

The sheriff shook his head. "Word will get around. Any dissenters should keep themselves in line after this. Besides, Paul and Henry were the two outspoken ones. No, you shouldn't have any more trouble."

"May we see him?"

"Yes," the sheriff said as he reached in a drawer in the desk and pulled out a set of keys on a ring. He unlocked a door to their left, which led into a hall, which housed four jail cells. Cletus Tooth was in the one furthest from the door, lying on a cot with his arm over his face, knees raised and crossed over each other. "Hey," the sheriff called. "You've got visitors."

Cletus stood up, grabbed hold of the cell bars, and peered out at them. "Oh, it's you. Come to convict me of more wrongdoing at your school?"

"No, I think you've done a pretty good job of convicting yourself," Catherine said, moving forward, followed by Samuel and the sheriff, who locked the door behind them.

"Tsk, if I would have known that you would have gone to this much trouble, I would have done a whole lot more," Tooth said.

Catherine stopped and screwed up her face. "Like what?"

"Like busted out all them windows."

"You did enough damage as it is," Samuel said.

"How long you gonna keep me in here?" Cletus asked the sheriff.

"As long as it takes."

"As long as it takes for what?"

"You still have to come up with the fine."

"Like I said, I don't got it."

"Then I guess you'll be in here a while."

"What are *you* looking at?" Tooth asked, directing his question at Catherine.

She shook her head. "Not much of anything. We're done here, Sheriff," she said, turning away from the cell back toward the door.

"Well, I'm not done with you," Tooth said, thrusting his arms out of the cell toward her. He made a grab for her and caught the sleeve of her dress. Samuel, as quick as anything, brought his strong arm down on the man's hands.

"Let her go," he yelled as Catherine screamed. Tooth's hold on her was broken. He flailed his arms in the air outside his cell as Catherine rushed into the safety of Samuel's arms.

"That's right. Run to your boyfriend." Tooth sneered.

Catherine picked up her skirts and hurried to the door, which the sheriff unlocked and threw open. She rushed out, followed by Samuel and the sheriff, who locked the door behind them.

"I sure am sorry. I didn't have an inkling that Cletus would try that," he said.

Catherine shakily pulled a handkerchief from her sleeve and dabbed at her pink face. Samuel's hand rested lightly on her shoulder.

"We better go," he said. "Thank you, Sheriff. We probably won't be bothering you again about the prisoner."

Samuel helped Catherine into the buggy and looked up into her face. "You all right?"

"As much as can be expected."

"You want me to take you home or to the school?"

"Home please," she said, stuffing the handkerchief back up her sleeve.

Samuel removed the reins from the hitching post and climbed in next to her. "Think you'll have school tomorrow?"

"Most certainly," she said and smiled.

Chapter 26

Over the course of the next few weeks, Catherine taught all the students with equal fervor. There were no more major disruptions, except for the occasional playground disagreements. Things began to settle into a normal routine. But as the months grew colder, the time was drawing near that Catherine would have to prove to the community that she should be allowed to continue teaching their children. The time for a school recital was now her top priority.

"Now, let's practice our program," Catherine said one fine December day. The potbelly stove heated the room to a comfortable level, while outside, the wind blew cold air and fallen leaves all around the lawn.

"You'll line up in the front of the classroom, and we'll start with the youngest to the oldest. Here, Dorthea, Zillah, Ruthie, and Elizabeth Harris, you stand there in front."

"Teacher, I'm not sure I know my part good enough," Dorthea moaned, standing at the front of the classroom.

"Dorthea." Catherine stooped down to the child's level. "We've been practicing reciting the poems for a while now. You've never faltered before. Why the lack of confidence now?"

"'Cause I'll be saying it in front of my ma and pa and everyone else."

"Those are just nerves talking. You'll be fine once you get going."

"Teacher." Elizabeth Harris raised her hand and danced from foot to foot.

"Yes, Elizabeth?"

"I gotta use the outhouse. My nerves are coming up on me, too."

"Go ahead. But hurry back. We need to practice your entrance." Catherine straightened.

"Entrance? What entrance?" Frank asked.

"When you arrive with your parents, you'll stand in the back of the room. I'll introduce our program, and then you'll walk in a single file line up here to the front of the room, where you'll give your recitation. I'll give you a cue as when to start." Catherine sat on the bench in the front row. "Ready?" The children nodded.

"Now, Dorthea, watch me, so you know when it's your turn." Catherine pointed to the child and gestured for her to step forward, which she did. "Okay, now you recite your poem."

Dorthea recited the poem she chose with gusto. When she finished, Catherine pointed to her again, and she stepped back into line. Catherine pointed to Zillah and then Ruthie. Elizabeth Harris hurried back into place beside Zillah just in time for her to step forward and recite her chosen poem. Next, Hershel Fields stepped forward and gave a recitation. Catherine went down the line, pointing to each child in turn, who stepped forward and recited either a poem or a story from their readers.

"Wonderful. You all did a wonderful job today. Now, let's hope you do as splendidly tonight for your parents. Remember, after the recital, we'll have refreshments provided by the board."

"What are refreshments?" Dorthea asked.

"We'll have punch and cookies."

Dorthea, Zillah, Ruthie, and Elizabeth looked at each other, their mouths wide with excitement and anticipation.

"Looks good," said a familiar voice from the back of the room.

"Preacher's here," Dorthea announced.

"Thank you, Dorthea," Catherine said. "You may all be dismissed, but make sure you arrive fifteen minutes before the program begins tonight." The children ran to gather their things and then headed out the door past Samuel, who greeted each one by name. Dorthea stopped and looked up at him.

"Preacher, when are you and Teacher getting married?"

Both Samuel and Catherine laughed as Easter scooted her sister out the door. "What's so funny about that? He's here an awful lot of the time," Dorthea stated.

"It isn't polite to say so," Easter scolded as they went out the door.

When they were alone, Catherine turned to erase the board to hide her flushed cheeks as Samuel limped further into the room.

"Catherine? I love you, and I want to marry you. I think you love me, too. What are you keeping from me?"

"There are things in my past that not even a preacher could forgive."

"Try me."

She shook her head and looked away.

"What's so terrible in your past that you think I couldn't forgive it?"

"It isn't something I want to discuss with you."

"Right now? Or ever."

"Ever."

"You know, when we were growing up, there wasn't anything you couldn't tell me."

"I know, but people change."

"I haven't. People tell me lots of horrible things, and I know the Lord forgives them for them all. There isn't a sin too deep that the Lord can't forgive it. Take me, for instance."

"What about you?" she said turning to face him.

"I left Isabella to die alone while I went and comforted another sick parishioner. I knew God could and I knew He would heal her if I just stepped out in faith. But when I returned home, I found her dead."

"Oh, Samuel." Tears welled up in Catherine's eyes and threatened to spill down her cheeks. She watched Samuel brush away his own tears. She started to reach out to him but then remembered where they were and pulled back.

"But I prayed and asked the Lord's forgiveness. I held her death against Him for so long. I felt He had failed me when she died. I asked for His forgiveness for keeping Him out of my life, and He forgave me. Now, you know my secret. What about yours?"

Catherine's stomach knotted. "It's not as simple as all that. I know the Lord can forgive you. You were stepping out in faith. I just don't think you would forgive me."

"As I tell all the parishioners, God is bigger than our problems. And we are to confess our faults one to another."

"Not right now. Maybe after the program."

"I'll hold you to it," he said, smiling.

After she cleaned the board of the assignments for the day, Catherine drew trees and a road leading to a house with mountains in the background. Stepping back, she surveyed her work.

"How does that look?"

"Wonderful. Looks like a place I'd like to live."

She laughed, putting the chalk down on her desk. "That *is* where we live."

Samuel motioned for her to go ahead of him out of the room. "Ready to drive home and get a bite to eat?"

"Yes, please." She swiped little stray hairs from around her face as she followed Samuel out to his buggy. Wrapping her gray, wool shawl about her shoulders tighter, he took her hand and helped her into the buggy. She felt a surge of warmth pass through his hand to hers. She gasped and looked at Samuel. Their eyes met. He narrowed his gaze and smiled. Catherine sighed.

"Yes," Samuel said.

"Yes, what?"

"Yes, I feel it, too."

She leaned toward him, still holding his hand.

"It's getting colder, and the wind has picked up. You sure you'll be warm enough with just a shawl?"

"Yes, it should be fine."

"Just wondering if I need to get out a wool blanket for our ride. Look at how the leaves are stirring about." Samuel pointed as he drove the buggy down the lane toward Catherine's home.

"The leaves are almost off all the apple trees. Soon, it will be bad weather."

"And snow. Will you stay in town when bad weather comes? Or have Harl drive you?"

"The winters here aren't so bad, and the snow isn't too deep. I'll put an extra layer of bear grease on my boots and walk. Maybe I can get a ride home from you after school every day?" she asked, her eyes on Samuel's face. He smiled, and his eyes crinkled at the corners.

"Of course, you can always get a ride home from me," he said, wrapping one arm around her shoulder.

"You've been so kind to give me a ride all this time. I appreciate it."

"It's no trouble at all. I'm glad to do it. I want to make sure you get home safe and sound."

Catherine looked out at the bare apple trees in the orchard and sighed. "I really miss summer."

"I know what you mean." Samuel pulled up in front of the house.

After eating, Catherine and Samuel headed back to the schoolhouse to set up for the program that night.

"The parents should be here around 6:45 p.m."

"We'll have everything set up by then. My mother is bringing the punch bowl, cups, and gallon jars of punch. She should be here shortly."

Sure enough, Maude and Benjamin Harris arrived at 6:30 p.m. with the items, as promised.

"We'll put the teacher's desk in the back corner by the outside door and serve the punch and cookies from that area," Maude instructed.

Benjamin and Samuel carried the desk to the corner of the room.

"Samuel, come help me arrange the table," his mother said as Benjamin and Catherine walked to the front of the room.

Maude laid out the glass punch cups and trays of delicate-looking cookies. Lowering her gaze to a tray of cookies, she asked, "How are you son?"

"Great."

"Have you forgiven yourself yet for Isabella's death?"

"Yes, I got that squared away with the Lord the other night."

"And how goes it with Catherine?"

"She's holding something back. Something she can't tell me just yet. I don't know what it is, but I'm here for her no matter what."

Maude raised her eyes to her son's face and smiled.

Catherine spun around at the front of the room and clapped her hands together, holding them to her mouth. "This is going to be a wonderful night," she declared.

"Yes, dear. We are all curious to see how well our students have been doing these last few months," Maude commented.

"Well, it looks fine, real fine." The sound of Henry Frazier's voice grated on Catherine's nerves as he stepped into the room.

"Mr. Frazier, how nice of you to come." Catherine feigned courtesy and stepped forward.

"Nice nothing. I wanted to see what you've been teaching our children all these months." He hooked his thumbs in his crushed red velvet vest. "I want to make sure my money's not going to waste."

"I can assure you, it isn't going to waste," Catherine said. "The students have worked very hard on the program, and I hope you'll appreciate their efforts."

"Uh-huh," he grunted. Moving past her, he took a seat on the end of a row up front as students and parents began arriving.

Catherine and Samuel greeted each one in turn and ushered them into the schoolhouse.

Maude and Benjamin Harris took seats across the aisle from Henry Frazier. Caleb and Lucy Harris arrived with Penelope, Jonathan, and Elizabeth. They took seats near the front. Last to arrive were the Richardson boys and their mother. Ezzard Fields stood outside by his wagon and waved Catherine away when she walked toward him to let him know the program would be starting. Her delicate nose picked up the distinct smell of hard liquor on his breath as she turned to go back into the schoolhouse. She hoped he wouldn't cause any trouble tonight.

Catherine looked at the children lined up in the back near the outside door. She motioned for them to follow her. Silently, they walked in a single-file line toward the front of the room.

Catherine took the seat next to Samuel on the front bench as each student jockeyed for a position in front of her. The students stood looking uncomfortably out at the faces of their parents and neighbors.

She nodded, smiled at them, and placed her finger to her lips. She stood and turned toward the waiting guests.

"Welcome, parents and friends, to our first school recital. We are glad you are here and welcome you. Listen as we review our lessons and the like." Turning back to face her students, she placed her finger to her lips and smiled. Moving her finger, she asked, "Ready?" All of the students nodded their heads.

Taking a seat next to Samuel, she raised her right hand and pointed at Dorthea Fields, who stepped forward and gave a recital of a brief poem about a duck splashing in water. When she finished, she stepped back in line as her mother and others clapped loudly. She bowed slightly. The crowd laughed at her awkward movement when she turned the bow into a clumsy curtsey.

Next, Zillah Williams stepped forward and recited her poem. On down the line it went until each child recited either a poem or a story from memory. Some of the students even calculated from memory as Catherine gave them problems to solve. At the end of the program, the crowd clapped loudly.

Rising, she turned to the crowd and said, "It's our pleasure if you would now join us for some refreshments at the back of the room.

Thank you for attending our program, and I hope you've enjoyed yourselves this evening."

She was met with tremendous applause as she dismissed the students to return to their parents. Catherine watched the Fields children as they found their mother.

Dorthea reached her mother first. "Did you see me? Did you see me?" she asked.

"I saw you. You done good." Margaret Fields smoothed her hand over her daughter's hair. "You all done good, and I'm right proud of you."

Easter turned a pleasing shade of pink as Hershel shoved his hands in his pockets and looked at the worn toes of his boots.

"Come on. Let's go get some of them refreshments. You all done so good."

Catherine followed them to the refreshment table, where she greeted each parent and friend as she handed out cups of punch and offered the tray of cookies. She glanced up and saw Samuel looking at her. Once all the guests had been served, she dipped out a cup of punch and placed a cookie on a napkin. Walking toward him, she offered it to him.

"I see you never made it to the refreshment table."

"You brought this for me? Had to fight the crowd for it, did you?" he teased.

"Yes, of course I did. I thought it might be hard for you to make it through the crowd with your leg."

"That was very thoughtful of you. Thank you." He smiled, taking the punch and offered cookie.

Once all the parents and children left the building, Catherine began tidying up. Maude Harris helped her.

"That was a lovely program, Catherine," Maude remarked. "I see the students have worked hard these months."

Catherine straightened. "Thank you so much. That means the world to me."

Maude smiled at her.

After placing the dirty punch cups into the bowl, Catherine swept the floor, while the Harris boys carried her desk back into its place at the front of the room. Maude straightened the rows of benches.

"It was a fine turn out," she said.

"Yes," Catherine agreed.

"It's getting late. Will Samuel take you home?"

"I believe he will."

"Samuel, make sure our teacher gets home all right," his mother instructed.

"Yes, Mother. I will."

"Benjamin will see me home. Well, good night, everyone," Maude said as she turned from the room. Benjamin returned to the room and picked up the punch bowl with the dirty cups and followed closely behind his mother.

"Good night," Catherine and Samuel called in chorus as his mother left.

"Are you ready to go?" he asked.

"Yes, everything seems to be in order."

Samuel went outside and waited beside the buggy to help her in.

Looking out at the night, Catherine felt the caress of the cold December breeze on her hot cheeks. The moon shone full and bright. It would light their way home. Many of the leaves of the trees surrounding the school had fallen and dried, crunching under her feet as she walked toward Samuel.

He held her hand as she climbed into the buggy. Again, she felt the warm, tingling pass from her hand to his. Limping around to the other side, he climbed in. Throwing a blanket over their legs, he spoke to the horse, and it moved forward.

"It is quite a lovely night," he observed after several minutes of silence. He placed his arm about her shoulders and pulled her closer to him.

"Yes," she said, feeling heat in her cheeks. After all this time of being so close to this man, why did she still feel shyness around him? Was it truly shyness that made her cheeks flame or something else? She cared for this man, but how deeply? Could she marry him? Was he the Lord's choice for her? Would she be happy with a man like Samuel? The answer resounded inside her—yes!

Why, then, couldn't she bring herself to accept him fully? One word stood in her way—Clair. She loved the child more than life itself, but could she bring herself to disclose her secret to her former friend and the town reverend? Would he understand her choice to keep such a secret? Would he keep her secret?

"You seem lost in thought. What are you thinking?"

"There's something you don't know about me that may change your opinion of me."

Samuel's brows knit together. "I doubt that, but go on."

It was several moments before Catherine spoke. "You know John and I had a long engagement after the war. I was in school."

"Yes, I remember."

"When I came home for Christmas break, he visited me." Her mouth went dry as she tried to think of her next words. "I was so glad to see him that we . . . " Her voice trailed away. "I mean, his parents were away, and we had the house to ourselves. So, we . . . well, that is to say . . . " She swallowed hard. "Clair was the outcome of us coming together out of wedlock."

Samuel drew in a sharp breath. "Oh. I see," he said shortly, removing his arm from around her.

She gazed at him, her face twisted, and she placed her hand on her heart.

"We were married shortly after that. I know. It doesn't make it right, but at least Clair had a home and a daddy who loved her."

Samuel nodded, keeping his eyes on the road ahead of him.

They continued in silence for the rest of the way to her mother's house. When they arrived, Samuel helped Catherine down. Gone was the warm tingling when their hands touched.

"Good night then, Mrs. Reed," he said. Before she stepped foot on the stairs leading into the house, he had turned the buggy around and was headed back the way he came.

Catherine stood at the foot of the stairs and watched him go. Her stomach knotted. Was she seeing the last of the preacher, her friend?

Her mother opened the door and stepped out onto the porch. Catherine's face twisted as she attempted to hold back her emotions.

"Catherine, honey, what's wrong?" she asked. "Why are you all out of sorts?"

Catherine could hold back the tears no longer and raced up the steps into her mother's arms. "Oh, Ma! I told him. I told him about what me and John did before we were married."

Chapter 21

"Well, it's about time." Her mother held her and stroked her hair. "Now, now, what's done is done. You gotta leave the outcome to the Lord."

Catherine sobbed against her mother's shoulder. "But what if he doesn't come back? I lost a good man tonight."

"Love always comes back if it is true love. If not, then it was something else and not worth your time."

"But I love him," Catherine sobbed.

"Of course, you do. Just give him time to process what you told him and watch and see if he doesn't come back after a while. Now, come on, honey," her mother said, leading the way into the house. "You've had a busy day and need your rest. I put Clair to bed hours ago. You just go on up and leave it in the Lord's hands and pay it no more mind."

Catherine nodded and dabbed at her cheeks and nose with the handkerchief she kept stuffed up her sleeve for occasions just like this one. She plodded up the stairs—weariness overtaking her.

In her room, she gazed down at the sleeping form of her child. Clair lay so still and peaceful under the quilt her mother made for her. She breathed in and out rhythmically. *What a sweet child.* Catherine smiled. She was the joy of her life. Clair was her one saving grace out

328   *Second Chance at Happiness*

of her relationship with John. It was because of Clair that Catherine could go on—wanted to go on—living. She gulped down a sob and unfastened several buttons on her bodice. Pulling the combs from her hair, she shook it loose. Looking in the mirror over the dresser, she smiled at herself. "You can get through this," she said.

Pulling back the covers on her bed, she sat down on it and unbuttoned her boots, kicking them off. Without removing her dress, she lay down and threw the blankets over her head and drifted into restless slumber.

In the morning, Clair woke her by crying out in her sleep. Catherine leaped out of bed and hurried over to the child. She held her on her lap and stroked her hair as she kissed the top of her head. "Don't worry, baby. It was just a dream. Mama is here."

Clair's little arms struggled to embrace her mother fully. Catherine rubbed the child's back and shushed her. Clair sighed as she lay in her mother's arms.

"Are you ready to get up and go see Grandma?"

Clair nodded. Catherine changed the child out of her nightgown into her day dress and apron. Catherine buttoned up her bodice and carried the child down the stairs and into the kitchen, where her grandmother stood over the hot stove stirring milk gravy.

"Land's sakes," Hazel said, looking from Clair to Catherine. "You slept in your clothing, honey?"

Catherine yawned and stretched. "Yes, I did," she said, placing Clair on the floor.

"I'll watch Clair while you go get ready for school."

"Thank you, Mama."

Catherine changed into a dark skirt and white button-up, high-necked blouse. She pinned the little watch over her heart and looked at her reflection in the mirror.

If Samuel was gone, he was gone. There was no bringing him back. She would face the day alone at school and thank the Lord for all His other kindnesses. Her thoughts were interrupted when her mother called to her that breakfast was ready.

When Catherine walked into the kitchen, her mother looked up. Placing her hands on her hips, Mother exclaimed, "Now, that's more like it. It's time you was out of them drab clothes and into something fresh with life."

Catherine's face broke into a wide grin.

"You feeling better about last night?"

"Yes, it's in the Lord's hands now."

Her mother nodded. "You heap your cares on Him 'cause He can carry them for you."

"I did a lot of heapin' this morning."

Her mother smiled. "The Lord's shoulders can carry a whole lot if we would just let Him."

"Thank you, Mama. It's good to be reminded of that."

After breakfast, Catherine kissed Clair goodbye and set off through the fallen leaves down the orchard path toward the schoolhouse. She listened intently for the jangle of the reins of Samuel's horse and buggy, but neither one broke the perfect stillness of the early morning. He promised her rides to school, but he wasn't there to pick her up.

Standing in the doorway to the schoolhouse, Catherine greeted her students as cheerily as she could muster. She glanced over to

Samuel's home but saw no flicker of light and no movement. Perhaps he was out. It was getting colder, and maybe one of the parishioners was ill or needed him and called him away in the night. Or maybe he didn't want to have anything else to do with her and was keeping his distance.

These thoughts tore at her heart as she instructed her students in their lessons. She tried to keep her mind on what she was doing, but her eyes strayed often to the little watch hanging over her heart.

Will Samuel greet me at the end of the day as he always does, or will I be forced to walk home alone?

At the end of the day, she dismissed the students and ushered them to the door. Waving goodbye to the last of her pupils, her heart sank. Samuel was nowhere to be seen.

She hurried to tidy the classroom, erase the board, and write the lessons for the next day on it. Surely, something or someone had kept Samuel away today, or he would have been here to drive her home in his buggy.

Ezra Williams, riding a mule with his children on the back of it, sauntered over to her. "You looking for the preacher?"

Catherine nodded.

"I seen the preacher with Doc Johnson tearing out across the countryside this morning. Appears to me, he is still indisposed of whatever called him away."

Catherine's heart soared. The corners of her mouth rose ever so slightly, and her eyes brightened. "Well, that makes me feel better knowing he isn't hurt somewhere."

"We'll see you tomorrow," Ezra said, tipping his hat to her.

The mule slowly plodded away out onto the road. Catherine stood watching until they were out of sight. Surely, someone must have fallen into a mishap if both the doctor and preacher were called out. There was no sense in waiting around for Samuel to return. It could be hours before he darkened his own doorway.

Resigned, she headed for home, kicking some of the fallen leaves that were swept into her path by the evening breeze. It was an emergency that kept Samuel away from her today, she repeated to herself.

At home, she ate a small supper and then played dollies with Clair and read the child two stories before putting her to bed.

As she watched Clair sleep, Catherine sat rocking slowly in the chair by the window. Would Samuel forgive her for her mistake? If he forgave her, could he forget the mistake she and John had made? Could he love Clair like his own? Suddenly, there was no question in her mind. If Samuel couldn't bring himself to forgive her, then there was no way he could ever love Clair like Catherine wanted. But if Samuel could forgive Catherine, then could he love Clair? Catherine changed into her nightgown and sat combing her long hair, thinking.

Maybe Samuel wasn't the best choice for a husband as she once thought. Sure, they grew up together and knew everything about each other, except for their lives after school. Samuel loved her—of that she was sure—but could he overlook such a blatant mistake? Wrestling with such a question in the window on a cloudy night would not bring her the answers she sought. It was best to sleep on it and ask the Lord to reveal what her choice should be.

When she finally fell asleep, her sleep was fitful and void of any dreams. In the morning, she woke groggy and uneasy. Would Samuel meet her at the school today?

She washed and dressed Clair and herself quickly. She ate like a woman on a mission and hurriedly kissed her mother goodbye. Her feet almost skipped as she hurried toward the schoolhouse and answers she hoped Samuel could provide about his disappearance the previous day.

Her insistent steps led her to the darkened schoolhouse. She glanced over to the equally darkened preacher's house. What could have happened that was so wrong to keep him away from his home for two days?

Catherine began to fret that Samuel could be laying somewhere in a ditch. But the doctor was with him, she soothed. Certainly, the doctor could take care of them both if something bad had happened. Since the preacher was still out, did that mean that the doctor was still with him? Ezra said he saw them both tearing over the road. Something bad happened, but what and to whom?

She pushed the negative thoughts out of her head as she opened the school. Lighting a lamp, she hurried to the wood stove and stirred the coals into flame. She added more wood, and soon, a nice fire blazed—something that Samuel could have done, and would have done, for her if he had been there. She shook her head—pushing the thoughts out as her first students arrived.

She stepped out onto the porch to greet them.

Dorthea, Easter, and Hershel were the first to arrive.

Catherine rang the hand bell, calling her children to line up before her. Catherine said the morning prayer and then invited the students to take their seats.

Looking around the room, Catherine was surprised to see that Minnie and Minerva Clark were not there. "Has anyone seen Minnie and Minerva?"

All the children shook their heads as they took their seats.

"Hmmm," she thought. Could the girls have taken ill? One yes, but both of them? She would pay a visit to Dosha Clark's home later to see if she could find out why the girls weren't in school.

Chapter 18

By lunchtime, each student recited their lessons to her and were instructed on the next set of assignments for the coming day. Catherine successfully kept her mind on her work and only once looked toward the preacher's house when she thought she heard the jingle of reins.

After lunch, she dismissed her class. Every student whooped as they left the building.

Catherine sat behind her desk and let her eyes drift over to the windows which faced the preacher's house. She clasped her hands under her chin and sighed. *Where could Samuel be? What was keeping him away?*

She decided to go see Doctor Johnson. If he was still out, that meant that the preacher could still be with him. She wanted to know. She *had* to know. She banked the fire, tidied the room, and then hurried out the door, locking it behind her.

The doctor's office was in the middle of town. She picked her way between wagons and carriages driving around until she reached the doctor's shingle. A wooden finger pointed toward the office entrance. She tried the door and was surprised and a little disheartened to find it open. Entering, she was greeted by a woman in a black dress wearing a white apron and a white lace cap—Mary Edwards.

"Hello. Can I help you?" Mary asked.

Catherine held her breath. "Is Doctor Johnson here?"

"I'm afraid not. He's been called away."

"For two days?" Catherine gasped.

"It's a very bad case, I'm afraid."

Ah, Catherine thought, *thus the need for the preacher.* "Well, I'm sorry to have bothered you."

"It's not a bother at all." Mary smiled warmly.

Catherine turned toward the door and then back again. "Do you know when to expect the doctor?"

Mary shook her head and shrugged. "When he returns is all I know."

Catherine nodded and headed out the door. Outside, she thought of returning to ask who was so ill that it had taken both the doctor and the preacher away from their homes but decided against it. The patient would probably want to remain anonymous, and it really wasn't any of her business.

As she walked down the wooden boards that served as a sidewalk, a glimmer of gold caught her eye. Turning her head, she saw Henry Frazier headed her way; his watch dangling from its fob caught and shimmered in the afternoon sunlight.

"What brings you out to town in the middle of the day? Everything all right at the school?"

The nerve of the man. It wasn't any of his business, but she didn't want to cause any more ill feelings between them, so she answered his question. "I was looking for the doctor."

Henry's face dropped, and genuine concern showed. "I hope nothing serious."

"No, it's not for me. I wanted to know where he was is all." She failed to add that where the doctor was, the reverend was, too. It wasn't any of Henry Frazier's business that she was looking for Samuel.

"Ah, yes, a very bad time."

"You know where they are?"

"The doctor and the preacher? Yes, I do. They went to Dosha Clark's home."

"What's happened? You must tell me." She took a step toward him.

"All right," Henry said coolly, hooking his thumbs into the pockets of his crushed red velvet vest. "But first, have dinner with me."

Catherine stepped back as if punched in the gut. "No," she blurted. "Just tell me where they are and what has happened."

"I don't know what has happened, but I know that Dosha Clark is in a bad way. That's why the preacher was called, too." He continued, "Minerva Clark came tearing into town on the back of that saddle mule they use. Ran into doc's office. Came back alone and then ran for the preacher. I caught up to her at the preacher's and asked what was the matter. She said her mother was bleeding out and was possibly dying."

Catherine took a step back, her mouth open and brows pinched. "Is anyone else with them?"

"Not that I know of." Henry rocked back on the heels of his boots. "I could drive you out there if you wanted to go."

"Thank you, but no. Excuse me, please." Catherine turned and hurried back toward the school.

She looked behind her and frowned. Henry Frazier was standing in the street watching her, his thumbs still stuck deep in his vest pockets.

When she reached the preacher's house—still dark and empty—the road rounded down toward the school and out of sight of the town. It was there that she picked up her skirts and ran. Her hair shook loose from the tight bun at the nape of her neck, but she didn't care. She needed to get home, fix a basket of food, and have Harl take her up to Dosha's place. Those poor children might not have anything to eat.

She arrived breathless at home some minutes later. Racing up the porch steps, taking them two by two, she burst in the door, but stopped to rest with her palms on the wooden kitchen table. Her mother, who was sitting peeling apples into a pan, jumped up when she saw her.

"What's happened?" she demanded. Clair looked up from playing dolls on the floor and started to cry.

"Here, here now, baby," her mother soothed, picking Clair up.

Once Catherine caught her breath, she explained, "Dosha Clark . . . bleeding out . . . maybe dying. Got to go." She hesitated between each word.

"I'll get Harl." Patting Clair's back, she handed her to Catherine before heading outside. "There, there, don't fret so, honey. See. Your mommy's all right."

Clair hugged her mother's neck. Catherine kissed her forehead and placed her back on the floor with her dolls. She searched around, picking up canned goods off the shelves that lined the room. She dumped the peeled apples into a sack and placed them into a large basket along with the canned goods.

Harl burst into the room, followed by their mother.

"I've got the mules and the wagon ready to go," he said.

Catherine motioned to the heavy basket. Harl hefted it up into his arms. Catherine followed him out the door. Turning, she saw her mother carrying Clair and coming behind them.

"No, this is a bad business. I don't want Clair to come."

"Well, we can't leave her here alone."

Catherine looked at her mother, questions in her eyes.

"I'm coming, too," she said. "Seems to me they may need as much help as they can get."

Catherine nodded.

"Clair can play with Dosha's girls, and we'll see what needs doing."

Harl helped Catherine and Clair into the back of the wagon. He helped their mother up onto the seat beside him. Speaking to the mules, the group set off.

It was a long, bumpy ride out to Dosha Clark's place, set back against one of the many hills that made up Harrisville. Catherine wound her hair back into a tight bun as they drove.

Cresting the last hill, Catherine's heart sank. There beside the doctor's carriage stood Samuel's. He was still there. The doctor still being there, Catherine could understand, but Samuel? Exactly how sick was Dosha?

Harl pulled the wagon up alongside the carriages, set the break, and then helped everyone dismount.

Minnie and Minerva Clark came out to greet their visitors with red, tear-stained faces. Her mother hugged each one and then hurried into the house.

Catherine took her time walking up to them. Clair ran to greet them, showing them her cloth dolly.

Catherine shook her head and broke into tears. She threw her arms around the girls and hugged each one in turn. Harl hung back and tended the mules. Catherine didn't need to ask how bad it was when their faces spoke volumes.

Inside the tiny log cabin, Catherine noticed the doctor speaking to her mother in hushed tones as she nodded and gasped. She, too, started to cry. Catherine joined them in time to hear the words that set her mother to crying—Dosha was dying.

"Isn't there anything that can be done?"

"She lost a lot of blood—a lot of blood," the doctor emphasized.

"Was there an accident or something to cause her to lose so much blood?" her mother asked.

"I think it is a form of cancer of the uterus," he said dryly.

Catherine looked around the room, expecting to see Samuel in one of its four corners, but did not see him.

"Where's Samuel?" she asked.

"In the bedroom with Dosha. I got the bleeding stopped hours ago."

"Show me to her bedroom," Catherine said.

As the doctor turned toward the hallway, one of the doors opened, and Samuel stepped out, white faced, Bible in his shaky hand.

Catherine gasped when she saw him.

When he saw her, his face twisted as if in pain. He raced to her and embraced her.

She was taken back by his open expression of emotion and held her breath as he whispered in her ear, "Forgive me."

A sob broke from his lips as he pressed them to her ear.

Catherine could hear her mother openly sobbing. She watched as the doctor turned to go check on his patient.

Samuel turned his face toward Catherine. "I'm so sorry. I've been such a fool," he whispered loud enough for only her to hear. "Can you forgive me?"

Catherine nodded her head as tears made their way down her cheeks and collected at her chin. Samuel reached in his back pocket and pulled out a handkerchief and wiped her tears away.

"Samuel," called Doctor Johnson.

"Coming," Samuel called. "Come with me. Comfort Dosha as best as you can. She's very weak."

Catherine nodded and followed Samuel. Minnie and Minerva sat on the bed beside their mother—her face ghostly white.

"Now listen, Preacher," Dosha said in a whisper. Samuel bent down to hear her. "I have relatives up in Lexington. The girls will be well taken care of by them."

Both Minnie and Minerva protested through their tears, but their mother held up her hand. "The doctor isn't sure I'm going to pull through. I've lost a lot of blood, and I'm weak. We have to plan for life's what-ifs." Spying Catherine, she reached her shaky hand out to her. Catherine took it. "I'd like to be laid out in my wedding dress. You'll see to that, won't you?"

Catherine nodded and gulped back tears.

"Now, don't you worry none. I'm going to a better place than this one ever was." Dosha heaved a sigh, and her eyes closed.

Doctor Johnson, who stood on the other side of the bed, shooed everyone out of the room. "She needs to conserve her strength and rest."

In the kitchen, her mother was making herself at home unpacking the basket full of canned goods. Minnie and Minerva watched. "You girls go gather some more wood for the fire, and I'll make us dinner."

Obediently, they left the room while her mother arranged cast iron skillets on the cold stove top. Catherine looked into the tinder box and saw that it was almost full. Her eyes met her mother's.

"They need to get their mind off their ma right now and be busy with a task," she explained.

Her mother started a fire in the stove and waited for it to heat.

The girls soon returned loaded down with wood. They helped her mother by setting the table and pouring milk for each person. The door to their mother's bedroom stood open, and they caught glimpses of her as they worked. Doc Johnson pulled a straight-back chair over to the bedside and held her wrist in his hand.

Samuel returned to the room and paced. His hands were clasped in prayer. Catherine helped her mother dish the food onto the plates.

When it was time to eat, Catherine slipped into the bedroom and motioned for both the preacher and the doctor to come and eat.

"You go first," Samuel said. "I'll keep watch on her."

The doctor nodded his weary head and rose. "I'll relieve you in a few minutes," he said. Samuel nodded in agreement.

Catherine looked at Dosha, so quiet and peaceful. She looked like death had overtaken her already, except for the rise and fall of her chest. "I'll sit with her," Catherine said to the doctor, who nodded his head as he passed her.

Catherine sat beside the bed in the chair the doctor vacated and watched Samuel pace. Dosha moaned softly, and her eyes fluttered open. Seeing Catherine beside her, she spoke. "Everybody makes mistakes, you know, honey. I made a big mistake before me and the girls' father was married, but I don't regret it one bit. She's been a good daughter to me and a good sister to Minnie. I already told the preacher, and I don't mind telling you my sin either. We need to confess our sin to one another and forgive each other."

Catherine reached for her hand and clutched it tightly.

"Made the preacher cry, it did, when I told him. Ain't none of us perfect, except the good Lord Himself. We got to remember that." Dosha's eyes closed, and she sighed heavily again.

Catherine looked up at the preacher, who held his clasped hands under his chin. "She confessed that to you?"

"Yes, she's right. Everyone makes mistakes—even me."

"I understand. I'll stay with you if you like."

Samuel's face softened, and he nodded his head through tears.

"I never thought I'd find another kind soul to care for after Isabella died. The Lord is good to us in spite of our sins."

Catherine rose and went to him. Throwing her arms around him, she squeezed his shoulders. "He gives us more than we deserve."

Doctor Johnson walked into the room, wiping his mouth with his handkerchief. "Why don't you two go have something to eat? It's my turn to keep watch."

"I might like a little cup of broth if you have it," Dosha's weak voice piped up.

"Of course," Catherine answered, hurrying from the room and into the kitchen.

Hazel had heard Dosha's request and was straining some broth off the meat in the Dutch oven for her before Catherine reached the stove. When she returned with the broth, the doctor was holding Dosha's wrist again.

Spooning the warm liquid into the woman's mouth, Dosha only took a few spoonfuls of the liquid before waving it away. "That's enough for now," she said.

Catherine looked at the doctor, who shook his head.

"Minnie and Minerva," he called. "Come be with your mother."

The girls rushed into the room.

In the kitchen, Catherine helped herself to some meat and vegetables. Samuel joined her at the table and ate quickly from the plate her mother set before him.

Before they finished their meal, the doctor came out shaking his head. "She's gone," he said.

Catherine gasped. Samuel rose and rushed into the bedroom, followed by Catherine.

Minnie sat on the bed at her mother's side. Minerva pressed her mother's hand to her face as she sat in a chair at the bedside. Both girls were bent over her pale, lifeless form weeping.

"There was nothing I could do," Doctor Johnson said from behind them.

Catherine nodded and let the tears flow.

"I'll go get the undertaker," the doctor said.

"I'll wait with the girls," Samuel said. Catherine nodded, brushing away tears.

"I'll stay, too."

Mother and Harl decided to stay as well, helping to clean up and keep the girls distracted.

"Oh, honey," her mother said to Minerva, coming into the room. "I'm so sorry about your mama."

Minerva and Minnie rose and hugged the woman and let their tears fall afresh.

Catherine wept openly and held her stomach as if that was where her grief was centered. She walked out into the yard and dropped to her knees. Why had the Lord allowed Dosha to die, leaving two young daughters? Why had He allowed John to die? If only John had lived, she wouldn't be here now. Witness to this family's pain and grief.

A firm hand pressed onto her shoulder. Turning, she saw her brother. "Oh, Harl!" she cried, throwing her arms around his neck.

"I know," he said, choking back tears in his voice. "I know."

They stood holding each other and crying as the doctor pulled up, followed by Ernest Bell, the town's undertaker. His business partner, Joseph Nelson, sat next to him on the wagon seat. In the back was a new pine coffin.

Catherine and Harl followed the men into the cabin. They went into the bedroom. Catherine and Harl stayed out. Her mother, with Minnie and Minerva pressed to her sides, walked out of the room, followed by Samuel.

"We'll need to sit up with her for the night. Are you prepared to do that?" he asked Catherine.

"Yes, of course."

"Let's arrange the chairs in here," Hazel said, pointing to the living room.

Catherine swallowed and nodded.

"I'll get them, Sis," Harl said.

"Here, let me help you," Samuel offered.

The men placed the chairs in the room across from the kitchen. Two of the chairs they sat in an open place facing each other.

The men came out of the room. Joseph walked out to the wagon.

"Would you ladies care to wash and dress her?" Ernest asked.

The group nodded.

"I'll get a pan of water with the soap," Hazel said.

"Come show me your mother's wedding dress," Catherine said to the girls.

In the room, Minnie and Minerva dug through the cedar chest at the bottom of the bed. They pulled out a baby blue dress and laid it on top of the chest.

Catherine and her mother washed Dosha and put the dress on her while Minnie and Minerva stood in the corner of the room crying.

"There now," her mother said, opening her arms to the girls. "Don't your mama look pretty?"

The girls gulped and nodded.

"Now, come on. Let's let the undertaker do his part," her mother said, moving the girls out of the room. Catherine followed them out into the kitchen. Looking over to the living room, she saw the coffin was set up on the two chairs facing each other.

Ernest and Joseph entered the bedroom carrying a pallet. They carefully placed Dosha onto it and carried her out into the living room where they lifted her up into the coffin.

"Oh, Mama," Minnie cried. Catherine put her arms around the girl and pressed her head to her shoulder.

The next day, Dosha was buried beside her husband in the family cemetery down the hill from the house. Samuel presided over the service.

When it ended, he caught Catherine's eye, and she stayed behind as the others walked to the cabin.

"Let's go get a bite to eat, and then I'll take you home."

"No, it's all right. I'll ride with Harl and my mother and Clair."

"We need to talk."

"Yes, we do but not right now."

Samuel nodded. They turned and walked back to the cabin.

After everyone had eaten, Harl helped his sister up into the back of the wagon.

Samuel watched.

"Goodbye," she said, holding out her hand. Samuel came forward and grasped it.

"No, I won't say goodbye. I'll say, until later."

"All right."

He dropped her hand as Harl spoke to the mules to walk on.

Catherine gazed at Samuel until the wagon turned a corner and he was out of sight.

It was several days before Samuel came by the school after it let out.

"We need to talk," he said, stepping in the door. "I thought a lot about what you told me, and I've come to a decision."

Catherine held her breath.

"I want you and Clair to be part of my life. I don't want to lose you. I promise to be a good husband and father as best as I know how to you and Clair—if you'll have me."

Catherine sobbed and threw her arms around the preacher. "Yes, yes, a thousand times yes," she cried.

Samuel's smile spread across his face like the sun out from behind the clouds. He clasped her hands in his and squeezed her fingers.

"When can we be married?" he asked.

"As soon as you like."

"Then let's go into Bakersfield and get married. I have a friend who is a traveling preacher holed up there right now. He can do the officiating."

"Let's go tell Mama and Clair and Harl."

Samuel pulled her close, looked into her eyes, and lifted her chin. She turned her head up expectantly as he lowered his. As their lips met, the electricity she had felt at each touch of their hands coursed all the way through to her toes. She smiled up at him as they pulled away, breathless.

Samuel took his time driving through the cool, late December afternoon.

"I'll send word tomorrow to my pastor friend. We can drive over tomorrow night and get married." Catherine slipped her arm around his and pressed her head against his shoulder.

"That sounds wonderful," she whispered in his ear.

"Where would you like to spend your honeymoon? I've got some money saved up. We could really do it up big," he said.

Catherine shook her head and sighed. "Anywhere with you will be fine. We don't need to go away. I wouldn't mind honeymooning in Harrisville."

"All right, then." Samuel smiled to himself, thanking God for a second chance at happiness.

For more information about
Greta Picklesimer
and
Second Chance at Happiness
please visit:

www.gretapicklesimer.com

For more information about
AMBASSADOR INTERNATIONAL
please visit:

www.ambassador-international.com

Thank you for reading, and please consider leaving us a review on Amazon, Goodreads, or our websites.

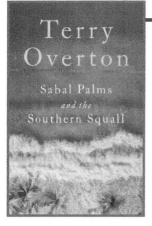

Elaine Smith lived in the small coastal town of Sabal Palms long enough to know when to worry about a squall and when to simply close the windows and wait for it to pass. This one would be significant. It would be significant in terms of damage, but that was to be expected. What no one expected was the profound effect it would have on the lives of people from the Texas coast to New York City.

When Dr. Sam Gray is sent to Africa as a volunteer physician, he is counting down the days until he can go home again. During a trip to the local school, he runs into the Cloverdales, a missionary family determined to win every soul in Africa to Christ. Try as he might, Dr. Sam can't seem to resist the family and finds himself being pulled into their midst again and again. As he battles his own beliefs, Dr. Sam begins to find that maybe he's in need of a Physician as well. Can anyone heal his hardened heart?

King Solomon is well-known as a wise man and the wealthiest king to have ever lived. But with great power often comes great corruption, and Solomon was no exception—including his collection of wives and concubines. But who were these women? What was life like for them in Solomon's harem? S.A. Jewell dives into a deeper part of Solomon's kingdom and shows how God is always faithful, even when we may doubt His plan.